"Unconquerable Night," the woman read. "It is a wish for his future victory against the god of fires. But that fight is far off. For now, he dwells in darkness and is at peace in his kingdom."

"Does he then," said Jaspre, "truly exist?"

"Yes. The King of the World, that is him. The Prince of Darkness, eternal adversary of the devil Lucifer, bringer of light and blinding. The Lord of Eternal Night. By some called Bel, and in the Roman tongue Arimanio, as it is carved here. But as you shall worship him now, he is named Angemal. Angel, demon and god."

"And I am to serve him?"

"For this you were born."

Slowly, the young girl's cheeks stained red with blood. The light in the eyes of the statue blazed and sang, as if he saw and smiled at it.

"Lee is one of the most powerful and intelligent writers to work in heroic fantasy."

—Publishers Weekly

RED AS BLOOD

Or

Tales from the Sisters Grimmer

Tanith Lee

DAW BOOKS, INC.
DONALD A. WOLLHEIM, PUBLISHER
1633 Broadway, New York, NY 10019

Cover art by Michael Whelan.
Interior illustrations by Tanith Lee.

ACKNOWLEDGMENTS

Paid Piper, from Fantasy & Science Fiction, © 1981 by Mercury Press, Inc. *Red As Blood*, from Fantasy & Science Fiction, © 1979, by Mercury Press, Inc. *Thorns*, from Young Winter's Tales, © 1972, by Macmillan, Ltd *When the Clock Strikes*, from Weird Tales, © 1980 by Lin Carter. *Wolfland*, from Fantasy & Science Fiction, © 1980 by Mercury Press, Inc.

FIRST PRINTING, JANUARY 1983

1 2 3 4 5 6 7 8 9

DAW TRADEMARK REGISTERED
U.S. PAT. OFF. MARCA
REGISTRADA, HECHO EN U.S.A.

PRINTED IN U.S.A.

Table of Contents

Paid Piper

In the late summer afternoon, the river lay thin and shallow among its smooth stones. A young girl kneeled there, washing her long dark hair. Her name was Cleci, and she was fourteen.

Up on the left-hand bank stood a group of lindens. Their leaves were powdered by the summer dust, which floated in the air like smoke. Beyond the lindens was the village of Lime Tree, which was called for them. It was a large, sprawling, prosperous village, of many narrow streets and open squares, that stood in the midst of its own wheat fields. While beyond the right-hand bank of the river, these fields ran off into Lime Tree's vineyards, where the red grapes ripened on their stocks.

Lime Tree understood why it was so prosperous. It wisely worshiped the rat god, Raur, and Raur therefore kept his folk in order. Other places might be plagued by vermin, who spoiled the crops and fouled the granaries, but not Lime Tree village. Lime Tree took gifts to Raur in his whitewashed temple by the ford. After the harvest, in thanks and homage, they would lay wheat sheaves, apples and wine on his altar.

Last Spring Festival, Cleci, along with thirty other young girls, had been made a Maiden of Raur. This happened to all the many daughters of the village when they were about fourteen or so. It meant that they were allowed into the sanctuary, to gaze on Raur for the first time. Cleci thought him very beautiful, for he was five feet tall, and carved in flawless marble, with rose-opal eyes. His rat's face was intelligent and amenable. The rich people of the village kept white fur rats in gilt cages, and Cleci had determined she too would have a white fur rat to talk to and to play with. She began to save up her coins, of which she got but few. She was the washerwoman's daughter, and her father was dead. She would fetch the washing, help wash it in the tubs of scalding water, help dry it in the yard, then carry it back to the houses it had come from. Already Cleci's hands were rough, and she put them behind her back now, when she went to the temple, in memory of Raur's soft silken paws.

Every fifth day Raur was worshiped, but in winter, spring and late summer, there was a great festival. Lime Tree would deck itself with ribbons and banners. There would be eating and drinking and dancing in the streets. And Raur's image would be taken out of its sanctuary, though veiled—the Lime Treeans were only permitted to look at him face to face on special occasions—and up and down the byways on the shoulders of his priests. Finally he would be borne through the fields to safeguard and bless them. When night fell, there would be bonfires and singing. Cleci was looking forward to the Summer Festival, which was now less than a day away.

That was why she had stolen the hair-washing hour away from her mother. The washerwoman cared more for the cleanliness of the garments of paying neighbors. But Cleci had now rinsed her hair, and sat combing it into a dry dark shining in the wide westering bars of the sun. As she did so, she mentally counted her coins. There were only ten, however, and counting did not increase them. Which was a pity, since she would need twenty times that number to purchase a white rat from the priests.

Suddenly, all the birds in the lime trees stopped singing. Then a new bird began to sing.

Cleci lifted her head, astonished, wondering what the bird could be. Its voice was much fuller and more mellow than that of any she had ever listened to. And, if possible, more sweet. Yet the trillings and flights of music must definitely be those of a bird, for only something natural could sound so primitive, strange and marvelous. Then the song broke into a double cascade of extraordinary harmonizing notes, took on, in addition, a wild, dancing rhythm, and began to come along the right-hand bank above her. She realized it could not be a bird after all. She stood up involuntarily, to see. And so she saw the Piper.

There had, once or twice, been minstrels—pipers, harpers—who had passed through Lime Tree. But never one who made music like this. Or who looked like this.

His hair grew to his shoulders, and it was a curious somber red, like no hair she had ever seen. There was a full, loose wave in it, too, like the shapes the wind made of grasses, clouds or smoke. . . . His skin was fair, not tanned at all, and his eyes were large, and blue as distance. His breeches were also blue, but the blue of a storm sky, and his sleeveless jacket the dark crimson of old wine. The pipe was of a pale plain wood and hung from a cord about his neck. He looked young, yet somewhere in his eyes he was much older. Yet his smile was the same age as Cleci.

"Who are you?" He said to Cleci, after he had smiled at her and filled her with a bizarre elation.

"I'm Cleci. Who are you?"

"Who do you think I am?"

"I thought it was a bird, singing."

"Ah," said the Piper. He tilted back his head on his young, strong neck, and looked up into the linden tops. And all at once three or four birds flew from the branches, dipped across the river, swooped to him and dropped, soft as leaves on to his shoulders.

"Oh," said Cleci. "Oh."

"Oh, yes," said the Piper. The birds kissed him on the lips with their sharp pointed beaks. Other birds were drifting down into the grass, hopping past his feet. A snake coiled round his ankle. A butterfly flickered in his red hair.

"*Oh*," sighed Cleci.

"I saw a temple by the ford," said the Piper. "Who do you worship there?"

Cleci blinked.

"Raur," she said with automatic pride. "The rat god."

"Why?" said the Piper.

A great stillness came when he asked her, as if the land listened too.

"Because. . . ." said Cleci. "Because he keeps his creatures from harming us. And because—he's beautiful."

"Is he?"

The Piper looked at her. Suddenly she felt ashamed. She did not know why. She stared at the ground and said, "Excuse me, please. I must be getting home."

And then she turned and ran, straight through the shallow river, up the slippery stones and up the bank. She ran under the lindens and toward the village. She was afraid.

When she got home to her mother's small house, the washerwoman scolded her. For running off, for washing her hair. All through the scolding, Cleci thought of the Piper. All through supper, Cleci thought of him. And as the day went down through a rift of swarthy red in the west, and the east closed to a shadowy blue, still Cleci thought of him. But by then her fear had gone, and a weird disappointment taken its place. She had begun to think she had dozed at the river and dreamed him. She dared not tell her mother, certainly, for her mother would scold her for that too. For dreaming, particularly for dreaming of a young man. Or was he so young as he looked? Could he possibly be as old as that something inside his eyes? "You," her mother would say, "you dreamed of being a princess when you were ten. *When I am a princess*, you would say. Doing the washing cured you of that. Then you wanted to be a priestess of Raur. As if they take anyone, boy or girl, who isn't from a rich man's house. Then, since you were Raur's Maiden, and saw a white rat in the miller's hall that day, all you would talk of was having a white rat we could never afford. And now you've met a beautiful young piper by the river. A likely tale!" No. Cleci would not tell her mother, for this was what her mother would say, and it was all true. It made Cleci despondent to think he had only been a dream. For there should be such people in the world.

"You've not eaten your supper," Cleci's mother scolded her. The washerwoman wrapped up the bread and cheese and put it away carefully for tomorrow.

Cleci went to the open door and looked out into the narrow street. The roofs leaned near to each other overhead, and the darkening sky rested on the gap between.

Suddenly all the dogs in Lime Tree, and there were a great many, began to bark and yelp and howl.

"Whatever's up?" said the washerwoman, as she lit the clay lamp. "They sound like a pack of wolves, they do."

But then the dogs fell silent. Down the street came floating, soft as the cool air, ripple on ripple of exquisite melody. It was an evening song, delicate yet piercing like the first stars coming out overhead. The pipe sounded deeper now, darker, old as the earth, or nearly.

A light fell over Cleci's shoulder onto the road. She realized her mother had come to the door, the lamp in her hand.

"Why—" said Cleci's mother, "whoever's that? He's a rare musician, whoever he is."

The Piper came walking along the street like a lynx, yet every fifth or seventh step, he would give a curious little skip, and the music would skip with him. He held the pipe sideways-on to his lips, and his cheeks scarcely altered their shape at all as he blew.

Other lights were falling out of doors and windows as people came to see. No one spoke at first, merely watched, and listened. But that changed presently. For behind the Piper, drifting like mist in his footsteps, came most of the dogs of Lime Tree, all that had been able to slip their ropes. And none of the dogs fighting, not even glancing at each other, a brindle, low-backed army, gliding to the tune of the pipe.

Cleci heard, along the way, the bursts of exclamation and oaths which marked their progress. Then the river of music came in again, filling the holes these sounds had punctured in the atmosphere. Cleci's mother did not speak, but she let out a great sigh, as if she had been holding her breath her entire life, and now could let it go. She set her free hand on Cleci's shoulder, and for once the contact was aware and gentle.

Just then, the Piper went by their door. He angled his head to look at them, but said nothing. Cleci wished she could touch him, to be sure he was real. Then he had gone.

Paws slid across Cleci's feet.

People stood in the street, staring, as the wonderful music faded like a scent.

"Where's he going?" she heard someone ask. They had not thought—or dared—to question the Piper himself.

"Toward the miller's house, looks like."

The miller was one of the important men of Lime Tree village, being one of the richest. His eldest son was a priest of Raur.

"Did you see the dogs?"

"The dogs were after some food he had, obviously."

"What does he want?"

"How do I know? Why are you asking *me*?"

"Tomorrow's Festival Day. Maybe he wants to play for the dancing. For a fat fee."

"Ah. That will be it."

"Ah."

Cleci felt a strange excitement under her ribs, like pain. She wanted to scream or laugh or sing. She wanted to be quiet as a stone.

"He's only another vagabond," her mother suddenly said, and Cleci turned and saw her mother, a worn, raw-handed stranger, her eyes tired to death, and greasy hair hanging in them. "Just another beggar." And Cleci hated her mother with a dull and grinding hate.

One last absconding dog rushed noiselessly up the street, pursuing the invisible tide of music that had flowed away there.

Cleci took her white Maiden's Dress out of the chest, and put it on. It was not yet light, and so she was able not to observe the whiteness of the Dress had faded. She tied a scarlet ribbon at her waist. The baker's wife had given it to her because it had a tear but, tied carefully, the tear was not apparent.

Her mother anxiously grumbled, because today she was not allowed to work.

All through the night, perhaps once every hour, at the moment when it turned over into every next hour, Cleci had woken. She had wondered what the miller and the baker and the smith, and the other important rich men, had said to the Piper. She had wondered if the Piper would lead Raur's Procession as, very occasionally, the most accomplished minstrels had been chosen to do.

Even before the sun was up, Lime Tree was hanging banners from its windows, but the colors did not show, or the paintings of magic scenes to do with the rat god: Raur turning a plague of rats and mice aside from the village; Raur battling a giant crow like a black dragon.

"I must go now," said Cleci to her mother.

"There'll be enough Maidens," said Cleci's mother disparagingly. "They won't miss *you.*"

But Cleci ran out of the door and along the street.

As she ran toward the temple, the sun rose above the winding clutter of houses, and all the banners burst open like flowers into green and crimson and violet. Gilt discs sang on streamers in the dawn wind, and little effigies of Raur, made of clay or pastry, bounced lightly on their strings.

The river was the color of the sky. Even the lindens were streaked by cool gold. Cleci picked a spray of blossom, thoughtlessly killing it, because it was beautiful, and put in in her hair.

Lime Tree was prosperous, and had many children, many young men and girls. All told, this year, there were a hundred Maidens, for a girl remained a Maiden till her wedding day, when she would be about fifteen. Then she became a Matron of Raur.

The Maidens came together on the bank above the ford, like a flock of white ducks. Next, the boys arrived, with their rat masks made of thin wood, their wooden swords, their skin tabors, and all their shouting. Raur would be carried out into the morning on the shoulders of the priests; the Maidens and the boys would follow Raur back into the streets, and the rest of the village would pour after them.

Sugar plums were being given out. The masked boy rats had some difficulty getting them through their mouth-holes. The Maidens ate with dainty self-consciousness, and wiped their sticky fingers on the grass. Today it did not matter so much that Cleci was the washerwoman's daughter. Some of the girls actually spoke to her. One of the baker's daughters even said loudly to her: "How nice that ribbon looks on you. I can't see the tear in it at all."

"Look! There's our illustrious daddy!" cried another daughter, more loudly still, over all the general noise.

Out of the temple walked Lime Tree's eminent men. The baker and the butcher came first, then the miller, the smith and the wainwright. Last, but not least, the vintner. Behind them, however, came only empty air. Cleci strained her eyes, trying to find the Piper in it. Perhaps, he would come out next, with the priests.

"He will *not*," said the baker's daughter, and Cleci realized she had spoken aloud.

"Indeed not," said the miller's daughter. "My father says he won't permit such lawless music to be played before the god. Not that he heard the fellow play, of course. but daddy's so clever, he didn't need to hear, to judge."

The sugar plum Cleci had eaten curdled in her stomach. Disappointment felt like toothache. Then she felt a wave of elation instead. And then the commotion began.

The Maidens turned in a snow-drop flurry. The boys turned their pointed handsome rat faces. The priests who were just starting to spill from the temple door, spilled faster, craning to see.

Out of Lime Tree came striding a wonderful young man in a sleeveless jacket of wine red, and storm-blue breeches. His hands balanced a pipe, held sideways-on to his lips, but you could not hear it over the crowd's hubbub. Only—only *feel* the music of it, that somehow pierced through air and light, bone and blood, and in at the walls of heart and mind.

His dark red hair blew back from his clear pale forehead, and he was smiling as he piped. Behind him came a flood tide of living creatures, dogs, a skitter of little lizards, a low-flying wing of birds, and a fizzing of insects even, dragonflies, butterflies and bees. There were all the village's twenty asses too, one with a saddle on it, the rest trailing chewed-through tethers. And there were *rats*; the tiny white bounding rats, that somehow—how?—had got out of their cages.

The sight of the rats, or maybe it was finally the unheard yet *experienced* glamour of the piping, caused the entire vociferous crowd to break into silence.

At which, of course, the music became audible.

But it was not like music anymore. It was like the river, the sky, the country. Like the pulses of the crowd beating, the drums of life itself, and the sun spinning on the blades of space and time. More music than a single piper could produce from the slender reed of a single pipe.

When suddenly the music stopped, everyone was left floundering, as if cast abruptly out of a great sea. Or as if they had all gone deaf.

Cleci became aware that the veiled statue of Raur had been carried out of the temple, and was shocked she had not previously noticed. Now Raur sat there on his garlanded stretcher, balanced on the priests' shoulders, still as everything else. As if he, too, had been entranced by the pipe.

The Piper lowered the instrument slowly. He looked about. Cleci could not help admiring him for his magnificent poise, assurance and charm with so many hundreds of eyes fixed on him. Then one of the rich men bellowed, and everyone instead looked at him. It was the miller.

"*How*," demanded the miller, choleric in the face, not poised at all, nor very assured, certainly not at all charming. "*How* did you steal our rats out of their cages?"

There was a small ripple of bemused agreement, and someone else shouted from the crowd: "And how did he loose my dads' riding-ass and all?"

Then a welter of voices. How this, how that.

The Piper just waited for them to finish. Which, inevitably, they did. Then the Piper said to the people of Lime Tree, in a voice that carried without shouting: "You try to lock everything up in a cage. Your animals and your hearts. But love will always get out. Love, or hate. Somehow."

Cleci shut her eyes. She held the words to her like a precious stone. She did not understand them, but she clung to them. Then she heard the Piper say, "So tell me now. Do I lead you in the dance, or not?"

And Cleci screamed, at the top of her lungs: "Yes! Yes! Yes!"

Then clapped her hands to her burning cheeks, opening wide her eyes in horror. But it was all right, for the whole crowd had cried out at exactly the same moment that she had, and the same words. Even the miller had, though he looked perplexed, and he turned immediately to the priests and spoke to them. The priest who was the miller's son nodded, and stepped forward, raising his hand for attention. He called to the Piper nervously.

"We're willing to elect you to play for us, to the honor of Raur. But what will you want paying?"

"Whatever you think I deserve," said the Piper.

"Oh, come now. That's an invitation to haggle."

"Don't be afraid," said the Piper. "I won't ask for anything you can't give me."

And he smiled that smile that was only fourteen years of age, and his eyes were several centuries old.

One of the priests squeaked, and Cleci saw the white rats

from the temple cages had also somehow got free. There were about fifty of them, and they were scampering through the priests' robes and over their toes, to get near the Piper.

"Raur himself, it seems has chosen you, pre-payment or not," said one of the older priests, and his face had relaxed. A slow warm sigh passed over the crowd, and at that moment the rim of the sun dazzled right up over the temple roof.

They carried Raur along every street, through every alley, across every square. By the doors and the bannered windows. Beneath arches, where ribbons and flowers danced with them. Round the two wells. Up the stairs. Not a treading place of Lime Tree was left untrod. The priests strode over it, and the men walked, and the Maidens and the women danced. The boys banged their tabors and the priestesses shook bells. And before them all, the Piper went, neither striding nor dancing nor walking, but something of all three. And the pipe sang like the voice of the day, like the voice of the earth itself.

By noon they came to the big square where the meat was roasting and the bread popping crisply out of the ovens. No one was tired. Somehow their feet kept tapping or making little dance steps. Then the jars of wine were brought. Even the Maidens drank the wine. A furry rat came and sat on Cleci's arm, and she fed it, loving the way it held discs of pastry in its paws, nibbling the food like a squirrel.

Birds lay thick as strange summer snow on the ledges and roofs. Dogs played chase and battle over each other's backs. Lizards basked fearlessly. No one quarrelled. The baker allowed the butcher should have the best cut of the meat. The butcher insisted the baker should have it. The miller's daughter said to Cleci, shyly, "You are much prettier than any other girl here." And she made Cleci take her own waist ribbon of blue silk, three inches broad, and quite flawless.

Then they went on, and the pipe, which somehow had never ceased to play—or had they only imagined it had not, for of course the Piper would have stopped playing to eat and drink too—soared up like a golden bird, and all the golden birds soared after it.

The sun lay on the streets in shining coins. Cleci ran dancing, hand in hand with the Miller's daughter and the baker's daughter.

When the Procession broke from the town and saw the fields, stretching like yellow forests away into the blue sky, they laughed for gladness. It was all so exotic, and so new to them. Though they had seen these things evey day of their lives, they saw them now for the first time.

They danced through the fields, garlanded with sunlight. Now the priests were dancing too, though all the marble weight of Raur was on their shoulders. Wild flowers were painted on the wheat. The Maidens brushed them with their fingers, but did not tear them up. Cleci touched the blossom in her hair, and her eyes filled with tears because she knew that, though it died, the blossom forgave her for plucking it without need. And she looked back for her mother in the great shimmering, dancing crowd that seemed to have been spangled with gold dust. When Cleci could not see the washerwoman, instead she called to her from inside her head: *I love you. I do.* And she visualized her mother's tired, irritable face smoothing out, as it had never really been smoothed since the day Cleci's father died. But then the dance whirled even individual caring from her mind.

Of all the paths among the fields that might be trodden, they did not miss one with their treading. They crossed the river, and the far fields were loud with their music and voices. And then they went up to the terraces where the vines bloomed in soft crimson rust, and the Piper led them between the stocks.

Baskets of sweets, of grapes, and skins of wine were passed along the Procession. They made no pretense of stopping now. They were less wearied than they had been at midday. Weariness was unknown to them. They could dance forever.

And the priests were laughing now. Everyone was. Or was it the pipe which laughed?

And then, the day began to go. It was curious, for it had seemed the day, too, would last forever. But still, it was a lovely departure, the sun folding itself under a wide pink wing, a violet light filling the enormous sky, and stars like bright birds coming to hover in that enormity.

Then the torches were lit. The Lime Treeans put their god down on the grassy slopes between the vineyards and the wheat fields. They lay on their elbows on the fragrant back of the world, and watched the last stain of sun linger on the river below, and the village beyond the river. And the village flamed softly like a burning rose in the moment before the dusk drank up the sun.

Do I live THERE? Cleci asked herself in wonder. *In so beautiful a place?*

A dog lay over her knee, and she kissed its head.

And then she thought about the music of the pipe, and how, rather than making them listen, it had made them see and feel and *know*. And now Cleci knew so much, she knew that the world belonged to her, and she must love it and cherish it so that it might love her also. And she knew she would live forever, even after her body had died. And she knew that she, and all men and women, and all beasts, and all forms of life, had been born simply in order to be happy.

Then the pipe stopped.

In the great stillness she heard the evening breeze flying low over the slopes. She sat on the grass, and smiled, as if she had just woken from a miraculous dream which she would never forget. And there was no face in all the crowd, wherever she glanced, that looked any different from her own. She felt then younger than the youngest child, and older than the hillside.

The Piper was standing about halfway up the hill, and he was clearly visible. The breeze lifted strands of his hair tenderly, and set them down. His face was radiant and still as the dusk. Yet his eyes, which were the dusk's color, glowed and shone. They were full of untold emotions. Emotions that perhaps no human had ever felt. And although he stood above her on the hill, Cleci was slightly puzzled as to how she could see all this so well from such a distance.

Some of the priests, and all Lime Tree's important men were walking slowly toward the Piper. They walked as they would have walked after a good dinner, contented, savoring.

Cleci heard their voices through the medium of the same intense clarity as had shown her the Piper's eyes.

"Well, Piper. I take it all back. You're a find, and no mistake. I've never known such piping."

"Never felt so good after the Procession, either. Where's the blisters I always get?"

"Ah. And where's my wife's swollen ankles?"

"On her feet?" innocently suggested the butcher, and the rich men burst out in childish guffaws, slapping each other on the back.

"There's more to come, more dancing yet," said the baker. "There's the bonfires to be lit, and the best wine to be drunk. But I say we should pay you now, to reward you for this fine day's work."

"Is that your only reason?" inquired the Piper. His head was raised, as if braced for a blow. There was a sudden strange tearing in his face, as if he knew an ancient, but well-remembered stab of pain.

"Oh, just for good measure," said the miller. "You know what they say: Once you've paid the piper, you can choose the tune."

"Not," said the miller's priest son, with anxious courtesy, "that the tunes you already played for us were not singularly splendid."

"State your fee," said the vintner. "Whatever you like. Gold if you want—I'm sure we're all agreed. I'll even throw in a jar of my best ruby."

"Yes, gold. And as much bread as you can carry."

"One hundred gold pieces, I say. And the pick of my forge."

"One hundred and fifty. And the pick of my stable—the best white ass for you to ride."

Then came a long nothing of soundlessness. The wind died, the dog sprang abruptly from Cleci's knee. She held her breath, and, as by the river in the westering sun the first time she met him, she felt a dreadful shameful fear.

She could hardly bear the Piper's face, so rare, so young, so old, so braced against agony. His whole body seemed braced against it now. As if slowly he were being wrenched apart, or beaten, or pierced by thorns, or iron nails.

At last he said, softly, his voice carrying to the edges of the sky, "I don't want any of that."

The rich men chuckled, uneasily now.

"You're not saying that you've played for *free*?"

"No. I'm not saying that."

"Never heard one turn his nose up at gold before."

"What I want is better than gold."

The priests seemed to draw together, their faces closing, their eyes watchful. The rich men still blustered.

"Well then," said the miller. "Come along, lad. What *do* you want?"

Everyone on the slope seemed to realize the miller's awful

gaffe. Even he. He should not have called the Piper "lad." But the Piper, in his slow invisible anguish, only said: "Don't you know what I want?" He turned his head, and looked at them gravely. In that vast crowd on the darkening hill, he seemed to miss no one. And when he looked in Cleci's eyes, she grew cold. "Do you truly not know? Are you truly so blind? Can you really only see commerce and cages? Only pray to save your goods or to fill your bellies? Could you never pray merely from the joy of being alive? *That*," he said and, turning, he pointed toward the veiled statue of Raur, which stood there shrouded and inanimate in the gathering darkness, "that is the symbol of your limitations. Don't you want to be free?"

"But Raur is beautiful," Cleci whispered under her breath. But she knew now he was not so beautiful as life, nor as the Piper, nor music, nor the land itself. Raur meant security, but not joy. Or not true joy, which only the Piper could teach them.

The crowd rustled. Some were getting to their feet, and some huddling down. Overhead the sky was almost black.

"Choose," said the Piper. "The cage, or the world."

The miller shouted at him: "Today was a festival. You're all right for Festival Days. But we can't carry on like this every day. There's work to do. Money to make."

"Look at the flowers," said the Piper, quietly. "Look at the stars. How gorgeous they are, and how well they live. And are they making money, do you suppose?"

His voice smiled, but you could hear there was a knife in him, in his very soul.

"Corrupter!" bawled one of the priests. "Blasphemer!"

Other priests took up the cry. All at once, most of the crowd was thundering. Only here and there someone wept, usually a woman.

"The fee I wished for," said the Piper, and even over the din they heard him, "was to win your love away from that statue of a rat, which is not any kind of god, whatever you may say."

Screams of outrage roiled on the slope. Again the Piper spoke, and again they heard him.

"But you won't pay my fee, will you? You won't open your cage and follow me."

From somewhere a stone whirled over the sky and aimed

to smash the Piper on the cheek, then another and another. A rain of stones and clods of earth flailed around him, and then ended, because none of the missiles had hit its mark. Like frightened wretches who have pulled the tail of a chained lion, only to find the chain is unfastened, the crowd collapsed on itself. The priests flung themselves down the hill to the feet of Raur the rat god. They tugged off his veil, and there he was, in all his marble magnificence, for the people to cling to. He would keep them sane and safe. He would drive off the rats and make sure that the granaries were full, and that some would get rich and all could dream of it. He would ensure there was always a profit to bicker over, someone better off to be jealous of, someone to cheat, someone to hate. And if any struck you in the face, Raur the rat would be sure to lesson you that you in turn must strike them back.

"Save us!" The priests and people yelled to Raur, clasping his chilly smooth sides.

Cleci remembered how she had hidden her rough hands from him, embarrassed to be poor.

The Piper watched the people on the hill, silently. And, just as before, his quiet spread to them, and their noise went out like the flames that were somehow going out on all the torches.

"I can't force you," he said at length. They all heard him, and most of them shuddered. "There would be no point in that."

"Our god is protecting us," someone screamed.

"Go away, you evil magician. Take your devil's music and go."

The Piper turned. It was odd. He appeared to be limping. Perhaps one of the stones had hit him after all.

All the stars seemed to die.

From the depths of the crowd, a woman squealed spitefully: "He's just a great tall insolent child. A wicked child that needs whipping."

At that, the Piper turned back. His face was a white blank that seemed to have no features.

"Am I to be wicked for you?" he said softly. "Yes, perhaps I can be. I'd forgotten that. As for children. . . . I couldn't lead you aside from your ugly rat god. But it seems a pity to me your children should be enslaved to him, as you are. I think I will take your children away from you."

On the hill, empty of day, of winds, of stars, of kindness, the crowd trembled.

"Yes," said the Piper. "My fee. Not your gold, and not your love. Your children I'll have."

Someone whimpered.

Cleci stared, but the Piper was not on the hill any more.

Then she felt a sharp pinch on her arm. The miller's daughter hissed at her: "Why, you little thief. You've stolen my ribbon. Give it back, or my daddy will have you ducked in the river."

Cleci tore the blue ribbon from her waist and threw it at the miller's daughter. Cleci jumped up before she knew what she was doing. She ran away, up into the night-black vineyards.

The only light in the vineyards seemed to be Cleci's own dull whitish dress. No moon showed, and no stars. The black sky must be choked by black clouds. The vines hung around her, also black. Once she turned her foot, and looked down and saw a silvery thing. One of the priestesses' bells, dropped during the Procession.

The day seemed a hundred miles away, and she knew he was nearer. She had only, it seemed to her, to wish to find him, and she would do so. But she was afraid. She could not bear to find the Piper, though she had come looking for him. She cried, and rubbed her eyes on her hair and her sleeves, till the scent of her tears blotted out the sweet tang of the grapes.

"Don't cry," he said to her eventually, out of the dark.

"Why not," she said. "You have spoiled everything."

She was so afraid of him, she did not become any more afraid from speaking to him in this way, though she understood by then he was supernatural, and a god.

"I regret the spoiling," he said from the darkness, "but I would do it again."

"Why must we love you, and not Raur?" she demanded. "Why?"

"You know why. Of them all, you know."

"Yes . . . because he's only a stone. But you are—"

"Yes. I am."

"Then, what difference does it make to you?" she asked him, sensing omnipotence, fire, aeons, and all of them his.

"Because, quite simply, unless I am believed in, I shall die. And when I die, Cleci, some part of the spirit of humanity dies with me."

"Yes," she said. She sighed, and sat on the grass between the stocks. She could not see the grapes, or his hair. If she had been able to, they would have been the same red. "Couldn't you," she said, "perform some magic to convince them?"

"The magic is everywhere. They're not convinced. Water can be turned into wine, or blood. I shall have to die for them, before they believe in me."

"I believe in you," she said.

"I know you do. That is why I am here."

"But the children," she said. "You mustn't take the children away."

"I'll spare you," he said.

She said hotly, "I'm not a child."

When he laughed gently, she knew for sure how dangerous he was. The others had been determined not to know, averting their eyes from the truth of him. He was like a snake, coiled in the shadows, smooth as amber, with the bite of death in his mouth which had made music.

"You spoke of love, but you're cruel," she said.

"Yes. Love is cruel, when denied. I'm sorry for your village, but I would do that again, too, if it were to be done. I will be remembered. Somehow."

"They'll remember wrongly." She looked away into the vines and the night. She knew she would not see him physically anymore. "How," she said, "will you take the children? Will you play the pipe and make them follow you, as the dogs and rats followed you? Will you pipe them into the deep water below the ford and make them drown?"

"No, Cleci," he said. "It's easier, and more vile, than that. But still, recollect when you are older, I promised I would spare you, and I shall. Because you believed in me, and through you I can exist. A while longer."

"How long have you lived?" she murmured, dazed.

"I was born on the day the first men thought of me. I shall die on the last day, when the last man forgets."

She beheld his loneliness then, like a pale mote in the night. She stared at it, and pictured him, a god who was lonely and dying. And somewhere in that staring, sleep came, and the night folded itself behind the world.

When the sun rose, she got up and looked about her, and saw only the fields and the vinestocks, the shallow river, the dusty lindens, and the sprawling village. And when she had gone home alone, she saw the poverty of her mother's house. And when her mother slapped and cuffed her for being gone all night, and called her horrible names, Cleci saw that, too. Yet through it all she dimly perceived, as if through smoke or water, how the earth had been, and how it still might be, under its veil of misery and lies.

In the days which followed, and in the weeks which followed these, the Piper was spoken of in fear and whispers, and later in noisy jibes and sneers. No one heard the pipe, and soon no one listened for it. The children ran about the streets and yards, and along the river bank. Despite his threat, he had not taken the sons and daughters of Lime Tree. Not only was he a vagabond and blasphemer, but a charlatan also.

Not until the first still-births occurred at the summer's end, did any nervous awe steal through the prosperous village. And then, when winter had come, and spring and summer, and another summer's end, and no fresh births with them, only then did a leaden horror blow through Lime Tree like the winter winds. And like the winds, which stripped the lindens of their leaves, so Lime Tree lay under the snow, stripped of its future. No new life was conceived, or born, and would never be. He had said he would take their children, in place of their love and their gold, and he had done it. Lime Tree withered among its wheat fields, and year by year its crops grew thin, its vines tarnished, and, one by one, its lindens died.

When Cleci was eighteen, the river mysteriously silted up. That was the year her mother died, too. She died of hard work more than anything, for hard work does actually kill, when it is too hard, too hopeless, and has too meager a reward.

Cleci went away to the south, and some years later, when she had borne her first child, she carried him to the shrine she had made, and laid an offering on the altar—grapes, and a lock of her own dark hair, and a flask of wine. And, as each of her children grew, she taught them who they must worship.

She did this not out of fear of him, but out of pity. Because she had come to see the ultimate terrible truth behind all others. Which was that the stupidity and avarice and hatred of mankind had finally begun to make him also stupid, avaricious, hating, and cruel beyond reason. Even though he was a god, a god of love.

Red As Blood

The beautiful Witch Queen flung open the ivory case of the magic mirror. Of dark gold the mirror was, dark gold like the hair of the Witch Queen that poured down her back. Dark gold the mirror was, and ancient as the seven stunted black trees growing beyond the pale blue glass of the window.

"*Speculum, speculum,*" said the Witch Queen to the magic mirror. "*Dei gratia.*"

"*Volente Deo. Audio.*"

"Mirror," said the Witch Queen. "Whom do you see?"

"I see you, mistress," replied the mirror. "And all in the land. But one."

"Mirror, mirror, who is it you do not see?"

"I do not see Bianca."

The Witch Queen crossed herself. She shut the case of the mirror and, walking slowly to the window, looked out at the old trees through the panes of pale blue glass.

Fourteen years ago, another woman had stood at this window, but she was not like the Witch Queen. The woman had black hair that fell to her ankles; she had a crimson gown, the girdle worn high beneath her breasts, for she was far gone with child. And this woman had thrust open the glass casement on the winter garden, where the old trees crouched in the snow. Then, taking a sharp bone needle, she had thrust it into her finger and shaken three bright drops on the ground. "Let my daughter have," said the woman, "hair black as mine, black as the wood of these warped and arcane trees. Let her have skin like mine, white as this snow. And let her have my mouth, red as my blood." And the woman had smiled and licked at her finger. She had a crown on her head; it shone in the dusk like a star. She never came to the window before dusk: she did not like the day. She was the first Queen, and she did not possess a mirror.

The second Queen, the Witch Queen, knew all this. She knew how, in giving birth, the first Queen had died. Her coffin had been carried into the cathedral and masses had been said. There was an ugly rumor—that a splash of holy water had fallen on the corpse and the dead flesh had smoked. But the first Queen had been reckoned unlucky for the kingdom. There had been a plague in the land since she came there, a wasting disease for which there was no cure.

Seven years went by. The King married the second Queen, as unlike the first as frankincense to myrrh.

"And this is my daughter," said the King to his second Queen.

There stood a little girl child, nearly seven years of age. Her black hair hung to her ankles, her skin was white as snow. Her mouth was red as blood, and she smiled with it.

"Bianca," said the King, "you must love your new mother."

Bianca smiled radiantly. Her teeth were bright as sharp bone needles.

"Come," said the Witch Queen, "come, Bianca. I will show you my magic mirror."

"Please, Mamma," said Bianca softly, "I do not like mirrors."

"She is modest," said the King. "And delicate. She never goes out by day. The sun distresses her."

That night, the Witch Queen opened the case of her mirror.

"Mirror. Whom do you see?"

"I see you, mistress. And all in the land. But one."

"Mirror, mirror, who is it you do not see?"

"I do not see Bianca."

The second Queen gave Bianca a tiny crucifix of golden filigree. Bianca would not accept it. She ran to her father and whispered, "I am afraid. I do not like to think of Our Lord dying in agony on His cross. She means to frighten me. Tell her to take it away."

The second Queen grew wild white roses in her garden and invited Bianca to walk there after sundown. But Bianca shrank away. She whispered to her father, "The thorns will tear me. She means me to be hurt."

When Bianca was twelve years old, the Witch Queen said to the King, "Bianca should be confirmed so that she may take Communion with us."

"This may not be," said the King. "I will tell you, she has not been Christened, for the dying word of my first wife was against it. She begged me, for her religion was different from ours. The wishes of the dying must be respected."

"Should you not like to be blessed by the Church," said the Witch Queen to Bianca. "To kneel at the golden rail before the marble altar. To sing to God, to taste the ritual Bread and sip the ritual Wine."

"She means me to betray my true mother," said Bianca to the King. "When will she cease tormenting me?"

The day she was thirteen, Bianca rose from her bed, and there was a red stain there, like a red, red flower.

"Now you are a woman," said her nurse.

"Yes," said Bianca. And she went to her true mother's jewel box, and out of it she took her mother's crown and set it on her head.

When she walked under the old black trees in the dusk, the crown shone like a star.

The wasting sickness, which had left the land in peace for thirteen years, suddenly began again, and there was no cure.

The Witch Queen sat in a tall chair before a window of pale green and dark white glass, and in her hands she held a Bible bound in rosy silk.

"Majesty," said the huntsman, bowing very low.

He was a man, forty years old, strong and handsome, and wise in the hidden lore of the forests, the occult lore of the earth. He could kill too, for it was his trade, without faltering. The slender fragile deer he could kill, and the moon-winged birds, and the velvet hares with their sad, foreknowing eyes. He pitied them, but pitying, he killed them. Pity could not stop him. It was his trade.

"Look in the garden," said the Witch Queen.

The hunter looked through a dark white pane. The sun had sunk, and a maiden walked under a tree.

"The Princess Bianca," said the huntsman.

"What else?" asked the Witch Queen.

The huntsman crossed himself.

"By Our Lord, Madam, I will not say."

"But you know."

"Who does not?"

"The King does not."

"Nor he does."

"Are you a brave man?" asked the Witch Queen.

"In the summer, I have hunted and slain boar. I have slaughtered wolves in winter."

"But are you brave enough?"

"If you command it, Lady," said the huntsman, "I will try my best."

The Witch Queen opened the Bible at a certain place, and out of it she drew a flat silver crucifix, which had been resting against the words: *Thou shalt not be afraid for the terror by night. . . . Nor for the pestilence that walketh in darkness.*

The huntsman kissed the crucifix and put it about his neck beneath his shirt.

"Approach," said the Witch Queen, "and I will instruct you in what to say."

Presently, the huntsman entered the garden, as the stars were burning up in the sky. He strode to where Bianca stood under a stunted dwarf tree, and he kneeled down.

"Princess," he said, "pardon me, but I must give you ill tidings."

"Give them then," said the girl, toying with the long stem of a wan, night-growing flower which she had plucked.

"Your stepmother, the accursed jealous witch, means to have you slain. There is no help for it but you must fly the palace this very night. If you permit, I will guide you to the forest. There are those who will care for you until it may be safe for you to return."

Bianca watched him, but gently trustingly.

"I will go with you, then," she said.

They went by a secret way out of the garden, through a

passage under the ground, through a tangled orchard, by a broken road between great over-grown hedges.

Night was a pulse of deep, flickering blue when they came to the forest. The branches of the forest overlapped and intertwined, like leading in a window, and the sky gleamed dimly through like panes of blue-colored glass.

"I am weary," sighed Bianca. "May I rest a moment?"

"By all means," said the huntsman. "In the clearing there, foxes come to play by night. Look in that direction, and you will see them."

"How clever you are," said Bianca. "And how handsome." She sat on the turf and gazed at the clearing.

The huntsman drew his knife silently and concealed it in the folds of his cloak. He stooped above the maiden.

"What are you whispering?" demanded the huntsman, laying his hand on her wood-black hair.

"Only a rhyme my mother taught me."

The huntsman seized her by the hair and swung her about so her white throat was before him, stretched ready for the knife. But he did not strike, for there in his hand he held the dark golden locks of the Witch Queen, and her face laughed up at him, and she flung her arms about him, laughing.

"Good man, sweet man, it was only a test of you. Am I not a witch? And do you not love me?"

The huntsman trembled, for he did love her, and she was pressed so close her heart seemed to beat within his own body.

"Put away the knife. Throw away the silly crucifix. We have no need of these things. The King is not one half the man you are."

And the huntsman obeyed her, throwing the knife and the crucifix far off among the roots of the trees. He gripped her to him and she buried her face in his neck, and the pain of her kiss was the last thing he felt in this world.

The sky was black now. The forest was blacker. No foxes played in the clearing. The moon rose and made white lace through the boughs, and through the backs of the huntsman's empty eyes. Bianca wiped her mouth on a dead flower.

"Seven asleep, seven awake," said Bianca. "Wood to wood. Blood to blood. Thee to me."

There came a sound like seven huge rendings, distant by the length of several trees, a broken road, an orchard, an underground passage. Then a sound like seven huge single footfalls. Nearer. And nearer.

Hop, hop, hop, hop. Hop, hop, hop.

In the orchard, seven black shudderings.

On the broken road, between the high hedges, seven black creepings.

Brush crackled, branches snapped.

Through the forest, into the clearing, pushed seven warped, mis-shapen, hunched-over, stunted things. Woody-black mossy fur, woody-black bald masks. Eyes like glittering cracks, mouths like moist caverns. Lichen beards. Fingers of twiggy gristle. Grinning. Kneeling. Faces pressed to the earth.

"Welcome," said Bianca.

The Witch Queen stood before a window of glass like diluted wine. She looked at the magic mirror.

"Mirror. Whom do you see?"

"I see you, mistress. I see a man in the forest. He went hunting, but not for deer. His eyes are open, but he is dead. I see all in the land. But one."

The Witch Queen pressed her palms to her ears.

Outside the window, the garden lay, empty of its seven black and stunted dwarf trees.

"Bianca," said the Queen.

The windows had been draped and gave no light. The light spilled from a shallow vessel, light in a sheaf, like pastel wheat. It glowed upon four swords that pointed east and west, that pointed north and south.

Four winds had burst through the chamber, and the grey-silver powders of Time.

The hands of the Witch Queen floated like folded leaves on the air, and through the dry lips the Witch Queen chanted:

"*Pater omnipotens, mitere digneris sanctum Angelum tuum de Infernis.*"

The light faded, and grew brighter.

There, between the hilts of the four swords, stood the Angel Lucefiel, somberly gilded, his face in shadow, his golden wings spread and glazing at his back.

"Since you have called me, I know your desire. It is a comfortless wish. You ask for pain."

"You speak of pain, Lord Lucefiel, who suffer the most

merciless pain of all. Worse than the nails in the feet and wrists. Worse than the thorns and the bitter cup and the blade in the side. To be called upon for evil's sake, which I do not, comprehending your true nature, son of God, brother of The Son."

"You recognize me, then. I will grant what you ask."

And Lucefiel (by some named Satan, Rex Mundi, but nevertheless the left hand, the sinister hand of God's design) wrenched lightning from the ether and cast it at the Witch Queen.

It caught her in the breast. She fell.

The sheaf of light towered and lit the golden eyes of the Angel, which were terrible, yet luminous with compassion, as the swords shattered and he vanished.

The Witch Queen pulled herself from the floor of the chamber, no longer beautiful, a withered, slobbering hag.

Into the core of the forest, even at noon, the sun never shone. Flowers propagated in the grass, but they were colorless. Above, the black-green roof hung down nets of thick green twilight through which albino butterflies and moths feverishly drizzled. The trunks of the trees were smooth as the stalks of underwater weeds. Bats flew in the daytime, and birds who believed themselves to be bats.

There was a sepulcher, dripped with moss. The bones had been rolled out, had rolled around the feet of seven twisted dwarf trees. They looked like trees. Sometimes they moved. Sometimes something like an eye glittered, or a tooth, in the wet shadows.

In the shade of the sepulcher door sat Bianca, combing her hair.

A lurch of motion disturbed the thick twilight.

The seven trees turned their heads.

A hag emerged from the forest. She was crook-backed, and her head was poked forward, predatory, withered and almost hairless, like a vulture's.

"Here we are at last," grated the hag, in a vulture's voice.

She came closer and cranked herself down on her knees and bowed her face into the turf and the colorless flowers.

Bianca sat and gazed at her. The hag lifted herself. Her teeth were yellow palings.

"I bring you the homage of witches, and three gifts," said the hag.

"Why should you do that?"

"Such a quick child, and only fourteen years. Why? Because we fear you. I bring you gifts to curry favor."

Bianca laughed. "Show me."

The hag made a pass in the green air. She held a silken cord worked curiously with a plaited human hair.

"Here is a girdle which will protect you from the devices of priests, from crucifix and chalice and the accursed holy water. In it are knotted the tresses of a virgin, and of a woman no better than she should be, and of a woman dead. And here—" a second pass and a comb was in her hand, lacquered blue over green— "a comb from the deep sea, a mermaid's trinket, to charm and subdue. Part your locks with this, and the scent of ocean will fill men's nostrils and the rhythm of the tides their ears, the tides that bind men like chains. Last," added the hag, "that old symbol of wickedness, the scarlet fruit of Eve, the apple red as blood. Bite, and the understanding of Sin, which the serpent boasted of, will be made known to you." And the hag made her last pass in the air and extended the apple, with the girdle and the comb, towards Bianca.

Bianca glanced at the seven stunted trees.

"I like her gifts, but I do not quite trust her."

The bald masks peered from their shaggy beardings. Eyelets glinted. Twiggy claws clacked.

"All the same," said Bianca, "I will let her tie the girdle on me, and comb my hair herself."

The hag obeyed, simpering. Like a toad she waddled to Bianca. She tied on the girdle. She parted the ebony hair. Sparks sizzled, white from the girdle, peacock's eye from the comb.

"And now, hag, take a little bit bite of the apple."

"It will be my pride," said the hag, "to tell my sisters I shared this fruit with you." And the hag bit into the apple, and mumbled the bite noisily, and swallowed, smacking her lips.

Then Bianca took the apple and bit into it.

Bianca screamed—and choked.

She jumped to her feet. Her hair whirled about her like a storm cloud. Her face turned blue, then slate, then white again. She lay on the pallid flowers, neither stirring nor breathing.

The seven dwarf trees rattled their limbs and their bear-shaggy heads, to no avail. Without Bianca's art they could not hop. They strained thier claws and ripped at the hag's sparse hair and her mantle. She fled between them. She fled into the sunlit acres of the forest, along the broken road, through orchard, into a hidden passage.

The hag reentered the palace by the hidden way, and the Queen's chamber by a hidden stair. She was bent almost double. She held her ribs. With one skinny hand she opened the ivory case of the magic mirror.

"*Speculum, speculum. Dei gratia.* Whom do you see?"

"I see you, mistress. And all in the land. And I see a coffin."

"Whose corpse lies in the coffin?"

"That I cannot see. It must be Bianca."

The hag, who had been the beautiful Witch Queen, sank into her tall chair before the window of pale cucumber green and dark white glass. Her drugs and potions waited ready to reverse the dreadful conjuring of age the Angel Lucefiel had placed on her, but she did not touch them yet.

The apple had contained a fragment of the flesh of Christ, the sacred wafer, the Eucharist.

The Witch Queen drew her Bible to her and opened it randomly.

And read, with fear, the words: *Resurgat.*

It appeared like glass, the coffin, milky glass. It had formed this way. A thin white smoke had risen from the skin of Bianca. She smoked as a fire smokes when a drop of quenching water falls on it. The piece of Eucharist had stuck in her throat. The Eucharist, quenching water to her fire, caused her to smoke.

Then the cold dews of night gathered, and the colder atmospheres of midnight. The smoke of Bianca's quenching froze about her. Frost formed in exquisite silver scrollwork all over the block of misty ice which contained Bianca.

Bianca's frigid heart could not warm the ice. Nor the sunless green twilight of the day.

You could just see her, stretched in the coffin, through the glass. How lovely she looked, Bianca. Black as ebony, white as snow, red as blood.

The trees hung over the coffin. Years passed. The trees sprawled about the coffin, cradling it in their arms. Their eyes wept fungus and green resin. Green amber drops hardened like jewels in the coffin of glass.

"Who is that, lying under the trees?" the Prince asked, as he rode into the clearing.

He seemed to bring a golden moon with him, shining about his golden head, on the golden armor and the cloak of white satin blazoned with gold and blood and ink and sapphire. The white horse trod on the colorless flowers, but the flowers sprang up again when the hoofs had passed. A shield hung from the saddle bow, a strange shield. From one side it had a lion's face, but from the other, a lamb's face.

The trees groaned and their heads split on huge mouths.

"Is this Bianca's coffin?" said the Prince.

"Leave her with us," said the seven trees. They hauled at their roots. The ground shivered. The coffin of ice-glass gave a great jolt, and a crack bisected it.

Bianca coughed.

The jolt had precipitated the piece of Eucharist from her throat.

In a thousand shards the coffin shattered, and Bianca sat up. She stared at the Prince, and she smiled.

"Welcome, beloved," said Bianca.

She got to her feet and shook out her hair, and began to walk toward the Prince on the pale horse.

But she seemed to walk into a shadow, into a purple room; then into a crimson room whose emanations lanced her like knives. Next she walked into a yellow room where she heard the sound of crying which tore her ears. All her body seemed stripped away; she was a beating heart. The beats of her heart became two wings. She flew. She was a raven, then an owl. She flew into a sparkling pane. It scorched her white. Snow white. She was a dove.

She settled on the shoulder of the Prince and hid her head under her wing. She had no longer anything black about her, and nothing red.

"Begin again now, Bianca," said the Prince. He raised her from his shoulder. On his wrist there was a mark. It was like a star. Once a nail had been driven in there.

Bianca flew away, up through the roof of the forest. She flew in at a delicate wine window. She was in the palace. She was seven years old.

The Witch Queen, her new mother, hung a filigree crucifix around her neck. "Mirror," said the Witch Queen. "Whom do you see?"

"I see you, mistress," replied the mirror. "And all in the land. I see Bianca."

Thorns

It was almost sunset when he met the dark woman on the road.

He'd been traveling for most of his eighteen years, across the dry orange lands in the west, the plains and green forests of the east and in wide-sailed ships on the back of uneasy, spiteful seas. Sometimes he rode with caravans and helped sell their wares, sometimes he'd stop at some great city or poor town and work for a bit, driving the chariot horses of lords, or else chopping up wood, whatever they'd pay him for. He had seen a good many strange things—huge beasts with gold towers on their backs, carrying kings, a serpent lady in a circus, scaled from chin to ankle; even once, in an Eastern city, a man brought back to life. But there was something about the dark woman standing on the road that tensed his muscles and shivered his spine.

She was all black cloak and black hair blowing on the chilly upland wind, and somehow, though he looked straight in her face, he could never seem to see it properly, although perhaps this was a trick of the westering light.

She was standing in his path, and when he came up level with her, one long pale hand snaked out and grasped his arm. He didn't like her touch, it was very cold. She said:

"Where are you going, Royal Born?"

At that, he knew he was in the presence of something supernatural, for there was no other way she could have known he had once been a king's son. Nevertheless he said lightly: "You're mistaken, madam. Take a look at my rags."

"There was a towered palace in the north, sacked by enemies, and a little prince carried to safety by a serving man. Now the prince travels the world, having no birthright left, and you are he."

The hair seemed to rise on his head and he looked down at her hand. On one long white claw burned a strange ring, made of silver, and shaped like a wheel.

"I shall give you land," she said, "and riches, if you go no farther. You shall be royal again. I promise you."

He looked up the road to that parting in the hills he had been making for since noon.

"Why?" he asked.

"There is a thing there I would rather were left alone."

He realized then, of course, that if she had been able to stop him by sorcery she would already have done so, and not be trying to dissuade him here. So he shook off her hand and said: "That's a thing I'd like to see."

She made no further move to detain him, but he never looked back till he reached the road's crest where the rocky uplands fell away into a narrow valley below. Then he turned, but there was nothing on the road behind—except for a tall black stone standing on the path.

As it turned out, it was a dismal and infertile valley. Perhaps if he'd not met the dark woman, he'd have left it alone, for it seemed to offer little.

The sky went up in a last blaze of scarlet, and a wood of dead trees wailed in the wind. He saw a few poor huts, but no sign of life in them, and the clouds changed from red to violet. Just then he heard the noise of water. He was thirsty, as well as hungry—hunger he was very used to. He came out of the wood, and found himself suddenly on the brink of a great slope. Here a stream flung itself off from its bed into the air, plunging down two hundred feet in a slender silver fall. Below stretched an inner secret valley, hidden from the hills above. And in the valley something gleamed like the ivory bones of a giant under the whitening moon.

The prince drank swiftly at the stream. There was a curious compulsion on him. As the night darkened and the moon brightened, he climbed down the treacherous slope. Eventually he stood on the outskirts of a ruined city.

It was the most beautiful city he had ever seen, perhaps because it was empty and desolate. The wind curled itself about the slim white towers and runneled down the colonades, and the stars glittered on fragments of colored glass still spiking in the narrow windows. At its center rose a low hill that seemed to be covered by a wood of some sort, he couldn't be sure, for the moon had slunk behind clouds—perhaps the place was a park or garden run wild.

He walked about in the city for an hour, and by then its beauty had begun to oppress him. Finally the sky clouded completely, thunder muttered and rain began to fall. He picked a way over toppled columns and emerged into a tangle of pine woods. All the trees seemed crippled and curiously leaning, but after a time he came on a straggling village, and there were lights showing.

The moment he got near, all the watch dogs started barking and snarling. Almost immediately doors opened and men ran out. Clearly they distrusted strangers. In the murky light he noticed something very odd. Not one of them had a knife, only thick wooden stakes angled at him.

He'd thought from his welcome they'd prove unfriendly and send him away, probably with the dogs to see him off, but they seemed satisfied by his explanation of himself, and when he offered to help with anything they might need doing—in their fields or their houses, or chopping their wood—they seemed to warm to him. He was shown into the headman's house—a rough botched affair like all the rest—and given food, and beer to drink.

But the longer he sat there, the stranger things seemed. They gave him no knife, either, to eat his meat with. The garments of the men and the women were made of animal skins, unmended and full of rents, and bundled round them and tied with tough grass stems, dried and plaited together. There was not a scrap of wool or cloth to be seen. Later on he got a look at their work tools and was astonished to find them made of stone, even to the blade of the axe—he saw now why they were so pleased to have someone else labor with it for a change. He asked the headman about this, and he looked puzzled, and said that it was the same all through the valley.

"Do traders never come here?" asked the prince.

"Oh, seldom, sir. You're the first we've seen in a year or more."

The headman's daughter said sullenly: "Once a man came with colored stones that sparkled and they were on a sharp little stick that would go through clothes like so—but Old Man told me it was bad luck, so I had to give it back."

The prince glanced aside at the one they called Old Man, a hunched-over grandfather sitting close to the fire. He had turned his wrinkled face to look at the girl when she spoke. Now he chanted in a dry, quavering tone: "No needle, no needle, no blade and no dart."

"It's just his way," said the headman uneasily. "He'll say that from time to time. But it's best to be careful. No sharp things must come into the valley—that's what all the old ones say."

The prince felt the hair stir again on his head. He looked about the room, and realized at last what was so wrong. Not only were there no knives, but no brooches on the women's dresses or ornamental pins in their hair. And there was not one sewn-up seam in their clothing. He saw, too, why they wore skins—somehow they had never learnt—or else they had forgotten. . . . He had recalled what was the most important item of every dwelling. You would always find it somewhere, in the corner of a village cot, in the upper rooms of the rich woman's house. A spinning wheel.

When they had gone to bed, the prince lay down by the fire on the hides they had lent him. But he couldn't sleep, and presently he heard the shuffling steps of the one they called Old Man coming back across the red-glowing room. Old Man stood over him and the prince sat up.

"Tell me, grandfather, why no spinning wheel to grace this house?"

"Nothing sharp, nothing sharp, no needle, no dart," Old Man chanted.

"Why not?"

"Death will come and the curse will fall, and the city will lie empty."

"Which curse is that, old man?"

"She will send it, the dark one, the Thirteenth Lady."

The prince grew very cold, despite the fire.

"It already came, grandfather."

"Thorns!" the old man suddenly cried out in a sharp and startling wail. "Thorns! Thorns! Thorns!" Then he bowed his head and whispered like a dry old leaf: "Seek the Oldest One, in the city. He will be there."

He turned then, and shuffled away. The prince lay down, and a black, dank shadow seemed to eat up the room. He fell at once into a deathlike and unbroken sleep.

In the morning he did what he could with the stone axe to repay them for his lodging. It was an icy but somehow airless day, and the pines craned about him like black shadows.

At noon he set off back through the trees towards the city, and, as he went, he heard every dog in the village begin to howl.

Why he went toward the city he was not sure. Perhaps he intended to search out in the ruins the 'Oldest One' the grandfather had whispered of—yet how he would find him he had no notion. Besides, he was uncertain altogether—he might have dreamed that dark conversation, even the black-haired woman on the road, the Thirteenth Lady with her silver wheel ring.

In the city everything was as before in the pale cold daylight, except that now he could see the colors of the glass in the windows, red and gold and indigo. Then he looked up, and stared again at that central hill, covered by its black, thickly-clustered growth. The sense of compulsion came once more. "There is a thing there I would rather were left alone," the sorceress had said to him on the road. He began to climb the slanting streets towards the hill.

Another storm came sweeping over the valley as he climbed. The sky went black, dazzling with green lightning forks, and he hurried with his head bowed against the rain. Turning a corner, he came upon a huge circular wall, the boundary of some great house or palace in earlier times. He moved along in its sheltering lee, and then there was a pair of rusty gates. He pushed at them and they slewed apart. As he went between, the lightning opened the sky, and its livid fire burst on a solid shining darkness, and threw over him a shadow as black as ink. Slowly he raised his head, and saw then what grew on the hill.

Thorns.

A vast, rearing stronghold of thorns, taller than tall trees, black as night, thick stems interwoven and sharp with blades. A tangle of daggers dripping the diamond rain. The prince gazed at it and his heart lurched. He felt the cold hand close again on his arm. Strewn among the knots and claws were white human bones, and further on a skull hung like an open rose. A mad impulse took hold of him when he saw the skull; he drew his knife and raised it to slash at the thorns. A voice came then, behind him.

"No, Royal Born. Not yet."

The prince turned about, still holding the knife. A man stood in the gateway. He wore skins like the people of the village, and he leaned on a wooden staff. He was old, older than Old Man. The flesh of his face and hands was like lizard skin or tree bark.

"I mean you no harm, Royal Born," he said in a voice as thin and as penetrating as the wind. "I am the Oldest One in the valley. I remember things, and I have waited for you."

"What is this place?" The prince cried out over the thunder.

"A place of thorns," said the Oldest One.

Then he turned and moved down the street without a word, and without a word the prince followed him.

He lived in the lowest room of a thin tower, and he had few belongings: a lamp, a pallet and a little wooden chest. The chest caught the prince's eye at once, for it was intricately carved and would have needed sharper tools than stone. A few pine branches burned on the hearth.

"You said you waited for me," the prince said, "yet how could you know me?"

"You are of no importance except that you are Royal Born. This I could see, having a gift for such things. One who is Royal Born was expected."

"Why? And for what?"

"To enter the place you saw, and to go in to what lies beyond the briars."

"What, then, lies there?"

"Ah," The Oldest One smiled, and his wrinkled skin moved on his face like sea waves. "I know only what was said, this being what my father told me. If you would care to listen, I'll tell you as much.

"Well then. I was born at sunset on a strange day. It was

the day the curse fell upon the valley. The nature of the curse is vague—it had to do with the Thirteenth Lady, the dark sorceress, and with a needle. For some sixteen years before my birth the king had allowed no sharp object into the valley—not an axe or a knife, not even a pin. And he had made a great bonfire and burned every spinning wheel in his kingdom on it. After which anyone who defied the law was put to death. I know nothing of the curse beyond this, except that on the day of my birth, at the very same moment that I arrived in the world, the curse came about, despite every precaution. Immediately a wall of thorns sprang up about the place. My father and his neighbours saw it happen. The thorns twisted and turned and threaded together until the topmost towers of the palace could no longer be seen. No one could get in, and no one out. The city sent for help. Kings' sons came, for it was said that only one Royal Born could cleave through the thorn wall. But the thorns impaled them and they died horribly. As you have seen, their bones hang there yet. After a few years the people abandoned the city. It was a place full of ghosts and fear. The walls cracked and the roofs fell in until it was as you find it now. Only my father and mother remained, and I, their child. I have outlived them, and I have known no other life than waiting for the last Royal Born."

"But how can you know who will be the last?" the prince asked, very low.

"That was the softening of the curse. After a hundred years it might be broken if there were any man here to dare it."

"You stayed my hand," the prince said.

"Yes, for it was not the time. When the sun sinks tonight beyond the hills, that will be as the hour of my birth and the hour of the curse. I shall be a hundred years old at sunset."

All through the afternoon the rain darted and rang on the stones of the city. But at last the sky cleared and turned golden, and the sun rested like a great red lamp on the crown of the hills.

"Now it is the time," said the Oldest One, and the prince rose. It was very chill and his arm burned coldly where the dark woman had touched it.

"What shall I find?" he asked, as he stood in the doorway.

"Suppose I should only turn away, and leave the valley by the quickest route?"

"You know you can never do that till you've seen. As to what you will find, they said something beautiful lies asleep there, but it was seldom spoken of. I scarcely know."

It was very silent when he walked back up the slanting street. He paused at the rusty gate, and the bones rattled on the briars. He drew his knife, as before, and took a step inside.

The great thorn stems writhed and twisted, though there was then no wind, and the barbs clashed together with a sound of battle.

He raised his blade and struck at them.

He'd come to expect, by that time, almost anything, and so was not surprised. The thorn wall broke apart before him and curled aside, forming a long avenue stretching away and away into a dim gloomy distance. He hesitated a moment. If he went up the path offered, the wall might easily spring back about him, and he would suffer the fate of all the rest. But something seemed to pull him on. He could no longer hang back. The shadow of the thorns fell over him but the avenue did not close up, though the stems thrashed about like angry serpents on either side.

Underfoot the soil was grey. The thorns had drained it. For a long time there were only the moving latticed shadows and the grey soil, and then a pale light glowed in front of him. It was the end of the briar tunnel. He ran toward it, and suddenly came out into the lavender gloaming. Immediately, with a terrible sound, the thorns closed ranks behind him, but there was no room left in him for alarm.

He was on a marble terrace which rose in marble steps to an incredible garden above. Dark green trees had been pruned into the shapes of birds and animals, fountains jetted into porphyry basins and a thousand roses bloomed. Not a leaf moved. The flowers were like things made of wax, and the water of the fountains stayed quite still like threads of crystal suspended in mid air. The prince climbed the steps and stood in the garden mystified and troubled, and ahead rose the vast pile of a palace with pointing milk-white towers. Taking one deep breath, he began to walk toward it.

On the trees birds sat, their beaks open in silent song. He came upon a garland of doves with spread wings simply hanging impossibly in the air, and on a lawn a springing cat with its paws several inches from the ground, quite motionless.

The doors of the palace were open as if something had rushed through them and blown them wide. Inside, soldiers with glaring eyes stood to attention down the length of the great hall. Pages were transfixed in the act of moving with their trays of sweets, and graceful women and proud men were posed in all manner of gestures, some laughing with their heads thrown back, the dim light glinting on their teeth, others frowning or yawning as they must have done for a hundred years. The prince noted that these people had kept their velvets and silks, though there were no hair pins or brooches, and the soldiers carried stone clubs at their belts.

He came to two thrones of gold, and here sat a king and a queen. Her face was sad and pale, his harsh and cruel. It seemed they had guessed at the last instant that the curse had fallen after all. Huge nets of cobwebs drifted over everything, caught between the golden chandeliers, the lion feet of the chairs, the fingers of the king. They alone moved. An enamel clock stood in a corner, but its hands had fallen off and lay on the floor, for in this place time had stopped.

The prince went from room to room, seeking something out, he didn't know what.

On the marble staircase a servant was lighting lamps, and the flare of his taper stood up like a piece of yellow ice, not flickering.

The prince came into the upper rooms, and here the twilight fell very thick, like the dust. He came to a strange, narrow, dark door, and pushed it open. There was a waiting lady here, her hands frozen at her mouth which was open on a soundless scream, and her eyes wide in terror. He looked where she was looking, up a twisting ugly stair to a half-open door at the top.

He ran up the steps and threw open the door.

It was a long narrow gallery, mostly pitch black, yet lit at the centre by a shivering grey light. The first thing he saw there was the spinning wheel which gave off this light. It was all silver, even to the wheel, which, as he took half a step into the room, began suddenly to whirl round so fast and so angrily that hissing white sparks flew off it and burst in the air. It gave out a sawing spitting noise, but he came on toward it, for like the thorns it seemed to have no power to harm him.

When he passed it by he glanced down and saw that on the tip of the wicked needle rested a single ruby—one drop of human blood.

A thick mesh of cobwebs hung behind the spinning wheel. He thrust through them and stopped dead still, for he knew he had found what he came for.

There was a great carved bed, hung with black velvet. On the curtains was embroidered many times the symbol of the silver wheel the sorceress had worn on her hand, and at the front of the canopy was a silver shield. Written on this shield in scarlet letters were the words:

MY FINAL GIFT TO HER

HER DEATH BED

His heart thudding in slow heavy hammer strokes, the prince walked up to the bed and looked down at what lay there.

She was more beautiful than anything he had ever seen.

She wore white silk, with diamonds at her throat, but she shone more brightly. Her hands were like white feathers on the black velvet bed, her skin like lampshine through alabaster, but her hair was light itself.

The prince stared at her and did not know what he must do. For she was quite still and unmoving, and more marvelous than any of the wonders he had ever seen. She did not even breathe.

Then it came to him, that miracle in an Eastern city, when he had seen a man brought back to life.

It seemed quite wrong that he should even touch her, she looked so peaceful. Yet it seemed also important that he had remembered at this moment how the thing was done. So he set his feelings aside and leaned down and placed his mouth on hers, and blew into her lungs the breath of life, as he had seen the priest do it. At first her ribcage rose and fell only with his breath, but presently she gave a deep sigh and he let her go. Her eyelids fluttered and lifted, and she looked at him and smiled.

"Welcome, Royal Born," she said. "So you came as they said you would."

At that the whirling thing shot off from the body of the spinning wheel and cracked in a thousand pieces like glass. It was strange. He had never really been afraid until she woke, and looked at him. Then fear began.

She led him down into the hall where now all the lamps flickered gold. The people moved rustily, and stared about like ghosts. They were so old, and yet they had hardly lived at all. The king and queen drew her into their embraces, moving like puppets, and then there was a feast.

They sat at the long tables, among the drifting cobwebs, and ate the roast meats and the peaches that had kept perfect for a hundred years, and they spoke in slow, hollow voices of all the things that had been a hundred years before and were no longer, though they did not know.

It filled the prince with terrible icy melancholy.

Even she, his princess, sitting at his side, seemed to be looking up at him out of her beautiful eyes through the dull waters of an ocean—the century which was between them.

Near dawn, when the sad weird figures still moved in their old forgotten dances in the hall, he drew her out into the garden. Beyond the animal trees and the fountains he saw that all the thorns had withered and fallen into dust, which now blew about the hill. For a long while the palace of the king would be surrounded by a desert of black dunes. He took her hand, which felt unreal, like the hand of a doll, and said, "Madam, I can't stay with you."

"This I know," she said. "I saw it in your face at once." She didn't weep, or frown, but she murmured: "After all, I am still asleep. I shall never be awake again."

He tried to comfort her, but it was no use and he saw it, and her pride, so he kissed her gently and went away as the sun was rising.

He didn't look for the Oldest Man in the city. He looked neither left nor right till he was out of the valley, and then he did not look back.

On the road the black stone was still standing up, and there was a raven perched on it which stared at him with silver eyes.

"So, after all, you had the last laugh, Thirteenth Lady," he said to it. "You were more clever than you thought."

But the bird flew up into the wide clear sky without a sound.

When The Clock Strikes

Yes, the great ballroom is filled only with dust now. The slender columns of white marble and the slender columns of rose-red marble are woven together by cobwebs. The vivid frescoes, on which the Duke's treasury spent so much, are dimmed by the dust; the faces of the painted goddesses look grey. And the velvet curtains—touch them, they will crumble. Two hundred years now, since anyone danced in this place on the sea-green floor in the candle-gleam. Two hundred years since the wonderful clock struck for the very last time.

I thought you might care to examine the clock. It was considered exceptional in its day. The pedestal is ebony and the face fine porcelain. And these figures, which are of silver, would pass slowly about the circlet of the face. Each figure represents, you understand, an hour. And as the appropriate hours came level with this golden bell, they would strike it the correct number of times. All the figures are unique, as you see. Beginning at the first hour, they are, in this order, a girl-child, a dwarf, a maiden, a youth, a lady and a knight. And here, notice, the figures grow older as the day declines: a queen and king for the seventh and eighth hours, and after these, an abbess and a magician and next to last, a hag. But the very last is strangest of all. The twelfth figure; do you recognize him? It is Death. Yes, a most curious clock. It was reckoned a marvelous thing then. But it has not struck for two hundred years. Possibly you have been told the story? No? Oh, but I am certain that you have heard it, in another form, perhaps.

However, as you have some while to wait for your carriage, I will recount the tale, if you wish.

I will start with what was said of the clock. In those years, this city was prosperous, a stronghold—not as you see it today. Much was made in the city that was ornamental and unusual. But the clock, on which the twelfth hour was Death, caused something of a stir. It was thought unlucky, foolhardy, to have such a clock. It began to murmured, jokingly by some, by others in earnest, that one night when the clock struck the twelfth hour, Death would truly strike with it.

Now life has always been a chancy business, and it was more so then. The Great Plague had come but twenty years before and was not yet forgotten. Besides, in the Duke's court there was much intrigue, while enemies might be supposed to plot beyond the city walls, as happens even in our present age. But there was another thing.

It was rumored that the Duke had obtained both his title and the city treacherously. Rumor declared that he had systematically destroyed those who had stood in line before him, the members of the princely house that formerly ruled here. He had accomplished the task slyly, hiring assassins talented with poisons and daggers. But rumor also declared that the Duke had not been sufficiently thorough. For though he had meant to rid himself of all that rival house, a single decendant remained, so obscure he had not traced her—for it was a woman.

Of course, such matters were not spoken of openly. Like the prophecy of the clock, it was a subject for the dark.

Nevertheless, I will tell you at once, there was such a descendant he had missed in his bloody work. And she was a woman. Royal and proud she was, and seething with bitter spite and a hunger for vengeance, and as bloody as the Duke, had he known it, in her own way.

For her safety and disguise, she had long ago wed a wealthy merchant in the city, and presently bore the man a daughter. The merchant, a dealer in silks, was respected, a good fellow but not wise. He rejoiced in his handsome and aristocratic wife. He never dreamed what she might be about when he was not with her. In fact, she had sworn allegiance to Satanas. In the dead of night she would go up into an old tower adjoining the merchant's house, and there she would say portions of the Black Mass, offer sacrifice, and thereafter practise witchcraft against the Duke. This witchery took a common form, the creation of a wax image and the maiming of the image that, by sympathy, the injuries inflicted on the wax be passed on to the living body of the victim. The woman was capable in what she did. The Duke fell sick. He lost the use of his limbs and was racked by excruciating pains from which he could get no relief. Thinking himself on the brink of death, the Duke named his sixteen-year-old son his heir. This son was dear to the Duke, as everyone knew, and be sure the woman knew it too. She intended sorcerously to murder the young man in his turn, preferably in his father's sight. Thus, she let the Duke linger in his agony, and commenced planning the fate of the prince.

Now all this while she had not been toiling alone. She had one helper. It was her own daughter, a maid of fourteen, that she had recruited to her service nearly as soon as the infant could walk. At six or seven, the child had been lisping the satanic rite along with her mother. At fourteen, you may imagine, the girl was well versed in the Black Arts, though she did not have her mother's natural genius for them.

Perhaps you would like me to describe the daughter at this point. It has a bearing on the story, for the girl was astonishingly beautiful. Her hair was the rich dark red of antique burnished copper, her eyes were the hue of the reddish-golden amber that traders bring from the East. When she walked, you would say she was dancing. But when she danced, a gate seemed to open in the world, and bright fire spangled inside it, but she was the fire.

The girl and her mother were close as gloves in a box. Their games in the old tower bound them closer. No doubt the woman believed herself clever to have got such a helpmate, but it proved her undoing.

It was in this manner. The silk merchant, who had never suspected his wife for an instant of anything, began to mistrust the daughter. She was not like other girls. Despite her great beauty, she professed no interest in marriage, and none in clothes or jewels. She preferred to read in the garden at the foot of the tower. Her mother had taught the girl her letters, though the merchant himself could read but poorly. And often the father peered at the books his daughter read, unable to make head or tail of them, yet somehow not liking them. One night very late, the silk merchant came home from a guild dinner in the city, and he saw a slim pale shadow gliding up the steps of the old tower, and he knew it for his child. On impulse, he followed her, but quietly. He had not considered any evil so far, and did not want to alarm her. At an angle of the stair, the lighted room above, he paused to spy and listen. He had something of a shock when he heard his wife's voice rise up in glad welcome. But what came next drained the blood from his heart. He crept away and went to his cellar for wine to stay himself. After the third glass he ran for neighbours and for the watch.

The woman and her daughter heard the shouts below and saw the torches in the garden. It was no use dissembling. The tower was littered with evidence of vile deeds, besides what the woman kept in a chest beneath her unknowing husband's bed. She understood it was all up with her, and she understood too how witchcraft was punished hereabouts. She snatched a knife from the altar.

The girl shrieked when she realized what her mother was at. The woman caught the girl by her red hair and shook her.

"Listen to me, my daughter," she cried, "and listen carefully, for the minutes are short. If you do as I tell you, you can escape their wrath and only I need die. And if you live I am satisfied, for you can carry on my labor after me. My vengeance I shall leave you, and my witchcraft to exact it by. Indeed, I promise you stronger powers than mine. I will beg my lord Satanas for it and he will not deny me, for he is just, in his fashion, and I have served him well. Now, will you attend?"

"I will," said the girl.

So the woman advised her, and swore her to the fellowship of Hell. And then the woman forced the knife into her own heart and dropped dead on the floor of the tower.

When the men burst in with their swords and staves and their torches and their madness, the girl was ready for them.

She stood blank-faced, blank-eyed, with her arms hanging at her sides. When one touched her, she dropped down at his feet.

"Surely she is innocent," this man said. She was lovely enough that it was hard to accuse her. Then her father went to her and took her hand and lifted her. At that the girl opened her eyes and she said, as if terrified: "How did I come here? I was in my chamber and sleeping—"

"The woman has bewitched her," her father said.

He desired very much that this be so. And when the girl clung to his hand and wept, he was certain of it. They showed her the body with the knife in it. The girl screamed and seemed to lose her senses totally.

She was put to bed. In the morning, a priest came and questioned her. She answered steadfastly. She remembered nothing, not even of the great books she had been observed reading. When they told her what was in them, she screamed again and apparently would have thrown herself from the narrow window, only the priest stopped her.

Finally, they brought her the holy cross in order that she might kiss it and prove herself blameless.

Then she knelt, and whispered softly, that nobody should hear but one—"Lord Satanas, protect thy handmaid." And either that gentleman has more power than he is credited with or else the symbols of God are only as holy as the men who deal in them, for she embraced the cross and it left her unscathed.

At that, the whole household thanked God. The whole household saving, of course, the woman's daughter. She had another to thank.

The woman's body was burnt, and the ashes put into unconsecrated ground beyond the city gates. Though they had discovered her to be a witch, they had not discovered the direction her witchcraft had selected. Nor did they find the wax image with its limbs all twisted and stuck through with needles. The girl had taken that up and concealed it. The Duke continued in his distress, but he did not die. Sometimes, in the dead of night, the girl would unearth the image from under a loose brick by the hearth, and gloat over it, but she did nothing else. Not yet. She was fourteen and the cloud of her mother's acts still hovered over her. She knew what she must do next.

The period of mourning ended.

"Daughter," said the silk merchant to her, "why do you not remove your black? The woman was malign and led you into wickedness. How long will you mourn her, who deserves no mourning?"

"Oh my father," she said, "never think I regret my wretched mother. It is my own unwitting sin I mourn." And she grasped his hand and spilled her tears on it. "I would rather live in a convent," said she, "than mingle with proper folk. And I would seek a convent too, if it were not that I cannot bear to be parted from you."

Do you suppose she smiled secretly as she said this? One might suppose it. Presently she donned a robe of sackcloth and poured ashes over her red-copper hair. "It is my penance," she said, "I am glad to atone for my sins."

People forgot her beauty. She was at pains to obscure it. She slunk about like an aged woman, a rag pulled over her head, dirt smeared on her cheeks and brow. She elected to sleep in a cold cramped attic and sat all day by a smoky hearth in the kitchens. When someone came to her and begged her to wash her face and put on suitable clothes and sit in the rooms of the house, she smiled modestly, drawing the rag or a piece of hair over her face. "I swear," she said, "I am glad to be humble before God and men."

They reckoned her pious and they reckoned her simple. Two years passed. They mislaid her beauty altogether, and reckoned her ugly. They found it hard to call to mind who she was exactly, as she sat in the ashes, or shuffled unattended about the streets like a crone.

At the end of the second year, the silk merchant married again. It was inevitable, for he was not a man who liked to live alone.

On this occasion, his choice was a harmless widow. She already had two daughters, pretty in an unremarkable style. Perhaps the merchant hoped they would comfort him for what had gone before, this normal cheery wife and the two sweet, rather silly daughters, whose chief interests were clothes and weddings. Perhaps he hoped also that his deranged daughter might be drawn out by company. But that hope foundered. Not that the new mother did not try to be pleasant to the girl. And the new sisters, their hearts grieved by her condition, went to great lengths to enlist her friendship. They begged her to come from the kitchens or the attic. Failing in that, they sometimes ventured to join her, their fine silk dresses trailing on the greasy floor. They combed her hair, exclaiming, when some of the ash and dirt were removed, on its color. But no sooner had they turned away, than the girl gathered up handfuls of soot and ash and rubbed them into her hair again. Now and then, the sisters attempted to interest their bizarre relative in a bracelet or a gown or a current song. They spoke to her of the young men they had seen at the suppers or the balls which were then given regularly by the rich families of the city. The girl ignored it all. If she ever said anything it was to do with penance and humility. At last, as must happen, the sisters wearied of her, and left her alone. They had no cares and did not want to share in hers. They came to resent her moping greyness, as indeed the merchant's second wife had already done.

"Can you do nothing with the girl?" she demanded of her husband. "People will say that I and my daughters are responsible for her condition and that I ill-treat the maid from jealousy of her dead mother."

"Now how could anyone say that?" protested the merchant, "when you are famous as the epitome of generosity and kindness."

Another year passed, and saw no huge difference in the household.

A difference there was, but not visible.

The girl who slouched in the corner of the hearth was seventeen. Under the filth and grime she was, impossibly, more beautiful, although no one could see it.

And there was one other invisible item—her power (which all this time she had nurtured, saying her prayers to Satanas in the black of midnight), her power was rising like a dark moon in her soul.

Three days after her seventeenth birthday, the girl straggled about the streets as she frequently did. A few noted her and muttered it was the merchant's ugly simple daughter and paid no more attention. Most did not know her at all. She had made herself appear one with the scores of impoverished flotsam which constantly roamed the city, beggars and starvelings. Just outside the city gates, these persons congregated in large numbers, slumped around fires of burning refuse or else wandering to and fro in search of edible seeds, scraps, the miracle of a dropped coin. Here the girl now came, and began to wander about as they did. Dusk gathered and the shadows thickened. The girl sank to her knees in a patch of earth as if she had found something. Two or three of the beggars sneaked over to see if it were worth snatching from her—but the girl was only scrabbling in the empty soil. The beggars, making signs to each other that she was touched by God—mad—left her alone. But, very far from mad, the girl presently dug up a stoppered clay urn. In this urn were the ashes and charred bones of her mother. She had got a clue as to the location of the urn by devious questioning here and there. Her occult power had helped her to be sure of it.

In the twilight, padding along through the narrow streets and alleys of the city, the girl brought the urn homewards. In the garden at the foot of the old tower, gloom-wrapped, unwitnessed, she unstoppered the urn and buried the ashes freshly. She muttered certain unholy magics over the grave. Then she snapped off the sprig of a young hazel tree, and planted it in the newly turned ground.

I hazard you have begun to recognize the story by now. I see you suppose I tell it wrongly. Believe me, this is the truth of the matter. But if you would rather I left off the tale . . . No doubt your carriage will soon be here—No? Very well. I shall continue.

I think I should speak of the Duke's son at this juncture. The prince was nineteen, able, intelligent, and of noble bearing. He was of that rather swarthy type of looks one finds here in the north, but tall and slim and clear-eyed. There is an ancient square where you may see a statue of him, but much eroded by two centuries, and the elements. After the city was sacked, no care was lavished on it.

The Duke treasured his son. He had constant delight in the sight of the young man and what he said and did. It was the only happiness the invalid had.

Then, one night, the Duke screamed out in his bed. Servants came running with candles. The Duke moaned that a sword was transfixing his heart, an inch at a time. The prince hurried into the chamber, but in that instant the Duke spasmed horribly and died. No mark was on his body. There had never been a mark to show what ailed him.

The prince wept. They were genuine tears. He had nothing to reproach his father with, everything to thank him for.

Nevertheless, they brought the young man the seal ring of the city, and he put it on.

It was winter, a cold blue-white weather with snow in the streets and countryside and a hard wizened sun that drove thin sharp blades of light through the sky, but gave no warmth. The Duke's funeral cortege passed slowly across the snow, the broad open chariots draped with black and silver, the black-plumed horses, the chanting priests with their glittering robes, their jeweled crucifixes and golden censers. Crowds lined the roadways to watch the spectacle. Among the beggar women stood a girl. No one noticed her. They did not glimpse the expression she veiled in her ragged scarf. She gazed at the bier pitilessly. As the young prince rode by in his sables, the seal ring on his hand, the eyes of the girl burned through her ashy hair, like a red fox through grasses.

The Duke was buried in the mausoleum you can visit to this day, on the east side of the city. Several months elapsed. The prince put his grief from him, and took up the business of the city competently. Wise and courteous he was, but he rarely smiled. At nineteen his spirit seemed worn. You might think he guessed the destiny that hung over him.

The winter was a hard one, too. The snow had come, and having come was loath to withdraw. When at last the spring returned, flushing the hills with color, it was no longer sensible to be sad.

The prince's name day fell about this time. A great banquet was planned, a ball. There had been neither in the palace for nigh on three years, not since the Duke's fatal illness first claimed him. Now the royal doors were to be thrown open to all men of influence and their families. The prince was liberal, charming and clever even in this. Aristocrat and rich trader were to mingle in the beautiful dining room, and in this very chamber, among the frescoes, the marbles and the candelabra. Even a merchant's daughter, if the merchant were notable in the city, would get to dance on the sea-green floor, under the white eye of the fearful clock.

The clock. There was some renewed controversy about the clock. They did not dare speak to the young prince. He was a skeptic, as his father had been. But had not a death already occurred? Was the clock not a flying in the jaws of fate? For those disturbed by it, there was a dim writing in their minds, in the dust of the street or the pattern of blossoms. *When the clock strikes*—But people do not positively heed these warnings. Man is afraid of his fears. He ignores the shadow of the wolf thrown on the paving before him, saying: It is only a shadow.

The silk merchant received his invitation to the palace, and to be sure, thought nothing of the clock. His house had been thrown into uproar. The most luscious silks of his workshop were carried into the house and laid before the wife and her two daughters, who chirruped and squealed with excitement. The merchant stood smugly by, above it all yet pleased at being appreciated. "Oh, father!" cried the two sisters, "may I have this one with the gold piping?" "Oh, father, this one with the design of pineapples?" Later, a jeweler arrived and set out his trays. The merchant was generous. He wanted his women to look their best. It might be the night of their lives. Yet all the while, at the back of his mind, a little dark spot, itching, aching. He tried to ignore the spot, not scratch at it. His true daughter, the mad one. Nobody bothered to tell her about the invitation to the palace. They knew how she would react, mumbling in her hair about her sin and her penance, paddling her hands in the greasy ash to smear her face. Even the servants avoided her, as if she were just the cat seated by the fire. Less than the cat, for the cat saw to the mice—Just a block of stone. And yet, how fair she might have looked, decked in the pick of the merchant's wares, jewels at her throat. The prince himself could not have been unaware of her. And though marriage was impossible, other less holy, though equally honorable contracts, might have been arranged to the benefit of all concerned. The merchant sighed. He had scratched the darkness after all. He attempted to comfort himself by watching the two sisters exult over their apparel. He refused to admit that the finery would somehow make them seem but more ordinary than they were by contrast.

The evening of the banquet arrived. The family set off. Most of the servants sidled after. The prince had distributed largesse in the city; oxen roasted in the squares and the wine was free by royal order.

The house grew somber. In the deserted kitchen the fire went out.

By the heart, a segment of gloom rose up.

The girl glanced around her, and she laughed softly and

shook out her filthy hair. Of course, she knew as much as anyone, and more than most. This was to be her night, too.

A few minutes later she was in the garden beneath the old tower, standing over the young hazel tree which thrust up from the earth. It had become strong, the tree, despite the harsh winter. Now the girl nodded to it. She chanted under her breath. At length a pale light began to glow, far down near where the roots of the tree held to the ground. Out of the pale glow flew a thin black bird, which perched on the girl's shoulder. Together, the girl and the bird passed into the old tower. High up, a fire blazed that no one had lit. A tub steamed with scented water that no one had drawn. Shapes that were not real and barely seen flitted about. Rare perfumes, the rustle of garments, the glint of gems as yet invisible filled and did not fill the restless air.

Need I describe further? No. You will have seen paintings which depict the attendance upon a witch of her familiar demons. How one bathes her, another anoints her, another brings clothes and ornaments. Perhaps you do not credit such things in any case. Never mind that. I will tell you what happened in the courtyard before the palace.

Many carriages and chariots had driven through the square, avoiding the roasting oxen, the barrels of wine, the cheering drunken citizens, and so through the gates into the courtyard. Just before ten o'clock (the hour, if you recall the clock, of the magician) a solitary carriage drove through the square and into the court. The people in the square gawped at the carriage and pressed forward to see who would step out of it, this latecomer. It was a remarkable vehicle that looked to be fashioned of solid gold, all but the domed roof that was transparent flashing crystal. Six black horses drew it. The coachman and postillions were clad in crimson, and strangely masked as curious beasts and reptiles. One of these beast-men now hopped down and opened the door of the carriage. Out came a woman's figure in a cloak of white fur, and glided up the palace stair and in at the doors.

There was dancing in the ballroom. The whole chamber was bright and clamorous with music and the voices of men and women. There, between those two pillars, the prince sat in his chair, dark, courteous, seldom smiling. Here the musicians played, the deep-throated viol, the lively mandolin. And there the dancers moved up and down on the sea-green floor.

But the music and the dancers had just paused. The figures on the clock were themselves in motion. The hour of the magician was about to strike.

As it struck, through the doorway came the figure in the fur cloak. And, as if they must, every eye turned to her.

For an instant she stood there, all white, as though she had brought the winter snow back with her. And then she loosed the cloak from her shoulders, it slipped away, and she was all fire.

She wore a gown of apricot brocade embroidered thickly with gold. Her sleeves and the bodice of her gown were slashed over ivory satin sewn with large rosy pearls. Pearls, too, were wound in her hair that was the shade of antique burnished copper. She was so beautiful that when the clock was still, nobody spoke. She was so beautiful it was hard to look at her for very long.

The prince got up from his chair. He did not know he had. Now he started out across the floor, between the dancers, who parted silently to let him through. He went toward the girl in the doorway as if she drew him by a chain.

The prince had hardly ever acted without considering first what he did. Now he did not consider. He bowed to the girl.

"Madam," he said. "You are welcome. Madam," he said. "Tell me who you are."

She smiled.

"My rank," she said. "Would you know that, my lord? It is similar to yours, or would be were I now mistress in my dead mother's palace. But, unfortunately, an unscrupulous man caused the downfall of our house."

"Misfortune indeed," said the prince. "Tell me your name. Let me right the wrong done you."

"You shall," said the girl. "Trust me, you shall. For my name, I would rather keep it secret for the present. But you may call me, if you will, a pet name I have given myself—Ashella."

"Ashella. . . . But I see no ash about you," said the prince, dazzled by her gleam, laughing a little, stiffly, for laughter was not his habit.

"Ash and cinders from a cold and bitter hearth," said she. But she smiled again. "Now everyone is staring at us, my lord, and the musicians are impatient to begin again. Out of all these ladies, can it be you will lead me in the dance?"

"As long as you will dance," he said. "You shall dance with me."

And that is how it was.

There were many dances, slow and fast, whirling measures and gentle ones. And here and there, the prince and the maiden were parted. Always then he looked eagerly after her, sparing no regard for the other girls whose hands lay in his. It was not like him, he was usually so careful. But the other young men who danced on that floor, who clasped her fingers or her narrow waist in the dance, also gazed after her when she was gone. She danced, as she appeared, like fire. Though if you had asked those young men whether they would rather tie her to themselves, as the prince did, they would have been at a loss. For it is not easy to keep pace with fire.

The hour of the hag struck on the clock.

The prince grew weary of dancing with the girl and losing her in the dance to others and refinding her and losing her again.

Behind the curtains there is a tall window in the east wall that opens on the terrace above the garden. He drew her out there, into the spring night. He gave an order, and small tables were brought with delicacies and sweets and wine. He sat by her, watching every gesture she made, as if he would paint her portrait afterward.

In the ballroom, here, under the clock, the people murmured. But it was not quite the murmur you would expect, the scandalous murmur about a woman come from nowhere that the prince had made so much of. At the periphery of the ballroom, the silk merchant sat, pale as a ghost, thinking of a ghost, the living ghost of his true daughter. No one else recognized her. Only he. Some trick of the heart had enabled him to know her. He said nothing of it. As the step-sisters and wife gossiped with other wives and sisters, an awful foreboding weighed him down, sent him cold and dumb.

And now it is almost midnight, the moment when the page of the night turns over into day. Almost midnight, the hour when the figure of Death strikes the golden bell of the clock. And what will happen when the clock strikes? Your face announces that you know. Be patient; let us see if you do.

"I am being foolish," said the prince to Ashella on the terrace. "But perhaps I am entitled to foolish, just once in my life. What are you saying?" For the girl was speaking low beside him, and he could not catch her words.

"I am saying a spell to bind you to me," she said.

"But I am already bound."

"Be bound then. Never go free."

"I do not wish it," he said. He kissed her hands and he said, "I do not know you, but I will wed you. Is that proof your spell has worked? I will wed you, and get back for you the rights you have lost."

"If it were only so simple," said Ashella, smiling, smiling. "But the debt is too cruel. Justice requires a harsher payment."

And then, in the ballroom, Death struck the first note on the golden bell.

The girl smiled and she said,

"I curse you in my mother's name."

The second stroke.

"I curse you in my own name."

The third stroke.

"And in the name of those that your father slew."

The fourth stroke.

"And in the name of my Master, who rules the world."

As the fifth, the sixth, the seventh strokes pealed out, the prince stood nonplussed. At the eighth and the ninth strokes, the strength of the malediction seemed to curdle his blood. He shivered and his brain writhed. At the tenth stroke, he saw a change in the loveliness before him. She grew thinner, taller. At the eleventh stroke, he beheld a thing in a ragged black cowl and robe. It grinned at him. It was all grin below a triangle of sockets of nose and eyes. At the twelfth stroke, the prince saw Death and knew him.

In the ballroom, a hideous grinding noise, as the gears of the clock failed. Followed by a hollow booming, as the mechanism stopped entirely.

The conjuration of Death vanished from the terrace.

Only one thing was left behind. A woman's shoe. A shoe no woman could ever have danced in. It was made of glass.

Did you intend to protest about the shoe? Shall I finish the story, or would you rather I did not? It is not the ending you are familiar with. Yes, I perceive you understand that, now.

I will go quickly, then, for your carriage must soon be here. And there is not a great deal more to relate.

The prince lost his mind. Partly from what he had seen, partly from the spells the young witch had netted him in. He could think of nothing but the girl who had named herself Ashella. He raved that Death had borne her away but he would recover her from Death. She had left the glass shoe as token of her love. He must discover her with the aid of the shoe. Whomsoever the shoe fitted would be Ashella. For there was this added complication, that Death might hide her actual appearance. None had seen the girl before. She had disappeared like smoke. The one infallible test was the shoe. That was why she had left it for him.

His ministers would have reasoned with the prince, but he was past reason. His intellect had collapsed as totally as only a profound intellect can. A lunatic, he rode about the city. He struck out at those who argued with him. On a particular occasion, drawing a dagger, he killed, not apparently noticing what he did. His demand was explicit. Every woman, young or old, maid or married, must come forth from her home, must put her foot into the shoe of glass. They came. They had not choice. Some approached in terror, some weeping. Even the aged beggar women obliged, and they cackled, enjoying the sight of royalty gone mad. One alone did not come.

Now it is not illogical that out of the hundreds of women whose feet were put into the shoe, a single woman might have been found that the shoe fitted. But this did not happen. Nor did the situation alter, despite a lurid fable that some, tickled by the idea of wedding the prince, cut off their toes that the shoe might fit them. And if they did, it was to no avail, for still the shoe did not.

Is it really surprising? The shoe was sorcerous. It constantly changed itself, its shape, its size, in order that no foot, save one, could ever be got into it.

Summer spread across the land. The city took on its golden summer glaze, its fetid summer smell.

What had been a whisper of intrigue, swelled into a steady distant thunder. Plots were being hatched.

One day, the silk merchant was brought, trembling and grey of face, to the prince. The merchant's dumbness had broken. He had unburdened himself of his fear at confession, but the priest had not proved honest. In the dawn, men had knocked on the door of the merchant's house. Now he stumbled to the chair of the prince.

Both looked twice their years, but, if anything, the prince looked the elder. He did not lift his eyes. Over and over in his hands he turned the glass shoe.

The merchant, stumbling too in his speech, told the tale of his first wife and his daughter. He told everything, leaving out no detail. He did not even omit the end: that since the night of the banquet the girl had been absent from his house, taking nothing with her—save a young hazel from the garden beneath the tower.

The prince leapt from his chair.

His clothes were filthy and unkempt. His face was smeared with sweat and dust . . . it resembled, momentarily, another face.

Without guard or attendant, the prince ran through the city toward the merchant's house, and on the road, the intriguers waylaid and slew him. As he fell, the glass shoe dropped from his hands, and shattered in a thousand fragments.

There is little else worth mentioning.

Those who usurped the city were villains and not merely that, but fools. Within a year, external enemies were at the gates. A year more, and the city had been sacked, half burnt out, ruined. The manner in which you find it now, is somewhat better than it was then. And it is not now anything for a man to be proud of. As you were quick to note, many here earn a miserable existence by conducting visitors about the streets, the palace, showing them the dregs of the city's past.

Which was not a request, in fact, for you to give me money. Throw some from your carriage window if your conscience bothers you. My own wants are few.

No, I have no further news of the girl, Ashella, the witch. A devotee of Satanas, she has doubtless worked plentiful woe in the world. And a witch is long-lived. Even so, she will die eventually. None escapes Death. Then you may pity her, if you like. Those who serve the gentleman below—who can guess what their final lot will be? But I am very sorry the story did not please you. It is not, maybe, a happy choice before a journey.

And there is your carriage at last.

What? Ah, no, I shall stay here in the ballroom where you

came on me. I have often paused here through the years. It is the clock. It has a certain—what shall I call it—power, to draw me back.

I am not trying to unnerve you. Why should you suppose that? Because of my knowledge of the city, of the story? You think that I am implying that I myself am Death? Now you laugh. Yes, it is absurd. Observe the twelfth figure on the clock. Is he not as you have always heard Death described? And am I in the least like that twelfth figure?

Although, of course, the story was not as you have heard it, either.

The Golden Rope

ONE

In the stone house amid the white wood, the woman sat and brooded on a power that only one might give her. She had wooed him long and diligently, and she had given her life over to learning and study that she might commune with him. But, like an unrequited love, so far she had been ignored.

All around the house the dead trees, a palisade, out-stared the moon. They were a constant reminder of her youth which she had given up, her vitality which had been drained. And yet, tonight, it seemed to her there was a strange stirring in the trees, and in her blood.

When loud knocking came on her gates, she was not amazed, nor quite calm. Very seldom did any seek admittance here. Those who knew of her—and she had not courted fame—understood her scholarship and disliked it. Others guessed her ambition, and feared her. Presently, her servant entered the room, a tall, dark-skinned man from the East, dressed in silken clothes, and tongueless. He bowed low, then indicated to her, in a gesture language she had taught him, and which none but she and he could comprehend, that a city fellow had sought her door. He was of the lowest urban class,

a rogue requiring her aid for his wife who, it seemed, was sick to the death.

Her normal practice, in such a case, was to dismiss the petitioner without seeing him. Now she instructed her servant to bring the man in. She gave the order with a curious excitment, and took care to compose herself that nothing of her mood should be detectable.

The man appeared a moment later. By her trained instincts and intelligence the woman told instantly much about him. He was a thief, one of the dregs of the world. That he cared so for his wife's health that he came seeking a witch implied no love, merely that his wife was some use to him. The woman noted, too, that her visitor was afraid of her. And that, under its filth, his hair was like new gold.

"So," she said. "What do you want?"

"My wife is with child. The condition does not suit her. I dread she may die."

The woman nodded coldly. He would never have known how her pulse had quickened.

"I understand. Your wife sells her body and brings you a fair wage from the enterprise. You suppose that when she grows big and cumbersome, her customers will dwindle."

The man faltered, then smiled at her ingratiatingly.

"I see I was a fool to try hiding anything from you, my lady. As you say. I find it hard to come by honest work. If we starve, it will do none of us any good. But if you could give me some of your clever herbs, so the trouble goes away—"

"And this child is yours, you think, that you will be rid of it so freely."

"I do not, alas, know."

"*I* know. It is. You are aware," she said, "I ask a price for any service."

He grinned and panted like an eager dog.

"When she is well, her first month's wages shall all be yours." The woman watched him. He grew uneasy. "We would never cheat you."

"Tell me, then, what that month's wage would be."

He shuffled, and named a sum.

The woman waited, concentrating, until she read from him the aura of thought which showed his wife. Though he had made a whore of her, this girl was beautiful.

The woman nodded again.

"I think you have halved the amount. No arguments, if you please. I shall be generous to you. I myself will double the coins, and you shall be given such a figure every twenty days. Providing your wife carries to term, and bears."

The cutpurse gaped.

"A wonderful bargain for you," she said. "You will benefit outrageously by it."

"But why—"

"Once the child is fit to travel, you will bring it here to me."

"But—"

"I will then settle upon you one last payment, to compensate your doleful loss."

"But—"

"Do not dare," she said, "to question me."

He balked. Clearly he was unsure if he was in luck, or if she was simply a lunatic who might renege, then harm him.

"Or," she said, "to doubt me."

"Ah no, *no*, my lady."

She rose, he cowered.

"Wait here, and touch nothing. There are safeguards on my property which prove injurious to meddlers. Do you believe me?" His pallor showed he did. "When I return, I will have for you your first payment. Also herbs and powders you must give your wife to strengthen her, so the child is robust."

She went from the room and along a passageway. She unlocked, in an unusual manner, a black lacquer door, and passed down a long flight of steps to the vast underground chamber that was her study and her insularium. As her fingers busied themselves in the preparation of those medicines she had prescribed, they trembled slightly.

Infallibly, she knew a golden rope had been placed in her hands. She had only, with patience and wisdom, to draw it in.

The child was born, and opened its unfocused eyes on dirt and squalor. Then, if it was even properly aware of such things, came an upheaval, a cessation of warmth, the dim wailing of a woman—someone was sorry to see it go after all. The child cried, then slept. Bundled in its covers it was taken to high gates, and given over to a pair of dark lean hands. Money rang inside a leather bag. As thin snow began to fall, a door thudded shut.

"A girl," said the woman. "That is very well. This wisp of hair is dark now, but will change inside a year. She is whole and will be lovely."

The world was altered.

The earliest memory, the first impression, did not linger, was wiped away. Life was this: A beautiful apartment which opened on a large garden. The walls about the garden were very tall; on three sides the stone piles of the house leaned over it. On the fourth a few dead branches, like a handful of white bones, were all that might be glimpsed of any other place. The ceilings of the beautiful apartment were themselves extremely lofty, but they sank a little closer as the years passed, just as the childish bed and chairs and desk were taken away, and adult furniture replaced them. There came to be an exquisite harpsichord, two guitars of dark and blond wood, with ivory frets. Tapestries and paintings came, and hand-painted books, sweeping pleated dresses of pale lemon silk and cream satin and blanched-almond brocade where there had hung little-girl dresses of similar materials and tints. In a box lined in velvet lay some pieces of priceless flawless jewelry, several of an Eastern cast.

The child, too, had changed, was no longer a child. She was thirteen, the age at which many a damsel of good house might already be contracted if not married. The girl had, however, never seen a man, save in a painting, never heard of one save in a book. She knew they existed, just as lions, wolves, unicorns existed, far beyond the walls, another species in another country. Yet from this same outer wonderland her toys, her furnishings, her books somehow transpired. Everything was delivered as she slept, or taken away as she slept—like magic. Sometimes shocking, and sometimes delightful, yet she was used to it. Magic, as with the apartment, the garden, was an everyday matter.

And beyond the walls of the house and the garden which divided her from the far-off mythology of the earth? The bones of the trees gave evidence of a waste. No other evidence was awarded her.

The woman, whom she did not call "Mother" but "my lady," was the only live thing the young girl saw, or had ever seen. It was a fact, as the ceilings drew lower, the woman became smaller, until she and the girl were almost of the same height. Otherwise, the woman seemed not to change at all. She wore plain clothes, dark and without ornament. Her face was colorless, expressionless. She offered neither love nor friendship, not even the shelter of another personality. Yet it was this woman who, without passion, without enthusiasm of any kind, taught the girl all she had come to know, and brought in to her, by those mysterious nocturnal means, the literature, the musical instruments, that were the accessories and gilding of knowledge; the elegant garments, and the jewels.

The young girl knew her origins, also. My lady had told her from the first. "You are not the child of my body. You are the child of a man and woman who did not want you. I wanted you, and so you were brought to me. You are named Jaspre, since I sent to your mother powders of jaspre to strengthen her while she carried you. Do not feel any regret or any betrayal. Your natural parents are nothing to you." And the girl named Jaspre felt nothing. The ideas of parentage, of love, even, were unconvincing, alien to her. In her world, such things did not exist.

Sometimes, Jaspre would wander through the large garden, among its avenues, of which there were many, between its uncannily manicured box hedges, in and out of its grottoes where nymphs of mossy stone played statically with each other but never with her. Occasionally birds flew over the garden. In some naive manner, she understood they represented freedom, but freedom held no particular allure. Jaspre's world was of the intellect and the spirit. Even her daydreams were contained within the garden. She had never seen a lion or a man or a forest or a mountain. She had never seen beyond the door of her apartment.

Nor, when she looked into her long mirrors, did she realize what looked back at her was the most beautiful thing in the beautiful room.

But the woman realized. She had nurtured Jaspre like a rare plant, its white stem, its bright petals. The woman, who had no lust for human flesh, who lusted only for one thing, had caught her breath, seeing the glowing creature drift toward her from the sunset shade of an ilex tree in the walled garden. The skin like pearl melting in the dress of pearl silk, scarcely any difference observable. The loosely plaited hair like a golden rope. . . .

"Do you recall how old you are, Jaspre?"

"Yes, my lady. I am thirteen years of age."

"You have never," said the woman, "asked me anything concerning the rest of the house."

"It is," said Jaspre, "the house." To this non-questioning the woman had molded her in subtle, gentle ways. It was not apathy. It was an intelligent disinterest in those things that could have no bearing on one's existence.

And yet now, "I will show you, today, a door. It has remained hidden, Jaspre, but now we shall use it, you and I."

Jaspre nodded calmly.

"Yes, my lady."

The door was concealed behind a section of the wall which moved. It gave on a stair. It was the stair to the insularium.

To the world of the apartment and the garden then, was added this new continent of marvels. In ranks, the tall stoppered vials, from which a pinch of powder dropped into air might burn, another produce sweet perfume. Slim flattened statues of bronze stood in the shadows, a bronze bull with wings. While on a platform reached by several narrow steps, was a great instrument which, when tilted up at an extravagant angle, pierced some opening in the side of the house, and by means of mirrors and lenses captured the stars and planets in the green evening sky.

Jaspre wandered in the vast room, windowless and lamplit, sipping from it, tasting of it. She had been nurtured and lessoned to gain much from the appearances of things, the sensations of their umbras, less from their functions. Hers was an intellect which dreamed and fantasized upon, rather than inquired into. So, she touched the statues, the telescope, gazed on the constellations, inhaled the sweet aroma of powders, and did not ask their natures, nor require to be informed.

Presently, the woman led her to a narrow alcove, and drew aside a curtain of smoky samite, and then another behind it of black velvet. Beyond the curtains was a gate of horn scrolled by black iron, and with a gilded iron lock. This lock the woman negotiated without a key, using strange pressures of her hands. As the gate opened, a third curtain was disclosed, but this of a dull brazen chain mail.

Although she did not know, and had been told nothing of what lay in store, the suspenseful drawings of curtain upon curtain, the unlocking of the gate, the metallic mesh, the unsuspected depth of the alcove itself—all this had worked upon the young girl's imagination. That some pinnacle of importance was about to be attained, and revealed to her, was apparent.

The woman paused, her hand resting on the drapery of brazen mail.

"That I took you in," she said, "was for a purpose. I did not, as you have seen, bring you here to serve me. And yet, I did take you, raise you, keep you, in peerlessness and in innocence, that you might serve—another. And now you are fit to learn of him and to look upon his image."

Jaspre's heart beat quickly, instinctually, and she waited, her eyes fixed only on the curtain. Which, in another instant, the woman drew aside.

Jaspre had never seen a man before. Inside the alcove stood a man. Then, as the lamplight beat on him, she beheld he was made of stone, a pale stone finely planed, fantastically burnished, colored with all the most convincing nuances of life.

His long and thickly curling hair was black, and lay seemingly loosely against his forehead, cheeks and shoulders. His features were chisled, of a faintly Eastern cast, singularly handsome even to the point of beauty. His flesh was pale, but not with the dead pallor of the stone, rather a curious dark whiteness flushed through with somber tinctures, as if ichors flowed directly under the skin. In the eyes, which most of all might display lifelessness in a statue, there had been set dark jewels that glimmered, that seemed possessed of actual sight.

The image was represented as garbed in a black outer mantle of the ancient Parsua, diagonally cut and fringed with silver, with a broad belt that flashed with large bloody gems. Gems of blood and ink and blue water also crusted the shoes carved on his feet, and stared from his long fingers. One hand lay relaxedly at his side. The left hand was gracefully uplifted in an ambiguous gesture of offering or beckoning.

The statue's feet rested upon a low plinth, and in the plinth some words had long ago been cut, their letters softened now by time that had, in no other form, impaired the freshness of the work. After a while, as if impelled, Jaspre looked at them and next leaned close.

Deo Arimanio, they read. *Nox Invictus.*

The woman spoke quietly at Jaspre's side.

"You have deciphered the writing. Do you translate it?"

"He is," said the girl, "a god, and this is his name. And here it says that night—"

The woman broke in, softly as before:

"Unconquerable Night, is what it says. It is a good wish for his future victory, against the god of fires."

Jaspre's eyes fell. Her heart beat so fast now the woman did not miss it.

"But that fight is far off. For now, he dwells in darkness and is at peace in his kingdom."

"Does he then," said Jaspre, "truly exist?"

"Yes. He is God. The King of the World, that is him. The Prince of Darkness, eternal adversary to the devil Lucifer, bringer of light and blinding. The Lord of Eternal Night. By some called Bel, and in the Roman tongue Arimanio, as it is carved here. But, as you shall worship him now, he is named Angemal. Angel, demon and god."

"And I am to serve him?"

"For this you were born."

Slowly, the young girl's cheeks stained red with blood. The lights in the eyes of the statue blazed and sang, as if he saw and smiled at it.

TWO

Into her world, then, of floral garden, of gracious room, of magical laboratory, a god had entered.

In miniature, a creation myth, Jaspre its feminine principle, her axis now fixed: A man who was also God. Who was also the Serpent.

She was thirteen, and everything spread before her, a glittering sea clothed in phantasmal mists, tossed by mystic gradual lights. On this her mind embarked, into the perpetual dawn of knowledge. And now knowledge was enhanced by that best accessory of all—desire.

Jaspre did not know that, in the person of the remarkable and lifelike statue, her desire and her love had come to reside, to put down tenacious roots, to burn into red blossom. But her feelings, senses, yearnings, these did the work for her. She did not need to think, to know, to reason. Her pulse and her spirit were now her guides.

The woman had been not only generous in the gifts of learning she had poured in on Jaspre's receptive intelligence; she had been also most selective. There from the first, always, was that which would enhance and increase this ultimate moment, the moments which succeeded it. Nothing to detract. Nothing to alarm, defame, erode.

Knowing nothing of this esoteric cult which now had been set shimmering before her, Jaspre knew no indecision and no doubt.

She had been born to magnify him. He had chosen her.

For a year then, she "served."

She brought her offerings, fruits and flowers from the walled garden, and laid them at his jeweled feet. She brought him wine, and music. She began to dream of him. Her dreams were lapped in fires, which were dark, heatless, sable, laval fires, such as burned in his kingdom, far, far beneath the earth.

Lord of Demons, Prince of Darkness. She began to hunger for him, for those things which were his. Less and less did she sleep by night. She slept by day, drawing her shutters and her curtains against the sun. At dusk, as if to blue morning, she woke. She sat among the closed night flowers, and played upon her guitars to the rising of the moon. She made her hymns to him then. And her skin grew moon-burned, she supposed, as was his.

For she too altered. Her hair hung long, to her waist, to the backs of her knees. She was taller, more slender. An ambient night-vision enabled her to perceive the silver apples on the tree, the nocturnal moths flying on their paper wings from the surface of the moon.

Angemal. Arimanio. Lord of winged things, lord of the panther and the black wolf, lord of quietude, lord of the silver caves a hundred miles beneath the ground.

Fruit and flowers she brought, her hymns she brought, and next her tears.

He lived. She worshiped. Should he never come to her? Would they never meet? Her mind, her spirit dreamed; her flesh spoke also—dreams were not enough.

"How old, Jaspre, are you now?"

"I am fourteen, my lady."

"I seldom see you in the garden, now, by day."

"I am there after dark, my lady. I abhor the sun. I love only the night."

"And he that is the night. You love him."

Jaspre's face, lovely, savage, a storm."

"Yes! I would give him more than ever I gave."

"You shall."

The hidden door, the stair, the insularium.

There was a difference to the room.

At its every angle, aromatics burned, bittersweet, rose, terebinth, camfre, myrrh. The lamps were out. A single blue cloud burned high up on a massive chandelier of candles let down from the ceiling. On the floor there were marks: The Circle, the Star of the Five Points, the figures of an arcane zodiac—Fish, Serpent, Bull, Virgin. . . . At various stations stood the symbols, the Chalice, the Sword, the Crown, the Veil and others.

The girl knew little of any of this. But what if her baroque world grew still more unfamiliar and bizarre? She checked at nothing.

"Now," said the woman, "I will tell you what you must do."

She did so, and Jaspre obeyed her.

Jaspre removed her gown of icy satin, her undergarments and her shoes. Unaware that nakedness meant shame and vulnerability, she went to the Circle naked, and naked she lay down in it, her hands and her feet extended to conform with four points of the five-pointed Star, her head conforming with the fifth, and her hair like pale golden snow frayed out about her everywhere.

The scents of the smokes made Jaspre drowsy and sad. Her heart beat in her very womb, and she lay listening to it.

The woman said to her out of a blue fire-cloud in the air:

"You have brought many offerings to the Lord Angemal. Do you fear to give him of your blood?"

"No," said Jaspre.

She did not know what she had said. Yet her soul knew and beat its wings within her, attempting, like the caged bird it was, to fly.

How beautiful she was. The woman, bending above her with the silver knife, comprehended without human lust this beauty. After all, had she not trained it, complimented it, nourished it, setting all things to inspire the enchantment of physical perfection? A child of golden light.

"Fix your thoughts," the woman said, "upon him. Do you consent to be his?"

Jaspre breathed. "I do."

She felt a flicker of pain. It did not trouble her, she rejoiced in it. Her pain, too, she would render him. Was it sufficient? She almost entreated to be hurt again.

The dream began subtly, first with a vague awareness, then with a still certainty, of where she was, and the reason and the logic of it.

Far down under the house, beneath the very surface of the ground, the insularium was a cellar. Only the telescope craned, and that merely by the means of a stone funnel and twisted lenses, upward into the sky. Now, however, some portion of the chamber, that magian centre at which Jaspre lay—the pivot of the Star—had become the head of a mighty tower.

The tower was stone. She could visualize it quite clearly, the roofed cup of its spire, which contained her, the perilous swooping descent of its sides. Slowly, Jaspre rose. She looked about. The room in the head of the tower was small, and, of course, pentagonal. In each of the five sides, a long window lacking glass framed an uncanny vaporous darkness, without form and void—indeed, as the first darkness of all, the dark of Chaos, had been described in the parchments of the Judaians.

Yet, Jaspre was not afraid of the void darkness, nor of the height of the tower. She went to the window before her, toward which formerly her own skull had pointed, and looked out of it.

The scentless, moistureless yet somber mists, disturbed a little, seemingly by human warmth, swirled and floated. Nothing else was visible before her, and so she turned her eyes to gaze downward.

The spire plummeted below her, it seemed, forever. She grasped at once, as if she had always been cognizant of the fact, that the sub-earth cellar of the insularium could be also the top of a tower because such a place thrust on, by sorcerous means, deep into the core of the world, to those nether regions, those buried caverns that had been named Hell, or Hades, or Tellus Occultus in explanatory, analogous legend. It seemed to fall miles below her, growing ever more slender as it fell, becoming eventually nothing larger or stronger than a needle, and on this the upper masonry balanced, and she within it, so she seemed to experience all at once a gentle swaying in the cup of the tower, rhythmic as that of a pendulum, mild as that of a flower-stalk in a breeze. And still, she was not afraid, either to sense this motion, or to stare downward into the formless abyss.

There were carvings in the sides of the tower, the magic symbols from the chamber as it had been, the zodiac, the Crown, the Sword, the Chalice—she knew such seals must hold the spire safely.

And then she became aware of the little fluttering at her left wrist. She looked, and a scarlet butterfly flew away from her, away down the length of the tower, and then another, another, an unraveling scarf of butterflies like winged blood. Jaspre watched them descend, and as she leaned there, strands of her unbound hair came streaming over her shoulder, and spilled away also, unfurling like a shining ribbon, down, down, down with the red ribbon of the butterflies, down, down into the dark below.

Jaspre was filled by wonder, but not by perplexity or questioning. The butterflies, which were born from her wrist, seemed spontaneous and natural. The way her hair trickled now from its fount, pouring over her, pouring down, a golden river, a silken rope, growing long and longer—as it had done in her life, but never so swiftly—this appeared also fitting, and right.

And then her very eyes, her very sight and spirit seemed to be freed of her body, and she herself, invisible, a thing of air, flowed down the tower.

She had no fear. She was exalted, glad.

Darkness before her, stone beside her, the falling of scarlet and gold. At length, she saw an ending to every descent: The base of the tower.

It was a doorless block of granite, high as the walls of the house had been. And cut in the stone in letters taller than

Jaspre, when she had been in her body, the words NOX INVICTUS.

The butterflies played around these letters, blooming like garnets in the dullness. The golden hair touched them, and so the ground, and poured no more, a trembling fountain that ran away into a thread above, and thus into nothing. Up there, in that fresh, inverted abyss, Jaspre's body leaned from its window, no longer to be seen.

About the base of the tower, a plain of smooth and empty rock glided away and away, also into an inchoate nothingness that was its only horizon.

Jaspre knew only gladness. Incorporeal and weightless as the winged creatures in their dance, she danced with them. Caught in a spiral of heatless laval fire, she beheld another thing, and paused transfixed.

On the horizon of nothingness, many days' journey as it seemed from the tower, a flicker of blue luster had evolved. And, in a few seconds, drew nearer. And in a few seconds more, much nearer.

As the light began to swell, Jaspre saw that it was not light at all, but the essence of the dark given clarity, *unlight*, more sumptuous, more lambent than any luminence of the world's.

From the brilliancy, bringing it, like great wings folded about him, a figure presently came.

He was like some picture from one of her books, animate, and imbued with all the qualities of life, and with some other thing which was not life at all, but more, perhaps, than life. He rode a horse blacker than the blackest material the earth was capable of, blacker than ebony, sable or jet. But its mane and tail were of an iridescent blueness, and it was accoutered in a blue and silver hail of sparkling stuffs, bells, gems. He, too, was garbed in the same black blackness as the flesh of the horse, as if he had stepped from some Avernal lake and its waters clung to him, becoming satin, and metal. His hair was the blackest thing of all. His face—but as he came closer, he turned his head. Some shadow then, the curling curtain of the hair, hid all his features from her. She did not need to see them. She knew they were the features of the statue in the insularium.

He had ridden now to the spot where the fountain of hair came down. The horse stopped at once. And he, the god-demon she was to call Angemal, stretched out one hand gloved in silvery mail and with one huge ring upon it, a fiery ring of an apricot color, the stone which was her name. He touched the golden rope of her hair with his fingers. And immediately Jaspre saw, without amazement, the hair twisted and refashioned itself. It became a ladder of silk—

She heard him laugh, then, a low sound, scarcely audible, musical as song and colder than frozen iron. Then, he was gone. It was not that he vanished. He was; he was *not.*

Jaspre felt a desolation and an agony, as if her psychic fibers tore and frayed at their insubstantial roots. Her spiritual sight went out, and in that fading, she glimpsed the butterflies raining like blood on the plain, while above her the golden hair was burning, shriveling, blowing away; black butterflies where there had been red. Even her soul, witnessing this, seemed to shrivel also, and to die.

Jaspre opened her eyes. She lay on the floor of the insularium. The chandelier smoldered, the color of thunder, most of its candles extinguished, and the woman bent close. For the only time in all their acquaintance, Jaspre beheld a glaze of ghostly excitement on my lady's face, but it was almost instantly spent, or hidden.

"And what did you see?"

"I saw—a tower," Jaspre faltered. She was weak, and dazzled by the feeble light. Her left wrist, bound tightly with cloth, hurt her.

"Yes. A tower. What else?"

Jaspre's eyes closed of themselves. The woman leaned nearer and she whispered, "Speak, or I shall be angry. *What else?*"

"I saw—red butterflies, and my hair falling to the rock like a shower of gold. I never knew my hair would shine and blaze. . . . Oh, my lady, I am so weary."

"Speak. Or I shall strike you."

Jaspre's eyes opened wide. She was shocked and afraid. Never before had she been threatened—there had been no need.

"I—" Jaspre sought for words, found them, "I left my body and drifted down the tower to the plain beneath. There a man came, all in black, riding a black horse."

"And was it he?"

"I think that it was. But he turned aside. And when he touched the rope of hair it became a silken ladder, and he laughed. Then my hair burnt and charred, and he was gone."

Jaspre, barely conscious that she did so, raised her hands, the left with pain and stiffness, and discovered her hair and that it was not charred, but whole, lying in a long swath all about her. Though it was not so long as it had been when she dreamed of it, and maybe not so golden.

The woman had gone away from her. In the darkest corner of the room she sat, rigid, silent. And then she said, "You have lain there enough. Dress. Go to your apartment." And her voice was like a frost.

Jaspre rose. Her sight clouded. She took up her clothes.

"Have I displeased you, my lady?"

"It is your master you have displeased, the princely lord Angemal. For he did not find you acceptable, it seems."

Jaspre wept as she clad herself in the gleaming garments which no longer gleamed.

"Why?" she murmured. "What have I done?"

"I do not know. You were reared to please him. A child of light consenting to the shadow. It should have delighted him, master of ironies that he is. But the emblem of the vision is blatant. He rejected you, and therefore the way into the world whereby he might have manifested."

Jaspre wept soundlessly, her heart, her spirit, breaking.

"*Go,*" hissed the woman.

Jaspre ran soundlessly away.

After a while, the woman came to her feet. She returned across the chamber and regarded the opened Pentacle, the bowl of blood.

"Do you deny me still?" she asked. "Or do you only make a test of me? You shall have more. You shall have all of her, as I vowed, the supreme gift, the willing sacrifice of a human life. She will die for you with ecstasy and joy, in all her beauty, virgin, innocent, and wise. As I have caused her to be, a matchless unplucked flower set down upon your altar. Have I not devoted the sum of my energies to your service? You know I hunger for the power that only you can deliver. You *know*. But you will bargain, as in the days of the First Earth. Yes, you shall have more, much more."

THREE

The moon rose late upon the walled garden. It hollowed the sky above to a milky blueness, and touched the formal walks below with dainty traceries like lace, and in the wilder grottoes found out the pale limbs of nymphs and the mirrors of water. Passing the sundial, making of it a moon-dial, the moon let fall a long veil on to a lawn hedged by the briers of a savage shrubbery, and so found Jaspre too. She sat upon the ground. Her hands, which had been dishes for her tears, now lay as if slain in her lap. Her eyes were dry, her heart a desert.

Her flight had brought her here, close to the outer wall, and she had glimpsed above it those claws of the blasted trees which were all she had ever seen of the outer world. A waste, wilderness must lie beyond the wall. And now, her life was such a wilderness. She could not mourn. She could no longer weep. Not grasping the essence of annihilation, she wished only to cease, to be no more, as if sunk in some profound sleep devoid of wakening.

It was unnecessary for her to search about herself. Even when the moon blushed through the garden, there was, for Jaspre's desolation, nothing to gaze on. And then some dormant nerve, rousing in spite of her, caused her to glance, to see the lawn, the dense shrubbery, and, seated between the two, the still shape that was neither plant nor statue.

Jaspre's hands revived and sprang together. She started up, young enough to experience terror even in her misery. But the shape ascended with her, steeped in moonlight. So she saw—not image, not dream—but an actual man, and scarcely seven paces away. His unknown features were handsome, even in the mezzotint of the moon, though drained by the moon as if seen through a fine gauze. His hair looked dark, his eyes brilliant. His clothes were quite alien to her, being classically functional—the wear of a woodsman or a hunter from one of her painted books.

She said nothing. Her sheer innocence did not provide for her the ready suspicion and the outcry of another. Yet she feared, feared till he spoke. And then his voice lulled her by its gentleness, by the curious words he offered.

"Sweet girl, your hair, which is like the sun by day, becomes the moon by night."

"How do you know me?" Jaspre asked, wonder easing her anxiety as anxiety had eased her despair.

"I do not know you. The witch's house is avoided. But once, I came through the wood, and heard melody and singing. It was not she. A creeper robes the wall. I climbed it. I saw you. I see you now. But know you I do not."

Jaspre turned a little way, toward the distant house from which the wide length of the garden separated her. It was an intuitive response, to evade him. And yet it was the house she now wished to evade, and all remembered and familiar things, tainted by her failure, the harsh and hating phrases of the woman this man named "the witch." She had flown here, and could not fly back into such dismal shelter. Entrapped, she shuddered. She had been kept from her own kind. She guessed this was a crime—to converse with a man. She had been offered to a god. Who had refused her. A fresh dawn of pain broke on her, a fresh river of tears.

"Why do you weep?" the man murmured. He had drawn closer and though she had turned from him, she did not move away. "Do you fear me so very greatly?"

"No," she said. Her tears were once more ceaseless.

"Is it then that hag who mistreats you?"

"I am worthless," said Jaspre. "I desire only to die."

"You are lovely," he said. "You must live."

"I was born for one purpose, and cannot hope for it."

"What strange purpose can that have been?"

Her tongue could not render all his titles, yet: "A lord," she sobbed, snared by the unique and final easement of confession, confiding. "A prince of a prince—and he does not want me. I am vile to him."

"He told you this?"

"My lady told me it was so."

His voice was already murmuring at her ear, and now his arm slid around her. In her grief and wretchedness she leaned against him, aware this was some further sin, yet unable to deny herself the comfort of it.

"Silver maiden," he said, and held her so she might rest, "Say I am a prince. Will you take me as your lord instead?"

But Jaspre, truthful in her naïveté, answered quietly,

"You are not a prince."

"Yes," he said, and laughed. His laugh was like warm music, and she recalled that other laughter in her dream, so terrible, so cold, and the destructive icy flame that leapt from it. "These are merely the clothes I wander in. Trust me, I have finery, I have horses flowered in metal and jewels. I have a kingdom, and rule there."

"No," she said, but she laid her head against his shoulder.

He smiled. His lips found her hair, her forehead, eyelids, lashes, and her tears ended.

"Will you take me, then, for myself alone?"

"Take you for yourself?" she whispered.

"As love, as lord. Your prince, if no other's, gorgeous Jaspre?"

"How do you know my name?"

"I heard her call you, the hag in the house."

Jaspre raised her eyes. She beheld him again, more sufficiently now. Remotely, the darkness of his hair calmed her, a reminiscence. And it seemed to her that, although he was not the statue, nor a god, yet he was more wonderful than the phantom she had been given to, his eyes like stars, his face like an angel's—and though she had been allowed her life that she should serve one alone, and that the demon prince Angemal, yet it came to her all at once that to love him had been her error. Then, the man who stood with her, holding her in his strong arms, warming and soothing her with his nearness and his own human beauty, kissed her mouth. The kiss was like no other touch, no other sensation ever before felt, or looked for. It seemed to her indeed she slept and had passed thereby into some other world. Or that, for the very first, she had awakened.

From the depths of this extraordinary state, as if beneath water, she heard him say, "You are imprisoned here. Come with me, I will release you from your jail."

Metaphysically she struggled then, with everything, and with herself. And was brought at last to say: "No. I may not leave this place."

"Yes. You may, you shall."

Jaspre hung her head, the comprehension of the wrong she did now awesome, almost pleasing, yet dreadful and to be dreaded.

And in that moment flame burst like lightning from the far

off shadow of the house. A lamp had been kindled in Jaspre's apartment.

"She searches for you," he said. "Go in to her. Tomorrow, at moonrise, return to this spot. You will find me here."

"No, I shall not return."

"It is a charm I set on you."

"No. No."

"I will draw you back to me. You shall see. By a chain of stars."

"No."

A footstep clacked upon a path.

His arms let her free, and Jaspre moved toward the footstep like a clockwork thing. Deception was new to her, a sword which cut her hands She did not look back, but beyond the clouded shrubbery, beyond a hedge, a walk, a tree with the moon like a white fruit in its branches, his voice stole once again to her ear, a moth of sound, no more, that replied only: *Yes.*

The woman stood, black on the lighted window, one foot on the paving which led into the garden, waiting. She spoke to Jaspre, toneless now, and cool, no longer harsh. There was in this mode a sort of forgiveness, a promise of leniency. Conjured before Jaspre's dazzled eyes, the image of Angemal in his black garments formed, and faded. The unknown lover's mortal kisses lingered on her skin.

The world was round and moved upon its axis, so the young girl knew quite well from her studies. The stars were fixed, it was the Earth which traveled, save for those wandering errants, the planets, which came and went on their own invisible roads across the dusks of morning and of evening and the enormous night of the outer spaces, which held everything. And yet, how contrary perception, which knew as well, and better, that the sun, the moon, the stars arose and set. The earth was flat beneath a dome of ether which flooded with light or dark only as the fire of the sun illumined it or went out.

And so with Jaspre's world, which had become two things: The impossible, which was reality, the reality which was impossible.

The witch's servant and doll, pressed now into rituals of fast and trance, into kneelings upon stone, crystals told like a rosary in her hands, incantations hymned, a pilgrimage along the inner path to him, the god of shadows, the prince of darknesses. Perfection to be made more perfect, fineness to be refined, until acceptable, until irresistible. This, the world as it was. And in the garden, the other earth, the landscape of truth growing every second more actual, making all else a ghost, and yet never to be realized. This, the deception, the mirage.

They walked under the black leaves, the silver branches. They leaned together on pillows of moss, only their hands linked, now and then their lips brushing, but as the leaves brushed overhead, like children. His patience in all seduction was inexhaustible, this stranger from beyond the wall. He spoke of the world's wonders, of seas and citadels, mountains, markets, the swarms of mankind, urging her to seek them with him. He mentioned a towered city and she knew he lied when he seemed to say that it was his. "I will not come away with you," she said. "Tomorrow, do not wait for me here." But always he returned, and Jaspre also. She came to gaze on him, to gaze and gaze, entranced by his features, the graceful gestures which he made. These trances were unlike the trances of the insularium. She fasted only in his absence. Like a certain flower, her love died in one area, sprang upward in another. To Jaspre now he was more handsome than the dream of Angemal. She worshiped at a human altar. The inspiration of the witch's god—Ahriman, Asmodeus, Bel, Satan—fell from her like charcoaled petals, and seemed done.

She felt no danger. Nor it seemed did her lover. His constant pleas, disciplined and never actually pleading, that she should escape with him at once, always *now* this night, this, or this, it had no slightest savor of panic. It seemed he thought time ever on his side, eternity before them in which he might persuade, in which she could decide.

And she, trained like a vine to the surface of her passions, heights but not depths, beheld all as it was, developing upon it her longings and her theme. She never checked at the sweep of a bird's wing over the moon, a shimmer of taloned briers, rustling among grasses. She had no guilt, no apprehension. She had a distant fear, but not of any subtle thing. She seemed to sense the abyss of the tower descending before her, and the great fall she must accomplish, and the ultimate rejection, no longer despair, but a terror past enduring. Yet, it was to come. It was the earth-turning sunset, moon-set. A fact that all evidence perceptible assured her was not so.

"How old are you, Jaspre?" the woman asked.

"I am fifteen years of age, my lady."

"You are pale and sullen. Do you mean to be?"

"No, my lady."

"Give me your hand. Do you see this faint scar on your wrist? Do you remember how it came there?"

"I remember a binding. When the binding was taken away, I saw the mark."

"Tonight you may not wander in the garden. In an hour, when the twilight is finished, you will enter the insularium."

The woman sat brooding in her stone house on fifteen years of power that had not yet come to her, on a statue with jeweled eyes, fingers, feet, until her servant advanced into the room, that tall man, the dark-skinned Eastern mute.

In his language of signs, which she had taught him and which only they knew, he spoke to her. He had watched the portico. It was ever the same. A young man would appear, slender, his movements catlike and elegant, his face in shadow, the moon at his back. And Jaspre would go to him. They would lie together, but not in carnality. She was a virgin yet, the pure child who was the price, the bargain, the golden rope into Hell the Underworld.

Demons had tempted maidens with apples. Peerless maidens, exquisite youths, these were the apples with which demons were tempted. Reared from birth to particular ways, definite forms, pliant, sweet, unblemished. Once bitten into, bruised, the spoiled fruit was useless and must be flung away.

Plucked then, but untasted. Perhaps only readied the more certainly. . . .

But the woman saw suddenly with her inner eye, the scavenging father, the lustrous whore, mother to the child. And these devils of the mind, cringing before her also jeered. "Why," the man said, filthy and golden, "he is one step from enjoying her, one minute away from getting her, maybe, full of a pair of twins—a son, a daughter. A powder then, a herb, to make the trouble go away—"

The woman dismissed him, this vision. Next, her flesh and

blood servant was sent out. Only then was one darkened window opened upon the night-bloomed garden.

Black before moon-rise, it stretched its vistas out for her, a carpet, a maze. Nothing stirred, no white figure, the too-early moon of Jaspre. Not even the foliage of a forbidden tree rippled in the low wind.

Presently the woman passed from black night to a black lacquer door, and down into her sorcerous cellar.

FOUR

Jaspre descended to the insularium, the first short prelude to that greater, abysmal descent. She knew, her very spirit guessed, that this night was the ending. And she was dull with terror, lax with it, she walked like one almost asleep.

Within, her mind turned drearily about and about.

Her blonde slippers on the stair, she thought of her lover, the moon's rising and his arrival in the garden to find, at last, she had not come to meet him. Her flaxen dress brushing over the occult threshold, she wondered how long he would linger before he went away. On each occasion of their parting she had said farewell to him as if forever, dimly acknowledging this last night would claim her finally, fold her away into its obscurity. From which, her instinct told her, she would not return. Her impulse was not to resist. Such seeds as resistance had never been planted in her character. She was just that creature her mentor had trained her to be—pliant, sweet—only he had left any imprint on her psyche, molding her gradually and mysteriously to other patterns. Yet he had been, it seemed, too gradual, too patient, too much an optimist. Seeing the shadow of the chamber spread like a deep well before her, Jaspre felt a moment's wilder fright, picturing how he might come to the house to seek her, batter on its doors, invite the wrath of the woman's cold and unstressed powers—but he, too, feared. *The witch* he had called her from the first. He had never gone close to the inner walls of the house. No, he would not risk himself in such a way. He would merely suppose the immaculate idyll ended, and so it was. He would hasten to safety. Jaspre mourned and she was glad it should be so.

She had never asked his name, even. In a year she, being

herself, had not thought to ask it. Yet, he had known her name, and might remember her, a little while, grieve for her, perhaps. And she, adrift in endless moonless, starless night, might sense that memory and tremulously burn like the palest spark, until he should utterly forget.

High in the vault of the chamber, the chandelier ignited into fire, not blue but purple. The witch stood waiting, straight and stony, her hands folded, each finger exactly fitted between two others.

"Come here, Jaspre. Disrobe."

Jaspre saw the marks upon the floor, the Circle, the Star of the Five Points, the figures of the zodiac—and other talismans, infinitely less clear and more inimical. The purple glare, while it showed all, seemed to give neither illumination nor dimension.

"Hurry," said the woman. "Why are you so reluctant? Have you mislaid who it is you serve? Yesterday, only then, you laid flowers at his feet and poured wine into the cup. You have been dutiful, but can you have omitted love?"

"No, my lady. Oh, no." If not to resist, she had learned somewhat to lie.

"For where else," mused the woman, "could you bestow your love? Not upon me, for sure. Not upon yourself, for yourself you do not know. Only Angemal is your motive and your lord. Remove your garments."

Jaspre shivered. Her hands hesitated over pearl buttons, satin lacings. Somehow she had also learned the vulnerability of nakedness.

But at length, naked, vulnerable, she lay down within the Circle, and it was closed upon her. Far away then she seemed to see her own luminous flesh, enmauvened by the ghastly candles, dashed with painted symbols, touched with oil and soot and water, and the unholy rosary of crystals pooled in chains between her breasts. The drugged resins uncurled their vapors. She floated in a syrupy sea of dread, her face beneath its surface, drowning.

The woman spoke aloud for a long while, but not at any time to her. It seemed the woman must be speaking to Angemal. And Jaspre felt his untrue beauty hover like a smoking star.

A knife slit the sea, the vapor, glittering.

"Kiss the blade."

Jaspre kissed the blade.

"Consent," said the woman. "Tell me so."

Jaspre shut her eyes. "I consent."

The pain licked out, her left wrist, her right wrist. Drums pounded in her veins. With abject horror, Jaspre felt herself commence to fall—

—And the dream began suddenly, and was appalling.

Jaspre hung from the fifth window of the great tower of stone, by her wrists. Two scarlet cords bound them, and she, depending from the cords, drew them tight. Her arms seared and throbbed so she moaned for their agony, while below, the endless drop of stone sheered down and down, and down and down. One other thing fell from the tower, a ladder of gold. Even as she looked at it, the ladder quivered. Its silken rungs sang out. Jaspre realized, even through her blinding hurt and fear, that something had sought the ladder's foot, something climbed toward her.

Angemal came to her, as he had been so ceaselessly invited to do. She recollected the black horse, the black-clad rider, who turned away his face. His face was not beautiful, then, but hideous, so hideous it could blast with fire as his laughter had blasted the fountain of her hair. But, how had such a notion claimed her? Pain and terror suggested it. The golden rope, enchanted from her hair and her soul, tingled, rang.

Jaspre writhed as she hung from the cords of her spilling blood, and the incredible tower swayed like a granite stalk. Jaspre screamed—

And woke as if she had been flung upward through the floor, the witch's face above her, malevolent and intent, its eyes alive, its lips parted.

"Ah," said the witch. "Go back—" and struck Jaspre across the cheek.

Cast from fear into fear, Jaspre was flung down again.

She felt herself, weightless as a feather, spinning, tumbling.

She lay at the tower's foot, and before her the shaft of it ran up and up, becoming a slender pole, an awl, a needle, nothing. A black cloud clung to the side of the tower where it had thinned to an awl. The cloud moved stealthily upward, and she believed it was the thing which now Angemal had become. No ladder of gold, no cascade of golden hair remained to aid its journey. Jaspre lay fluttering on the rock plain beneath the tower, and found herself a white butterfly.

Her body hung far away, out of her sight, screaming no longer, already dead.

Jaspre's wings flickered. She flew up into the air. She flew across the vacant rock, leaving the tower, the miasmic climbing cloud, the remembrance of her own self hung out for it, an empty vessel of flesh.

There was no more pain, and as she drew further and further from the immensity of the tower, very little sensation of any kind. She herself had already half forgotten herself. No longer did she have a name, or any care. Only love remained with her, though love was also nameless now, love and sorrow both, and both limitless and inexplicable. The void and its mists enveloped her. The tower was only a colossal specter at her back. The rocky plain ran on and on, barren of everything. And she, a shining flake of snow, sailed on her tiny tissue wings into the formless dark.

The woman stood, and experienced the enormous energy that seemed now to drive toward her. Its center was the girl who bled slowly to death in the heart of the Pentagram. But its source lay deeper down. The atmosphere of the insularium was charged and murmurous. Vials and vases shifted softly in their cabinets, the telescope rattled, the chandelier vibrated, splashing the floor and the inert body with wax, as if an earth tremor went on under the house.

The woman drew her breath thickly. Her dead eyes were quickened, her mask face almost galvanized to expression. Prepared and ready, her stance never altered as one by one the lights sank and bloodied to extinction.

A vast blackness, impenetrable and complete, brimmed upward through the chamber.

Seeing nothing, hearing no sound, still the woman knew some fabric of dimension gave way. A presence like a cool heat, invisible, untouchable, passed through, and was in that place with her.

The woman kneeled.

"Lord of lords," she said. "You are welcome, at last."

The voice which answered spoke within her head. It answered with one word, a word in a language obsolete and lost, a word no longer capable of any meaning. And yet the woman was granted a total understanding of that word, of all its myriad and profound convolutions, its nuances, its embryo.

She started instantly and involuntarily to her feet in a terror worse than any terror Jaspre had ever known.

And at once a hundred articles fell from their shelves and smashed all about, and the room was garishly lit by burning powders, so not a trace of darkness remained.

Darkness had failed, the desire of all one life had failed. Great fear stole in behind failure, shadow of a shadow.

Yet the woman walked from the insularium, straight as a rule, and in her cold unimpassioned voice, she called the mute servant to her. She instructed him on the cleansing and clearing of the chamber. One further item must be removed from it. The wrists of the girl were to be tightly bound, she was to be found some rag of clothing to put on. Then the servant should carry her outside the walls of the house, among the bone trees, and throw her down there. From her apartment then all the furnishings must be stripped, broken and burned. The bed, the chairs, the rich garments, the harpsichord. Even the jewels must be thrust into a fire, consumed.

The man gestured that he grasped what should be done, and went about it silently.

The woman proceeded through the house. As she moved beneath the many candelabra and the lamps, a silken thing glowed brightly in her hand. With one last stroke of her knife she had severed Jaspre's hair. She had stripped her of everything, her life, even her death—which now was purposeless.

Stiffly, the woman stepped into the avenues of the long garden, into darkness that was not darkness.

Among the pavilions of these trees, Jaspre had played as a child, here she had wandered into her young womanhood, shut from the world. And here he too had come, the intruder, the ruiner of all, who should in turn be ruined.

The moon poised on the peak of an unseen mountain in the sky, as white as fear.

The woman reached the lawn ringed by its savage shrubbery, the spiked and twining briers, and there she saw him immediately, now seated, idle and dismayed, now springing up alarmed. The moon chalked in his pale face, the leaves rained black lights across it. The woman saw him as if he were some cipher only, the humble garb, wild hair, wide eyes. Here it was, that which had cheated her after all, had married the delicious fruit in some insidious manner the woman neither knew nor cared to know. He was the ultimate of all Jaspre's treasures that would be destroyed.

"Come seeking love?" the woman said. "Here it is then."

And she tossed to him the golden rope of hair like a spray of silver water over the night.

Then she spoke swiftly to the garden.

At once the shrubbery came alive, lifting on its stems to seize and tangle, and the long briers like spined serpents thrashed and fell down on him. She did not hear him shout or cry aloud. She did not even stay to witness what she had wrought on him, his body whipped, clawed, flayed, his eyes scratched out. She turned and retraced her way briskly toward the house and into it, not glancing back.

Directly returning to the insularium, she found the mess of misadventure already tidied; and the half-dead useless thing had been dragged from her sight. While perhaps only psychologically perceived, there swirled the smell of burning silk, the sharp cracks of splintering wood.

All that she must do, she had done. Yet, she had importuned him, angered him, and now he had withheld at last what she had asked and schemed to get life-long—but still she must propitiate him, Angemal who was Arimanio, Prince of Darkness.

So, her rage in check, her anguish reined, she drew back the curtain of samite, the curtain of velvet, unlocked the door of horn and iron. Spat upon, degraded, his word of denial twisting in her brain, she would kneel and worship him, atoning all her days for ever once imploring him. And maybe he would be merciful. Then she pulled aside the curtain of mail and a brazen beast shrieked in her very soul, although the witch gazed in upon the alcove and therefore in upon herself as pitilessly as she gazed upon all other persons.

She never changed, although she felt, soft as a kiss, the curse he set on her, some future of blight, disease or madness, felt it begin within her at that very instant she beheld the statue. There were marks of claws upon it, the precious tintings ripped away and the stone gouged to ugliness beneath. While from the blind bowls of its eyes, the sable jewels had been torn out.

And so she was made aware of the full measure of his jest,

and his fastidious disdain, the one she had tempted with a rope of gold.

Jaspre had flown, a weightless butterfly in a waste of granite. Then, there came a waste of coldness, where frost formed on her wings. They presently snapped off from her like broken shutters, and she smote the stony floor of Hell and crawled about there. But then there came the waste of a great and blazing light, and Jaspre opened her eyes upon a blanched sun with the face of a skull, and against this sun huge fleshless hands stretched out in supplication or in hate.

She had been cast out into the wood of dead trees, which seemed to her to be all the world there was for her now. Her hair had been sheared, coarse sacking covered her skin. Bracelets of agony held her wrists. Her hands were numb and flaccid, and there was no strength in her, not even the strength to lament. So she lay and watched the white sun creep across the fingertips of the trees. The earth was not as he had told her, her lover, yet she loved him only the more for his lies which had been beautiful and kind. And if she must die here in the wilderness of the bone trees, she did not care, if he should only continue to live happily in some dream, or magic place he had conjured.

"But I will take you there, my child," he said, his voice, for her, like music.

And she smiled with joy, supposing she imagined it, until he lifted her in his arms.

For a few moments she lay against him as the pain melted from her wrists and body and a warmth and strength flowed like wine through her limbs, her heart, her reverie, and then she raised her head and looked at him. She knew him immediately, no other but the wanderer who had found her in her garden, the young man she had loved. She knew him also as he truly was, since now he had set aside the screen of illusion. Tall and pale, his hair blacker than blackness, apparelled in the dark of the moon and gemmed with its light, his eyes the oceans and the shores of night, his face no longer hidden, more wonderful than the face of any statue. She was not afraid. Love cannot fear. She asked him nothing.

But as he held her now, the bandaging upon her healed wrists turned to jewels, the sacking robe to velvet. And, as in her dream, her hair grew like a wind and poured over like a tide, a streaming silver that was gold, until it brushed the ground.

The bleached trees parted and darkness ran through. A black horse, flamed with a sapphire mane and tail, and hung with stars, stood against the sinking moon.

He mounted Jaspre before him.

"The soil, the roots of the trees, will open," he said. "My land lies there, beneath the earth. Whatever the woman told you of it you must unremember. The country is not as once it was, nor as you have seen it."

Then the horse danced on the ground and the ground gave way. Far off, Jaspre glimpsed—not darkness—but a glimmering multi-colored luminescence, the flowering trees of an endless spring, the towers of a rainbow city, more beautiful than in any book, and winged with a gilded morning, there in the black pit of the world.

"And this is your kingdom," the young girl sighed.

"This is my kingdom," said the Prince of Darkness.

And to this they went.

The Princess And Her Future

Down in the deep darkness of the green water of the cistern, where no reflection and no sunlight ever come, Hiranu waits. Not with patience, for patience is not a virtue to such as he. Nor with resignation, nor with despair. Hiranu knows, as he has always known, known from the actual instant of his binding, that at last his waiting must come to an end. Some hundreds of years have passed, in the emerald mud of the cistern's bottom. Above, far above, the temple has been crumbling to pink powder, and the great trees of the jungle-forest have woven a parasol against the sky. None of this is of any consequence of Hiranu, neither does it dismay him. He is immortal. He is incorrigibly optimistic. He understands that on one burning day or on one star-watered night—both of which have no meaning in the cistern—he will hear a step on the marble paving, loud as thunder, soft as a leaf. And that step will be for him. That step will be the release of Hiranu.

So he waits. And he waits.

The palace of the Ruler poised at the summit of a down-pouring of gardens. The palace was modest, for the Kingdom was small; however, the gardens were very beautiful, the product of great devotion on the part of the Ruler's slaves. At their farther end was a high wall, and in the wall a little door that gave on an overgrown pathway. The path led into the jungle-forest, and so to the clearing where an ancient temple stood. Creepers bound the pillars of the temple and flowers grew among its myriad carvings. Portions of the roof had collapsed. Harmless jewel-like snakes lived in the courts. Long ago, the rulers in the palace would leave the gardens by the little door, take the private pathway, seek the temple and worship there. But no longer. Somehow, the temple had fallen from its good repute.

The Ruler's daughter, Jarasmi, discovered the unused door as a child, and learned where it led. She was also told by her nurse that a demon haunted the temple, one of the *Rakshasas*, which could take any form it chose: lovely, to entice; fearsome—to terrify.

When Jarasmi was sixteen, she was attended by two maids. Her nurse was dead, and Jarasmi no longer believed the tale.

Jarasmi knew that in half a year's time she was to be married, and she thought a great deal of this, sometimes with pleasure, and sometimes with doubt. One day, as she passed through the marketplace in her litter, a man prostrated himself before it, begging that he might show the princess his wares. Jarasmi's maids spoke haughtily, but Jarasmi, looking out, caught a hint of gold and heard protestations of magic.

"Bring him to me at once," cried Jarasmi.

So he was brought.

He was a strange person, and she did not like him. He wore rags, and humbled himself, yet he had the bearing of one of importance. His eyes, which he kept mostly lowered, were very old. Rather than dark, they were yellow, and the pupils were not round, but slotted, like a serpent's. Surely, he was not quite human. He spoke.

"Some while before," he said, "I served a mighty prince, but I have come down in the world. Now I am a seller of sorcerous toys. Nevertheless, I dare approach the Ruler's daughter. Not that I may sell my goods, but that I may bring her a gift."

Jarasmi drew back, for she was uncertain now. But the man of the serpent's eyes held out to her a ball of golden glass, so clear the sun passed through it in a bolt of light.

"See," he said. "It is a thing of prophecy. If the princess wishes to know her future, she has only to cast the ball upon the ground with sufficient force to break it. What is to be found within will tell her all she desires."

Next instant, he had placed the glass ball in Jarasmi's hand. Uncannily, he slipped aside into the crowd and was immediately invisible.

Jarasmi's maids fluttered about her, all curiosity, but Jarasmi ordered her attendants to conduct her home to the palace. There, she sat alone in her chamber, and brooded upon the magical gift.

It was surely true, she wished to find out the secrets of her future, what her husband might be, and if she should love him and if he should love her, and whether she would bear him sons, and if her sons might become heroes. Such things she had pondered often. At first, she was almost afraid to try the golden ball in case it failed her, showing nothing. Then she grew more afraid, supposing it would show everything.

At length, her need for enlightenment outweighed her alarm. She raised her hand to throw the ball upon the floor—and checked. She had thought so long on the matter it seemed to her the whole palace might guess her intent. The moment any heard the splintering of glass, they would realize what she had done. Jarasmi became nervous and abashed at such a notion. She did not want her Father, the Ruler, to discover what she was about.

Finally, she stole out into the gardens. Here, she again prepared to throw the ball of golden glass. But glancing up, she saw a bird floating in the sky, watching her. She hid herself under a cinnamon tree, but the noon breeze ruffled its branches, and played with her hair—she was not alone.

Bronze fish stared from the pools. Shadows stirred. The flowers whispered as if someone were walking between them.

After some time, Jarasmi found herself beside the high wall of the gardens, and before her was the unguarded little door, which led a short distance through the forest to the old and unfrequented temple.

Jarasmi hesitated for the duration of ten heartbeats. Then she unbarred the door, and stepped out into the deep green shade of the jungle

Down in the dark of the cistern, where it is neither night nor day, Hiranu stirs. He senses his bonds, which are incorporeal and therefore not to be felt—and yet which he feels with great intensity—shiver, like strings that have been brushed by fingernails.

Then the step falls upon the paving. It is soft as a leaf.

The princess found herself uneasy at being in the temple. The hollow intensity of a deserted building hung about it. The bright snakes glinted from the walls. Here and there a spear of sunlight clove the dark, but mostly there was no light at all. And yet she had somehow found her way into a sunken court where there was a large cistern, still full of water, let into the marble pavement. Not a glimpse of sun entered this place, nor into the well, for the temple roofs leaned close and the trees bound up the sky in their veils.

Jarasmi knew a sudden fear, remembering her nurse's tale of the *Rakshasa*. But such an idea was foolish.

"Come," she said to herself, aloud but very low, wary of echoes, "throw the golden ball and learn the secret, if there is one to be learned. Then hurry home."

So, without further compunction, she cast the ball of glass down against the paving.

But it seemed her temerity had marred her aim. Rather than strike the marble and shatter, the ball skimmed over the cistern's rim, and fell into the water.

With a sharp cry of distress, that strangely roused not a single echo, Jarasmi ran to the cistern, and gazed into it. The ball was gone for sure. Not one bright trace could she see of it. Nor any other thing beneath the surface.

For a moment, her princess's vexation outweighed her nervousness, and Jarasmi smote the water with her ringed fist. "Give it me," she whispered foolishly to the cistern. "Am I never to know my future? Give back the glass ball."

And then she turned to fly, for a peculiar surge ran through the pool, another and another. Yet, reaching the doorway of the court, some extraordinary shrinking inquisitiveness made her hesitate, and look over her shoulder.

Something lay now on the skin of the water, round and glittering—the golden ball. It had been returned as she demanded.

Jarasmi hurried near, and stretched out her hand to retrieve the ball. But no sooner did she touch the glass than it broke into a thousand fragments, small as grains of dust, which showered in a sparkling pollen all across the water. Jarasmi screamed—and screamed a second time, for now her outstretched hand was caught fast in the grip of something cold and glutinous that had trapped it just beneath the surface. She could not see what held her so; her hand had vanished at the wrist in green water, as if severed, and struggled as she would, she could not pull away.

And then, as abruptly as it had taken her prisoner, the unseen creature let her go.

Half blind with horror, and stunned by a curious weakness, Jarasmi stumbled from the court and away through the ruined temple.

There seemed now a thunderous silence hung there, and in the forest beyond the outer doorway a silence like deafness. But the Ruler's daughter did not heed it as she fled. Nor did she note the jewelry serpents hid, as it seemed, from her. While the monkeys, which had scrambled amid the boughs above the path, were gone. At last she reached the door in the high wall and dashed through it, shutting and barring it behind her.

As she knelt by a fountain, rinsing her hands over and over, the bronze fish quivered, and darted under stones. But her two maids ran toward her laughing. The sun was low, and soon she must dine beside her Father, the Ruler, in his palace.

The red light on the hills beyond the forest came through the windows and splashed the fine plates, the goblets.

The musicians, mindful of Jarasmi's wedding half a year away, played music that had to do with bridal processions.

The Ruler was in a good humor. He urged his daughter to eat. "See," he said, "how tenderly the meats have been cooked to please you, and how cunningly the spices have been prepared. And how the gold flashes on your fingers as you move them. While, only too soon, I shall lose you to a fine and wealthy lord, who will carry you away to his own palace and make you mistress of it. What can have stolen your appetite with so much of joy and success about you?"

"Pardon me, my Father," said Jarasmi, "I do not know."

But she did.

The sun on the western hills changed from clear red to dark red. Servants came, drawing down the ornate lamps to light them.

The musicians played a bridal dance.

The sun sank.

The hills, the jungle-forest, and finally all the long windows turned black as ebony.

There came a strange sound, audible even above the music, though plainly it was far away.

"Now, what can that be?" inquired the Ruler, growing testy, for the evening was not as carefree as he had envisaged—his grateful daughter sullen and uneasy, his musicians faltering, and weird rappings echoing up from his garden like stony blows at the bottom of a cistern.

Just then a servant entered, and prostrated himself.

"Master-of-the-Palace, someone knocks for admittance—not at the great gate, but at the little door in the high wall of your garden."

The Ruler plucked at his robe, examined a ruby ring.

"It will be some beggar."

"No, Master-of-my life, no beggar. For when one of your guard questioned who knocked, a voice answered from the darkness: *'The Princess summoned me.'* "

"What is this?" demanded the Ruler angrily.

"I do not know," said Jarasmi.

But she did.

And now the dire rapping sounded again, hollow, far away, filling up the night.

"Tell them," said the Ruler, "they must not open the door."

But it was too late. One of the young guard had opened it, and stepping out on the jungle path, had challenged the depths of the silent forest and the tall pillars of the trees. No one was there.

"The noise has stopped now," said the Ruler. "All is quiet."

Indeed it was. A river of quiet was in the gardens, rolling toward the lighted palace. And as it came, the leaves grew still on the bushes, and the night-flying insects lay heavy as drops of moisture in the bowls of flowers. The fountains fell spent and did not rise again.

Quite suddenly, the birds in the cages about the room stopped twittering. The musicians' hands slid from their instruments.

Something smote upon the palace door. Again, and again and again. Cold the blows were, as if smitten under water, where sunlight had never once penetrated.

"This is too much," said the Ruler.

Rising, he drew his rich robe about him. He walked into the glittering vestibule, his servants round him, his slaves throwing themselves respectfully down, his guards massed, threatening with their leaf-headed spears.

All confronted the door, which rang and shook.

"Who dares to knock?" cried the Ruler.

From the soundless gardens beyond the door came a voice: "The Princess summoned me."

"You lie," said the Ruler. "Be gone, and I shall act leniently. Knock once more, and I will set my guard upon you."

The knock came. The palace vibrated at it.

"Open the door," thundered the Ruler, "and kill whatever is out there."

"No!" cried Jarasmi. "Do not open the door."

"Why do you say this?"

"I do not know," said Jarasmi.

But she did.

Next minute, the palace door stood wide, and the guard burst out upon the terrace. Only the black of night was waiting to be let in, and the motionless shrubs that did not stir in the windless air. The wind had crept instead into the palace. It blew upon the lamps and they flickered. It shook the draperies.

"Who is there?" shouted the Ruler.

But no one answered.

Then, returning to the table, one of the servant-women exclaimed. Jarasmi's untouched plate had been emptied. Her untouched cup was drained.

The Princess went to her apartment, and her steps were slow. She sat on a little stool while her maids brushed and anointed her hair, took from her her finger-rings and earrings, and clad her in a loose robe for sleep.

Below, two sorcerers were busy in the palace, and smoke rose. A priest discussed the nature of demons reassuringly with the Ruler. The young guard, who had opened the garden door, had been savagely beaten, and hung from a post, groaning.

"How strangely cold the chamber is," said one of Jarasmi's maids.

"It must be the season," said the other.

Unlike the Princess, they had hurried, and now hurried to leave, the anklets clinking on their dainty feet. Bowing low, they were gone.

Jarasmi sat motionless as a figurine upon the stool.

Jarasmi waited.

But it was not long before the voice spoke to her, from behind her left shoulder.

"You know that I am here, Princess."

"Yes," murmured Jarasmi, "I do."

And she did.

"Why not turn about, then, and see what you called from the cistern in the temple."

Jarasmi wept. She felt a dreadful, drawing weakness.

The voice, however, laughed gently.

"But what could I be that is so fearsome, if a small cistern can have held me?"

"Oh, you are something monstrous," cried Jarasmi wildly. "A beast like a fish, or a frog, thick-scaled and dripping slime, with talons and the teeth of a tiger, and the bulging eyes of a lizard."

The voice laughed again.

"So much? Oh, Jarasmi—a fish? A frog? A tiger? Turn and see."

Then her fear became so vast she was powerless to deny any command of her tormentor's, and she did turn and she did see. And so she beheld Hiranu.

There in the lamplight was a young and handsome Prince, clothed in beautiful garments, and burning jewels, his dark eyes burning more fiercely than any of them.

"I," said Hiranu, "was bound by the spell of an enemy, to abide in the mud of the well until an innocent girl might free me by some inadvertent deed, such as desiring a favor of me. How unlikely this seemed. But never once did I lose my faith that one turn of the wheel should bring reprieve."

Then the handsome prince came to her, and took Jarasmi's hand. His touch was delightful, and all her strength seemed to flow away.

"And now, exquisite Princess, I wish only that you will come with me to my Kingdom, and rule with me. And I will love you all your life."

At which, he kissed her, and every lamp in the chamber died.

In the pale azure hour before sunrise, the Ruler gave his only daughter to a foreign prince, to be his wife.

Presently, a wonderful carriage was driven into the court before the great gate of the palace. It was hung with scarlet, and fringed with gold, while silver discs made rippling music from each drape and fold. The window-spaces were filled by screens of carved ivory, and their eyelets closed with precious gems, so none might look in—or out. Reddish horses pulled the carriage, and the moment they stopped, their driver leapt down and ran to Hiranu, kneeling at his feet.

"This is my loyal servant," said Hiranu, "who all these years has patiently awaited my return."

And he embraced the man, and sent him to kneel also to Jarasmi. This the servant did, placing in her hands a white flower. When he rose, she saw his eyes were bright yellow as a snake's.

Jarasmi entered the carriage with her bridegroom, and the carriage was closed.

The Ruler stood before the palace door and watched the carriage rush away. He caressed the huge emerald the young Prince had given him, which was larger than a pigeon's egg, and the diamond that was even larger. The Ruler's face was sallow and his hands trembled so that soon he dropped both jewels. His slaves scrambled to retrieve them, as, from the halls of the Palace, there lifted the notes of a dreadful lamentation.

In the darkened carriage, Hiranu is almost done, now, with waiting.

Beyond the scarlet, gold and ivory, the day begins to blossom, but he will not see it; day and night are all one within the dark. He can, of course, see his bride perfectly well. And if she sees him less perfectly in the blackness, she may at last be glad of it.

How swiftly they travel through the jungle-forest. Perhaps, by moonrise, he will have reached his home. His bride, unfortunately will not. But it was true, he will love her all her life.

Hiranu turns to her, the means of his deliverance. She is finding it hard to smile at him; her smiles resemble, more often than not, winces of terror. Yet, garnished by her flower, she attends. She is here, and no one can come to her aid at all.

Hiranu ceases to wait. He assumes, very quickly, and with a degree of simple pleasure, his other form.

The sealed carriage does not reveal it. While Jarasmi's frenzied shrieks are muffled, and in any case, do not continue long.

Wolfland

1

When the summons arrived from Anna the Matriarch, Lisel did not wish to obey. The twilit winter had already come, and the great snows were down, spreading their aprons of shining ice, turning the trees to crystal candelabra. Lisel wanted to stay in the city, skating fur-clad on the frozen river beneath the torches, dancing till four in the morning, a vivid blonde in the flame-bright ballrooms, breaking hearts and not minding, lying late next day like a cat in her warm, soft bed. She did not want to go traveling several hours into the north to visit Anna the Matriarch.

Lisel's mother had been dead sixteen years, all Lisel's life. Her father had let her have her own way, in almost everything, for about the same length of time. But Anna the Matriarch, Lisel's maternal grandmother, was exceedingly rich. She lived thirty miles from the city, in a great wild château in the great wild forest.

A portrait of Anna as a young widow hung in the gallery of Lisel's father's house, a wicked-looking bone-pale person in a black dress, with rubies and diamonds at her throat, and in her ivory yellow hair. Even in her absence, Anna had always had a say in things. A recluse, she had still manipulated like a puppet-master from behind the curtain of the forest. Periodic instructions had been sent, pertaining to Lisel. The girl must be educated by this or that method. She must gain this or that accomplishment, read this or that book, favor this or that cologne or color or jewel. The latter orders were always uncannily apposite and were often complemented by applicable—and sumptuous—gifts. The summons came in company with such. A swirling cloak of scarlet velvet leapt like a fire from its box to Lisel's hands. It was lined with albino fur, all but the hood, which was lined with the finest and heaviest red brocade. A clasp of gold joined the garment at the throat, the two portions, when closed, forming Anna's personal device, a many-petaled flower. Lisel had exclaimed with pleasure, embracing the cloak, picturing herself flying in it across the solid white river like a dangerous blood-red rose. Then the letter fell from its folds.

Lisel had never seen her grandmother, at least, not intelligently, for Anna had been in her proximity on one occasion only: the hour of her birth. Then, one glimpse had apparently sufficed. Anna had snatched it, and sped away from her son-in-law's house and the salubrious city in a demented black carriage. Now, as peremptory as then, she demanded that Lisel come to visit her before the week was out. Over thirty miles, into the uncivilized northern forest, to the strange mansion in the snow.

"Preposterous," said Lisel's father. "The woman is mad, as I've always suspected."

"I shan't go," said Lisel.

They both knew quite well that she would.

One day, every considerable thing her grandmother possessed would pass to Lisel, providing Lisel did not incur Anna's displeasure.

Half a week later, Lisel, was on the northern road.

She sat amid cushions and rugs, in a high sled strung with silver bells, and drawn by a single black-satin horse. Before Lisel perched her driver, the whip in his hand, and a pistol at his belt, for the way north was not without its risks. There were, besides, three outriders, also equipped with whips, pistols and knives, and muffled to the brows in fur. No female companion was in evidence. Anna had stipulated that it would be unnecessary and superfluous for her grandchild to burden herself with a maid.

But the whips had cracked, the horses had started off. The runners of the sled had smoothly hissed, sending up lace-like sprays of ice. Once clear of the city, the north road opened like a perfect skating floor of milky glass, dim-lit by the fragile winter sun smoking low on the horizon. The silver bells sang, and the fierce still air through which the horses dashed broke on Lisel's cheeks like the coldest champagne. Ablaze in her scarlet cloak, she was exhilarated and began to forget she had not wanted to come.

After about an hour, the forest marched up out of the ground and swiftly enveloped the road on all sides.

There was presently an insidious, but generally perceptible change. Between the walls of the forest there gathered a new silence, a silence which was, if anything, *alive*, a personality which atended any humanly noisy passage with a cruel and resentful interest. Lisel stared up into the narrow lane of sky above. They might have been moving along the channel of a deep and partly frozen stream. When the drowned sun flashed through, splinters of light scattered and went out as if in water.

The tall pines in their pelts of snow seemed poised to lurch across the road.

The sled had been driving through the forest for perhaps another hour, when a wolf wailed somewhere amid the trees. Rather than break the silence of the place, the cry seemed born of the silence, a natural expression of the landscape's cold solitude and immensity.

The outriders touched the pistols in their belts, almost religiously, and the nearest of the three leaned to Lisel.

"Madame Anna's house isn't so far from here. In any case we have our guns, and these horses could race the wind."

"I'm not afraid," Lisel said haughtily. She glanced at the trees. "I've never seen a wolf. I should be interested to see one."

Made sullen by Lisel's pert reply, the outrider switched tactics. From trying to reassure her, he now ominously said: "Pray you don't, m'mselle. One wolf generally means a pack, and once the snow comes, they're hungry."

"As my father's servant, I would expect you to sacrifice yourself for me, of course," said Lisel. "A fine strong man like you should keep a pack of wolves busy long enough for the rest of us to escape."

The man scowled and spurred away from her.

Lisel smiled to herself. She was not at all afraid, not of the problematical wolves, not even of the eccentric grandmother she had never before seen. In a way, Lisel was looking forward to the meeting, now her annoyance at vacating the city had left her. There had been so many bizarre tales, so much hearsay. Lisel had even caught gossip concerning Anna's husband. He had been a handsome princely man, whose inclinations had not matched his appearance. Lisel's mother had been sent to the city to live with relations to avoid this monster's outbursts of perverse lust and savagery. He had allegedly died one night, mysteriously and luridly murdered on one of the forest tracks. This was not the history Lisel had got from her father, to be sure, but she had always partly credited the more extravagant version. After all, Anna the Matriarch was scarcely commonplace in her mode of life or her attitude to her granddaughter.

Yes, indeed, rather than apprehension, Lisel was beginning to entertain a faintly unholy glee in respect of the visit and the insights it might afford her.

A few minutes after the wolf had howled, the road took a sharp bend, and emerging around it, the party beheld an unexpected obstacle in the way. The driver of the sled cursed softly and drew hard on the reins, bringing the horse to a standstill. The outriders similarly halted. Each peered ahead to where, about twenty yards along the road, a great black carriage blotted the white snow.

A coachman sat immobile on the box of the black carriage, muffled in coal-black furs and almost indistinguishable from them. In forceful contrast, the carriage horses were blonds, and restless, tossing their necks, lifting their feet. A single creature stood on the track between the carriage and the sled. It was too small to be a man, too curiously proportioned to be simply a child.

"What's this?" demanded the third of Lisel's outriders, he who had spoken earlier of the wolves. It was an empty question, but had been a long time in finding a voice for all that.

"I think it is my grandmother's carriage come to meet me," declared Lisel brightly, though, for the first, she had felt a pang of apprehension.

This was not lessened, when the dwarf came loping toward them, like a small, misshapen, furry dog and, reaching the sled, spoke to her, ignoring the others.

"You may leave your escort here and come with us."

Lisel was struck at once by the musical quality of his voice, while out of the shadow of his hood emerged the face of a fair and melancholy angel. As she stared at him, the men about her raised their objections.

"We're to go with m'mselle to her grandmother's house."

"You are not necessary," announced the beautiful dwarf, glancing at them with uninterest. "You are already on the Lady Anna's lands. The coachman and I are all the protection your mistress needs. The Lady Anna does not wish to receive you on her estate."

"What proof," snarled the third outrider, "that you're from Madame's château? Or that she told you to say such a thing. You could have come from any place, from hell itself most likely, and they crushed you in the door as you were coming out."

The riders and the driver laughed brutishly. The dwarf paid no attention to the insult. He drew from his glove one delicate, perfectly formed hand, and in it a folded letter. It was easy to recognize the Matriarch's sanguine wax and the imprint of the petaled flower. The riders brooded and the dwarf held the letter toward Lisel. She accepted it with an uncanny but pronounced reluctance.

Chère, it said in its familiar, indeed its unmistakable, characters, *Why are you delaying the moment when I may look at you? Beautiful has already told you, I think, that your escort may go home. Anna is giving you her own escort, to guide you on the last laps of the journey. Come! Send the men away and step into the carriage.*

Lisel, reaching the word, or rather the name, Beautiful, had glanced involuntarily at the dwarf, oddly frightened at its horrid contrariness and its peculiar truth. A foreboding had clenched around her young heart, and, for a second, inexplicable terror. It was certainly a dreadful dilemma. She could refuse, and refuse thereby the goodwill, the gifts, the ultimate fortune her grandmother could bestow. Or she could brush aside her silly childish fears and walk boldly from the sled to the carriage. Surely, she had always known Madame Anna was an eccentric. Had it not been a source of intrigued curiosity but a few moments ago?

Lisel made her decision.

"Go home," she said regally to her father's servants. "My grandmother is wise and would hardly put me in danger."

The men grumbled, glaring at her, and as they did so, she got out of the sled and moved along the road toward the stationary and funereal carriage. As she came closer, she made out the flower device stamped in gilt on the door. Then the dwarf had darted ahead of her, seized the door, and was holding it wide, bowing to his knees, thus almost into the snow. A lock of pure golden hair spilled across his forehead.

Lisel entered the carriage and sat on the somber cushions. Courageous prudence (or greed) had triumphed.

The door was shut. She felt the slight tremor as Beautiful leapt on the box beside the driver.

Morose and indecisive, the men her father had sent with her were still lingering on the ice between the trees, as she was driven away.

She must have slept, dazed by the continuous rocking of the carriage, but all at once she was wide awake, clutching in alarm at the upholstery. What had roused her was a unique and awful choir. The cries of wolves.

Quite irresistibly she pressed against the window and stared out, impelled to look for what she did not, after all, wish to see. And what she saw was unreassuring.

A horde of wolves were running, not merely in pursuit, but actually alongside the carriage. Pale they were, a pale almost luminous brownish shade, which made them seem phantasmal against the snow. Their small but jewel-like eyes glinted, glowed and burned. As they ran, their tongues lolling sideways from their mouths like those of huge hunting dogs, they seemed to smile up at her, and her heart turned over.

Why was it, she wondered, with panic-stricken anger, that the coach did not go faster and so outrun the pack? Why was it the brutes had been permitted to gain as much distance as they had? Could it be they had already plucked the coachman and the dwarf from the box and devoured them—she tried to recollect if, in her dozing, she had registered masculine shrieks of fear and agony—and that the horses plunged on. Imagination, grown detailed and pessimistic, soon dispensed with these images, replacing them with that of great pepper-colored paws scratching on the frame of the coach, the grisly talons ripping at the door, at last a wolf's savage mask thrust through it, and her own frantic and pointless screaming, in the instants before her throat was silenced by the meeting of narrow yellow fangs.

Having run the gamut of her own premonition, Lisel sank back on the seat and yearned for a pistol, or at least a knife. A malicious streak in her lent her the extraordinary bravery of desiring to inflict as many hurts on her killers as she was able before they finished her. She also took space to curse Anna the Matriarch. How the wretched old woman would grieve and complain when the story reached her. The clean-picked bones of her granddaughter had been found a mere mile or so from her château, in the rags of a blood-red cloak; by the body a golden clasp, rejected as inedible. . . .

A heavy thud caused Lisel to leap to her feet, even in the galloping, bouncing carriage. There at the door, grinning in on her, the huge face of a wolf, which did not fall away. Dimly she realized it must impossibly be balancing itself on the running board of the carriage, its front paws raised and somehow keeping purchase on the door. With one sharp determined effort of its head, it might conceivably smash in the pane of the window. The glass would lacerate, and the scent of its own blood further inflame its starvation. The eyes of it, doused by the carriage's gloom, flared up in two sudden pupilless ovals of fire, like two little portholes into hell.

With a shrill howl, scarcely knowing what she did, Lisel flung herself at the closed door and the wolf the far side of it. Her eyes also blazed, her teeth also were bared, and her nails raised as if to claw. Her horror was such that she appeared ready to attack the wolf in its own primeval mode, and as her hands struck the glass against its face, the wolf shied and dropped away.

In that moment, Lisel heard the musical voice of the dwarf call out from the box, some wordless whoop, and a tall gatepost sprang by.

Lisel understood they had entered the grounds of the Matriarch's château. And, a moment later, learned, though did not understand, that the wolves had not followed them beyond the gateway.

2

The Matriarch sat at the head of the long table. Her chair, like the table, was slender, carved and intensely polished. The rest of the chairs, though similarly high-backed and angular, were plain and dull, including the chair to which Lisel had been conducted. Which increased Lisel's annoyance, the petty annoyance to which her more eloquent emotions of fright and rage had given way, on entering the domestic, if curious, atmosphere of the house. And Lisel must strive to conceal her ill-temper. It was difficult.

The château, ornate and swarthy under its pointings of snow, retained an air of decadent magnificence, which was increased within. Twin stairs flared from an immense great hall. A hearth, large as a room, and crow-hooded by its enormous mantel, roared with muffled firelight. There was scarcely a furnishing that was not at least two hundred years old, and many were much older. The very air seemed tinged by the somber wood, the treacle darkness of the draperies, the old-gold gleams of picture frames, gilding and tableware.

At the center of it all sat Madame Anna, in her eighty-first year, a weird apparition of improbable glamour. She appeared, from no more than a yard or so away, to be little over fifty. Her skin, though very dry, had scarcely any lines in it, and none of the pleatings and collapses Lisel generally associated with the elderly. Anna's hair had remained blonde, a fact Lisel was inclined to attribute to some preparation out of a bottle, yet she was not sure. The lady wore black as she had done in the portrait of her youth, a black starred over with astonishing jewels. But her nails were very long and discolored, as were her teeth. These two incontrovertible proofs of old age gave Lisel a perverse satisfaction. Grandmother's eyes, on the other hand, were not so reassuring. Brilliant eyes, clear and very likely sharp-sighted, of a pallid silvery brown. Unnerving eyes, but Lisel did her best to stare them out, though when Anna spoke to her, Lisel now answered softly, ingratiatingly.

There had not, however, been much conversation, after the first clamor at the doorway:

"We were chased by wolves!" Lisel had cried. "Scores of

them! Your coachman is a dolt who doesn't know enough to carry a pistol. I might have been killed."

"You were not," said Anna, imperiously standing in silhouette against the giant window of the hall, a stained glass of what appeared to be a hunting scene, done in murky reds and staring white.

"No thanks to your servants. You promised me an escort—the only reason I sent my father's men away."

"You had your escort."

Lisel had choked back another flood of sentences; she did not want to get on the wrong side of this strange relative. Nor had she liked the slight emphasis on the word "escort."

The handsome ghastly dwarf had gone forward into the hall, lifted the hem of Anna's long mantle, and kissed it. Anna had smoothed off his hood and caressed the bright hair beneath.

"Beautiful wasn't afraid," said Anna decidedly. "But, then, my people know the wolves will not harm them."

An ancient tale came back to Lisel in that moment. It concerned certain human denizens of the forests, who had power over wild beasts. It occurred to Lisel that mad old Anna liked to fancy herself a sorceress, and Lisel said fawningly: "I should have known I'd be safe. I'm sorry for my outburst, but I don't know the forest as you do. I was afraid."

In her allotted bedroom, a silver ewer and basin stood on a table. The embroideries on the canopied bed were faded but priceless. Antique books stood in a case, catching the firelight, a vast yet random selection of the poetry and prose of many lands. From the bedchamber window, Lisel could look out across the clearing of the park, the white sweep of it occasionally broken by trees in their winter foliage of snow, or by the slash of the track which broke through the high wall. Beyond the wall, the forest pressed close under the heavy twilight of the sky. Lisel pondered with a grim irritation the open gateway. Wolves running, and the way to the château left wide at all times. She visualized mad Anna throwing chunks of raw meat to the wolves as another woman would toss bread to swans.

This unprepossessing notion returned to Lisel during the unusually early dinner, when she realized that Anna was receiving from her silent gliding servants various dishes of raw meats.

"I hope," said Anna, catching Lisel's eye, "my repast won't offend a delicate stomach. I have learned that the best way to keep my health is to eat the fruits of the earth in their intended state—so much goodness is wasted in cooking and garnishing."

Despite the reference to fruit, Anna touched none of the fruit or vegetables on the table. Nor did she drink any wine.

Lisel began again to be amused, if rather dubiously. Her own fare was excellent, and she ate it hungrily, admiring as she did so the crystal goblets and gold-handled knives which one day would be hers.

Presently a celebrated liqueur was served—to Lisel alone—and Anna rose on the black wings of her dress, waving her granddaughter to the fire. Beautiful, meanwhile, had crawled onto the stool of the tall piano and begun to play wildly despairing romances there, his elegant fingers darting over discolored keys so like Anna's strong yet senile teeth.

"Well," said Anna, reseating herself in another carven throne before the cave of the hearth. "What do you think of us?"

"Think, Grandmère? Should I presume?"

"No. But you do."

"I think," said Lisel cautiously, "everything is very fine."

"And you are keenly aware, of course, the finery will eventually belong to you."

"Oh, Grandmère!" exclaimed Lisel, quite genuinely shocked by such frankness.

"Don't trouble yourself," said Anna. Her eyes caught the fire and became like the eyes of the wolf at the carriage window. "You expect to be my heiress. It's quite normal you should be making an inventory. I shan't last forever. Once I'm gone, presumably everything will be yours."

Despite herself, Lisel gave an involuntary shiver. A sudden plan of selling the château to be rid of it flitted through her thoughts, but she quickly put it aside, in case the Matriarch somehow read her mind.

"Don't speak like that, Grandmère. This is the first time I've met you, and you talk of dying."

"Did I? No, I did not. I spoke of *departure*. Nothing dies, it simply transmogrifies." Lisel watched politely this display of apparent piety. "As for my mansion," Anna went on, "you mustn't consider sale, you know." Lisel blanched—as she had feared, her mind had been read, or could it merely be that Anna found her predictable? "The château has stood on this land for many centuries. The old name for the spot, do you know that?"

"No, Grandmère."

"This, like the whole of the forest, was called the Wolfland. Because it was the wolves' country before ever men set foot on it with their piffling little roads and tracks, their carriages and foolish frightened walls. Wolfland. Their country then, and when the winter comes, their country once more."

"As I saw, Grandmère," said Lisel tartly.

"As you saw. You'll see and hear more of them while you're in my house. Their voices come and go like the wind, as they do. When that little idiot of a sun slips away and the night rises, you may hear scratching on the lower floor windows. I needn't tell you to stay indoors, need I?"

"Why do you let animals run in your park?" demanded Lisel.

"Because," said Anna, "the land is theirs by right."

The dwarf began to strike a polonaise from the piano. Anna clapped her hands, and the music ended. Anna beckoned, and Beautiful slid off the stool like a precocious child caught stickying the keys. He came to Anna, and she played with his hair. His face remained unreadable, yet his pellucid eyes swam dreamily to Lisel's face. She felt embarrassed by the scene, and at his glance was angered to find herself blushing.

"There was a time," said Anna, "when I did not rule this house. When a man ruled here."

"Grandpère," said Lisel, looking resolutely at the fire.

"*Grandpère*, yes. *Grandpère*." Her voice held the most awful scorn. "Grandpère believed it was a man's pleasure to beat his wife. You're young, but you should know, should be told. Every night, if I was not already sick from a beating, and sometimes when I was, I would hear his heavy drunken feet come stumbling to my door. At first I locked it, but I learned not to. What stood in his way he could always break. He was a strong man. A great legend of strength. I carry scars on my shoulders to this hour. One day I may show you."

Lisel gazed at Anna, caught between fascination and revulsion. "Why do I tell you?" Anna smiled. She had twisted

Beautiful's gorgeous hair into a painful knot. Clearly it hurt him, but he made no sound, staring blindly at the ceiling. "I tell you, Lisel, because very soon your father will suggest to you that it is time you were wed. And however handsome or gracious the young man may seem to you that you choose, or that is chosen for you, however noble or marvelous or even docile he may seem, you have no way of being certain he will not turn out to be like your beloved grandpère. Do you know, he brought me peaches on our wedding night, all the way from the hothouses of the city. Then he showed me the whip he had been hiding under the fruit. You see what it is to be a woman, Lisel. Is that what you want? The irrevocable marriage vow that binds you forever to a monster? And even if he is a good man, which is a rare beast indeed, you may die an agonizing death in childbed, just as your mother did."

Lisel swallowed. A number of things went through her head now. A vague acknowledgement that, though she envisaged admiration, she had never wished to marry and therefore never considered it, and a starker awareness that she was being told improper things. She desired to learn more and dreaded to learn it. As she was struggling to find a rejoinder, Anna seemed to notice her own grip on the hair of the dwarf.

"Ah," she said, "forgive me. I did not mean to hurt you."

The words had an oddly sinister ring to them. Lisel suddenly guessed their origin, the brutish man rising from his act of depravity, of necessity still merely sketched by Lisel's innocence, whispering, gloatingly muttering: Forgive me. I did not mean to hurt.

"Beautiful," said Anna, "is the only man of any worth I've ever met. And my servants, of course, but I don't count them as men. Drink your liqueur."

"Yes, Grandmère," said Lisel, as she sipped, and slightly choked.

"Tomorrow," said Anna, "we must serve you something better. A vintage indigenous to the château, made from a flower which grows here in the spring. For now," again she rose on her raven's wings; a hundred gems caught the light and went out, "for now, we keep early hours here, in the country."

"But, Grandmère," said Lisel, astounded, "it's scarcely sunset."

"In my house," said Anna, gently, "you will do as you are told, m'mselle."

And for once, Lisel did as she was told.

At first, of course, Lisel did not entertain a dream of sleep. She was used to staying awake till the early hours of the morning, rising at noon. She entered her bedroom, cast one scathing glance at the bed, and settled herself to read in a chair beside the bedroom fire. Luckily she had found a lurid novel amid the choice of books. By skimming over all passages of meditation, description or philosophy, confining her attention to those portions which contained duels, rapes, black magic and the firing squad, she had soon made great inroads on the work. Occasionally, she would pause, and add another piece of wood to the fire. At such times she knew a medley of doubts concerning her grandmother. That the Matriarch could leave such a novel lying about openly where Lisel could get at it outraged the girl's propriety.

Eventually, two or three hours after the sun had gone and the windows blackened entirely behind the drapes, Lisel did fall asleep. The excitements of the journey and her medley of reactions to Madame Anna had worn her out.

She woke, as she had in the carriage, with a start of alarm. Her reason was the same one. Out in the winter forest of night sounded the awesome choir of the wolves. Their voices rose and fell, swelling, diminishing, resurging, like great icy waves of wind or water, breaking on the silence of the château.

Partly nude, a lovely maiden had been bound to a stake and the first torch applied, but Lisel no longer cared very much for her fate. Setting the book aside, she rose from the chair. The flames were low on the candles and the fire almost out. There was no clock, but it had the feel of midnight. Lisel went to the window and opened the drapes. Stepping through and pulling them fast closed again behind her, she gazed out into the glowing darkness of snow and night.

The wolf cries went on and on, thrilling her with a horrible disquiet, so she wondered how even mad Anna could ever have grown accustomed to them? Was this what had driven grandfather to brutishness and beatings? And, colder thought, the mysterious violent death he was supposed to have suffered—what more violent than to be torn apart by long pointed teeth under the pine trees?

Lisel quartered the night scene with her eyes, looking for shapes to fit the noises, and, as before, hoping not to find them.

There was decidedly something about wolves. Something beyond their reputation and the stories of the half-eaten bodies of little children with which nurses regularly scared their charges. Something to do with actual appearance, movement: the lean shadow manifesting from between the trunks of trees—the stuff of nightmare. And their howlings—! Yet, as it went on and on, Lisel became aware of a bizarre exhilaration, an almost-pleasure in the awful sounds which made the hair lift on her scalp and gooseflesh creep along her arms—the same sort of sensation as biting into a slice of lemon—

And then she saw it, a great pale wolf. It loped by directly beneath the window, and suddenly, to Lisel's horror, it raised its long head, and two fireworks flashed, which were its eyes meeting with hers. A primordial fear, worse even than in the carriage, turned Lisel's bones to liquid. She sank on her knees, and as she knelt there foolishly, as if in prayer, her chin on the sill, she beheld the wolf moving away across the park, seeming to dissolve into the gloom.

Gradually, then, the voices of the other wolves began to dull, eventually falling quiet.

Lisel got up, came back into the room, threw more wood on the fire and crouched there. It seemed odd to her that the wolf had run *away* from the château, but she was not sure why. Presumably it had ventured near in hopes of food, then, disappointed, withdrawn. That it had come from the spot directly by the hall's doors did not, could not, mean anything in particular. Then Lisel realized what had been so strange. She had seen the wolf in a faint radiance of light—but from where? The moon was almost full, but obscured behind the house. The drapes had been drawn across behind her, the light could not have fallen down from her own window. She was turning back unhappily to the window to investigate when she heard the unmistakable soft thud of a large door being carefully shut below her, in the château.

The wolf had been in the house. Anna's guest.

Lisel was petrified for a few moments, then a sort of fury

came to her rescue. How dared the old woman be so mad as all this and expect her civilized granddaughter to endure it? Brought to the wilds, told improper tales, left improper literature to read, made unwilling party to the entertainment of savage beasts. Perhaps as a result of the reading matter, Lisel saw her only course abruptly, and it was escape. (She had already assumed Anna would not allow her grandchild to depart until whatever lunatic game the old beldame was playing was completed.) But if escape, then how? Though there were carriage, horses, even coachman, all were Anna's. Lisel did not have to ponder long, however. Her father's cynicism on the lower classes had convinced her that anyone had his price. She would bribe the coachman—her gold bracelets and her ruby eardrops—both previous gifts of Anna's, in fact. She could assure the man of her father's protection and further valuables when they reached the city. A vile thought came to her at that, that her father might, after all, prove unsympathetic. Was she being stupid? Should she turn a blind eye to Anna's wolfish foibles? If Anna should disinherit her, as surely she would on Lisel's flight—

Assailed by doubts, Lisel paced the room. Soon she had added to them. The coachman might snatch her bribe and still refuse to help her. Or worse, drive her into the forest and violate her. Or—

The night slowed and flowed into the black valleys of early morning. The moon crested the château and sank into the forest. Lisel sat on the edge of the canopied bed, pleating and repleating the folds of the scarlet cloak between her fingers. Her face was pale, her blonde hair untidy and her eyes enlarged. She looked every bit as crazy as her grandmother.

Her decision was sudden, made with an awareness that she had wasted much time. She flung the cloak round herself and started up. She hurried to the bedroom door and softly, softly, opened it a tiny crack.

All was black in the house, neither lamp nor candle visible anywhere. The sight, or rather lack of it, caused Lisel's heart to sink. At the same instant, it indicated that the whole house was abed. Lisel's plan was a simple one. A passage led away from the great hall to the kitchens and servants' quarters and ultimately to a courtyard containing coachhouse and stables. Here the grooms and the coachman would sleep, and here too another gateway opened on the park. These details she had either seen for herself as the carriage was driven off on her arrival or deduced from the apparent structure of the château. Unsure of the hour, yet she felt dawn was approaching. If she could but reach the servants' quarters, she should be able to locate the courtyard. If the coachman proved a villain, she would have to use her wits. Threaten him or cajole him. Knowing very little of physical communion, it seemed better to Lisel in those moments, to lie down with a hairy peasant than to remain the Matriarch's captive. It was that time of night when humans are often prey to ominous or extravagant ideas of all sorts. She took up one of the low-burning candles. Closing the bedroom door behind her, Lisel stole forward into the black nothingness of unfamiliarity.

Even with the feeble light, she could barely see ten inches before her, and felt cautiously about with her free hand, dreading to collide with ornament or furniture and thereby rouse her enemies. The stray gleams, shot back at her from a mirror or a picture frame, misled rather than aided her. At first her total concentration was taken up with her safe progress and her quest to find the head of the double stair. Presently, however, as she pressed on without mishap, secondary considerations began to steal in on her.

If it was difficult to proceed, how much more difficult it might be should she desire to retreat. Hopefully, there would be nothing to retreat from. But the ambience of the château, inspired by night and the limited candle, was growing more sinister by the second. Arches opened on drapes of black from which anything might spring. All about, the shadow furled, and she was one small target moving in it, lit as if on a stage.

She turned the passage and perceived the curve of the stair ahead and the dim hall below. The great stained window provided a grey illumination which elsewhere was absent. The stars bled on the snow outside and pierced the white panes. Or could it be the initial tinge of dawn?

Lisel paused, confronting once again the silliness of her simple plan of escape. Instinctively, she turned to look the way she had come, and the swiftness of the motion, or some complementary draught, quenched her candle. She stood marooned by this cliché, the phosphorescently discernible space before her, pitch-dark behind, and chose the path into the half-light as preferable.

She went down the stair delicately, as if descending into a ballroom. When she was some twenty steps from the bottom, something moved in the thick drapes beside the outer doors. Lisel froze, feeling a shock like an electric volt passing through her vitals. In another second she knew from the uncanny littleness of the shape that it was Anna's dwarf who scuttled there. But before she divined what it was at, one leaf of the door began to swing heavily inwards.

Lisel felt no second shock of fear. She felt instead as if her soul drifted upward from her flesh.

Through the open door soaked the pale ghost-light that heralded sunrise, and with that, a scattering of fresh white snow. Lastly through the door, its long feet crushing both light and snow, glided the wolf she had seen beneath her window. It did not look real, it seemed to waver and to shine, yet, for any who had ever heard the name of wolf, or a single story of them, or the song of their voices, here stood that word, that story, that voice, personified.

The wolf raised its supernatural head and once more it looked at the young girl.

The moment held no reason, no pity, and certainly no longer any hope of escape.

As the wolf began to pad noiselessly toward Lisel up the stair, she fled by the only route now possible to her. Into unconsciousness.

3

She came to herself to find the face of a prince from a romance poised over hers. He was handsome enough to have kissed her awake, except that she knew immediately it was the dwarf.

"Get away from me!" she shrieked, and he moved aside.

She was in the bedchamber, lying on the canopied bed. She was not dead, she had not been eaten or had her throat torn out.

As if in response to her thoughts, the dwarf said musically to her: "You have had a nightmare, m'mselle." But she could tell from a faint expression somewhere between his eyes, that he did not truly expect her to believe such a feeble equivocation.

"There was a wolf," said Lisel, pulling herself into a sitting position, noting that she was still gowned and wearing the scarlet cloak. "A wolf which *you* let into the house."

"I?" The dwarf elegantly raised an eyebrow.

"You, you frog. Where is my grandmother? I demand to see her at once."

"The Lady Anna is resting. She sleeps late in the mornings."

"Wake her."

"Your pardon, m'mselle, but I take my orders from Madame." The drawf bowed. "If you are recovered and hungry, a maid will bring *petit déjeuner* at once to your room, and hot water for bathing, when you are ready."

Lisel frowned. Her ordeal past, her anger paramount, she was still very hungry. An absurd notion came to her—*had* it all been a dream? No, she would not so doubt herself. Even though the wolf had not harmed her, it had been real. A household pet, then? She had heard of deranged monarchs who kept lions or tigers like cats. Why not a wolf kept like a dog?

"Bring me my breakfast," she snapped, and the dwarf bowed himself goldenly out.

All avenues of escape seemed closed, yet by day (for it was day, the tawny gloaming of winter) the phenomena of the darkness seemed far removed. Most of their terror had gone with them. With instinctive immature good sense, Lisel acknowledged that no hurt had come to her, that she was indeed being cherished.

She wished she had thought to reprimand the dwarf for his mention of intimate hot water and his presence in her bedroom. Recollections of unseemly novelettes led her to a swift examination of her apparel—unscathed. She rose and stood morosely by the fire, waiting for her breakfast, tapping her foot.

By the hour of noon, Lisel's impatience had reached its zenith with the sun. Of the two, only the sun's zenith was insignificant.

Lisel left the bedroom, flounced along the corridor and came to the stairhead. Eerie memories of the previous night had trouble in remaining with her. Everything seemed to have become rather absurd, but this served only to increase her annoyance. Lisel went down the stair boldly. The fire was lit in the enormous hearth and blazing cheerfully. Lisel prowled about, gazing at the dubious stained glass, which she now saw did not portray a hunting scene at all, but some pagan subject of men metamorphosing into wolves.

At length a maid appeared. Lisel marched up to her.

"Kindly inform my grandmother that I am awaiting her in the hall."

The maid seemed struggling to repress a laugh, but she bobbed a curtsey and darted off. She did not come back, and neither did grandmother.

When a man entered bearing logs for the fire, Lisel said to him, "Put those down and take me at once to the coachman."

The man nodded and gestured her to follow him without a word of acquiescence or disagreement. Lisel, as she let herself be led through the back corridors and by the hub-bub of the huge stone kitchen, was struck by the incongruousness of her actions. No longer afraid, she felt foolish. She was carrying out her "plan" of the night before from sheer pique, nor did she have any greater hope of success. It was more as if some deeply hidden part of herself prompted her to flight, in spite of all resolutions, rationality and desire. But it was rather like trying to walk on a numbed foot. She could manage to do it, but without feeling.

The coachhouse and stables bulked gloomily about the courtyard, where the snow had renewed itself in dazzling white drifts.The coachman stood in his black furs beside an iron brazier. One of the blond horses was being shod in an old-fashioned manner, the coachman overseeing the exercise. Seeking to ingratiate herself, Lisel spoke to the coachman in a silky voice.

"I remarked yesterday, how well you controlled the horses when the wolves came after the carriage."

The coachman did not answer, but hearing her voice, the horse sidled a little, rolling its eye at her.

"Suppose," said Lisel to the coachman, "I were to ask you if you would take me back to the city. What would you say?"

Nothing, apparently.

The brazier sizzled and the hammer of the blacksmithing

groom smacked the nails home into the horse's hoof. Lisel found the process disconcerting.

"You must understand," she said to the coachman, "my father would give you a great deal of money. He's unwell and wishes me to return. I received word this morning."

The coachman hulked there like a big black bear, and Lisel had the urge to bite him viciously.

"My grandmother," she announced, "would order you to obey me, but she is in bed."

"No, she is not," said the Matriarch at Lisel's back, and Lisel almost screamed. She shot around, and stared at the old woman, who stood about a foot away, imperious in her furs, jewels frostily blistering on her wrists.

"I wish," said Lisel, taking umbrage as her shield, "to go home at once."

"So I gather. But you can't, I regret."

"You mean to keep me prisoner?" blurted Lisel.

Grandmother laughed. The laugh was like fresh ice crackling under a steel skate. "Not at all. The road is snowed under and won't be clear for several days. I'm afraid you'll have to put up with us a while longer."

Lisel, in a turmoil she could not herself altogether fathom, had her attention diverted by the behavior of the horse. It was bristling like a cat, tossing its head, dancing against the rope by which the second groom was holding it.

Anna walked at once out into the yard and began to approach the horse from the front. The horse instantly grew more agitated, kicking up its heels, and neighing croupily. Lisel almost cried an automatic warning, but restrained herself. Let the beldame get a kicking, she deserved it. Rather to Lisel's chagrin, Anna reached the horse without actually having her brains dashed out. She showed not a moment's hesitation or doubt, placing her hand on its long nose, eying it with an amused tenderness. She looked very cruel and very indomitable.

"There now," said Anna to the horse, which, fallen quiet and still, yet trembled feverishly. "You know you are used to me. You know you were trained to endure me since you were a foal, as your brothers are sometimes trained to endure fire."

The horse hung its head and shivered, cowed but noble.

Anna left it and strolled back through the snow. She came to Lisel and took her arm.

"I'm afraid," said Anna, guiding them toward the château door, "that they're never entirely at peace when I'm in the vicinity, though they are good horses, and well-trained. They have borne me long distances in the carriage."

"Do they fear you because you ill-treat them?" Lisel asked impetuously.

"Oh, not at all. They fear me because to them I smell of wolf."

Lisel bridled.

"Then do you think it wise to keep such a pet in the house?" she flared.

Anna chuckled. It was not necessarily a merry sound.

"That's what you think, is it? What a little dunce you are, Lisel. *I* am the beast you saw last night, and you had better get accustomed to it. Grandmère is a werewolf."

The return walk through the domestic corridors into the hall was notable for its silence. The dreadful Anna, her grip on the girl's arm unabated, smiled thoughtfully to herself. Lisel was obviously also deliberating inwardly. Her conclusions, however, continued to lean to the deranged rather than the occult. Propitiation suggested itself, as formerly, to be the answer. So, as they entered the hall, casting their cloaks to a servant, Lisel brightly exclaimed:

"A werewolf, Grandmère. How interesting!"

"Dear me," said Anna, "what a child." She seated herself by the fire in one of her tall thrones. Beautiful had appeared. "Bring the liqueur and some biscuits," said Anna. "It's past the hour, but why should we be the slaves of custom?"

Lisel perched on a chair across the hearth, watching Anna guardedly.

"You are the interesting one," Anna now declared. "You look sulky rather than intimidated at being mured up here with one whom you wrongly suppose is a dangerous insane. No, *ma chère,* verily I'm not mad, but a transmogrifite. Every evening, once the sun sets, I become a wolf, and duly comport myself as a wolf does."

"You're going to eat me, then," snarled Lisel, irritated out of all attempts to placate.

"Eat you? Hardly necessary. The forest is bursting with game. I won't say I never tasted human meat, but I wouldn't stoop to devouring a blood relation. Enough is enough.

Besides, I had the opportunity last night, don't you think, when you swooned away on the stairs not fifty feet from me. Of course, it was almost dawn, and I *had* dined, but to rip out your throat would have been the work only of a moment. Thereafter we might have stored you in the cold larder against a lean winter."

"How dare you try to frighten me in this way!" screamed Lisel in a paroxysm of rage.

Beautiful was coming back with a silver tray. On the tray rested a plate of biscuits and a decanter of the finest cut glass containing a golden drink.

"You note, Beautiful," said Madame Anna, "I like this wretched granddaughter of mine. She's very like me."

"Does that dwarf know you are a *werewolf?*" demanded Lisel, with baleful irony.

"Who else lets me in and out at night? But all my servants know, just as my other folk know, in the forest."

"You're disgusting," said Lisel.

"Tut, I shall disinherit you. Don't you want my fortune any more?"

Beautiful set down the tray on a small table between them and began to pour the liqueur, smooth as honey, into two tiny crystal goblets.

Lisel watched. She remembered the nasty dishes of raw meat—part of Anna's game of werewolfery—and the drinking of water, but no wine. Lisel smirked, thinking she had caught the Matriarch out. She kept still and accepted the glass from Beautiful, who, while she remained seated, was a mere inch taller than she.

"I toast you," said Anna, raising her glass to Lisel. "Your health and your joy." She sipped. A strange look came into her strange eyes. "We have," she said, "a brief winter afternoon before us. There is just the time to tell you what you should be told."

"Why bother with me? I'm disinherited."

"Hardly. Taste the liqueur. You will enjoy it."

"I'm surprised that you did, Grandmère."

"Don't be," said Anna with asperity. "This wine is special to this place. We make it from a flower which grows here. A little yellow flower that comes in the spring, or sometimes, even in the winter. There is a difference then, of course. Do you recall the flower of my excutcheon? It is the self-same one."

Lisel sipped the liqueur. She had had a fleeting fancy it might be drugged or tampered with in some way, but both drinks had come from the decanter. Besides, what would be the point? The Matriarch valued an audience. The wine was pleasing, fragrant and, rather than sweet as Lisel had anticipated, tart. The flower which grew in winter was plainly another demented tale.

Relaxed, Lisel leant back in her chair. She gazed at the flames in the wide hearth. Her mad grandmother began to speak to her in a quiet, floating voice, and Lisel saw pictures form in the fire. Pictures of Anna, and of the château, and of darkness itself. . . .

4

How young Anna looked. She was in her twenties. She wore a scarlet gown and a scarlet cloak lined with pale fur and heavy brocade. It resembled Lisel's cloak but had a different clasp. Snow melted on the shoulders of the cloak, and Anna held her slender hands to the fire on the hearth. Free of the hood, her hair, like marvelously tarnished ivory, was piled on her head, and there was a yellow flower in it. She wore ruby eardrops. She looked just like Lisel, or Lisel as she would become in six years or seven.

Someone called. It was more a roar than a call, as if a great beast came trampling into the château. He was a big man, dark, all darkness, his features hidden in a black beard, black hair—more, in a sort of swirling miasmic cloud, a kind of psychic smoke: Anna's hatred and fear. He bellowed for liquor and a servant came running with a jug and cup. The man, Anna's husband, cuffed the servant aside, grabbing the jug as he did so. He strode to Anna, spun her about, grabbed her face in his hand as he had grabbed the jug. He leaned to her as if to kiss her, but he did not kiss, he merely stared. She had steeled herself not to shrink from him, so much was evident. His eyes, roving over her to find some overt trace of distaste or fright, suddenly found instead the yellow flower. He vented a powerful oath. His paw flung up and wrenched the flower free. He slung it in the fire and spat after it.

"You stupid bitch," he growled at her. "Where did you come on that?"

"It's only a flower."

"Not only a flower. Answer me, where? Or do I strike you?"

"Several of them are growing near the gate, beside the wall; and in the forest. I saw them when I was riding."

The man shouted again for his servant. He told him to take a fellow and go out. They must locate the flowers and burn them.

"Another superstition?" Anna asked. Her husband hit her across the head so she staggered and caught the mantel to steady herself.

"*Yes,*" he sneered, "another one. Now come upstairs."

Anna said, "Please excuse me, sir. I am not well today."

He said in a low and smiling voice:

"Do as I say, or you'll be worse."

The fire flared on the swirl of her bloody cloak as she moved to obey him.

And the image changed. There was a bedroom, fluttering with lamplight. Anna was perhaps thirty-five or six, but she looked older. She lay in bed, soaked in sweat, uttering hoarse low cries or sometimes preventing herself from crying. She was in labor. The child was difficult. There were other women about the bed. One muttered to her neighbor that it was beyond her how the master had ever come to sire a child, since he got his pleasure another way, and the poor lady's body gave evidence of how. Then Anna screamed. Someone bent over her. There was a peculiar muttering among the women, as if they attended at some holy ceremony.

And another image came. Anna was seated in a shawl of gilded hair. She held a baby on her lap and was playing with it in an intense, quite silent way. As her hair shifted, traceries became momentarily visible over her bare shoulders, and arms, horrible traceries left by a lash.

"Let me take the child," said a voice, and one of the women from the former scene appeared. She lifted the baby from Anna's lap, and Anna let the baby go, only holding her arms and hands in such a way that she touched it to the last second. The other woman was older than Anna, a peasant dressed smartly for service in the château. "You mustn't fret yourself," she said.

"But I can't suckle her," said Anna. "I wanted to."

"There's another can do that," said the woman. "Rest yourself. Rest while he is away." When she said "he" there could be no doubt of the one to whom she referred.

"Then, I'll rest," said Anna. She reclined on pillows, wincing slightly as her back made contact with the fine soft silk. "Tell me about the flowers again. The yellow flowers."

The woman showed her teeth as she rocked the baby. For an instant her face was just like a wolf's.

"You're not afraid," she said. "*He* is. But it's always been here. The wolf-magic. It's part of the Wolfland. Wherever wolves have been, you can find the wolf-magic. Somewhere. In a stream or a cave, or in a patch of ground. The château has it. That's why the flowers grow here. Yes, I'll tell you, then. It's simple. If any eat the flowers, then they receive the gift. It comes from the spirit, the wolfwoman, or maybe she's a goddess, an old goddess left over from the beginning of things, before Christ came to save us all. She has the head of a wolf and yellow hair. You swallow the flowers, and you call her, and she comes, and she gives it you. And then it's yours, till you die."

"And then what? Payment?" said Anna dreamily. "Hell?"

"Maybe."

The image faded gently. Suddenly there was another which was not gentle, a parody of the scene before. Staring light showed the bedchamber. The man, his shadow-face smoldering, clutched Anna's baby in his hands. The baby shrieked; he swung it to and fro as if to smash it on some handy piece of furniture. Anna stood in her nightdress. She held a whip out to him.

"Beat me," she said. "Please beat me. I want you to. Put down the child and beat me. It would be so easy to hurt her, and so soon over, she's so small. But I'm stronger. You can hurt me much more. See how vulnerable and afraid I am. Beat *me*."

Then, with a snarl he tossed the child onto the bed where it lay wailing. He took the whip and caught Anna by her pale hair—

There was snow blowing like torn paper, everywhere. In the midst of it a servant woman, and a child perhaps a year old with soft dark hair, were seated in a carriage. Anna looked at them, then stepped away. A door slammed, horses broke into a gallop. Anna remained standing in the snow storm.

No picture came. A man's voice thundered: "Where? Where did you send the thing? It's mine, I sired it. My property. *Where?*"

But the only reply he got were moans of pain. She would not tell him, and did not. He nearly killed her that time.

Now it is night, but a black night bleached with whiteness, for a full moon is up above the tops of the winter pines.

Anna is poised, motionless, in a glade of the wild northern forest. She wears the scarlet cloak, but the moon has drained its color. The snow sparkles, the trees are umbrellas of diamond, somber only at their undersides. The moon slaps the world with light. Anna has been singing, or chanting something, and though it can no longer be heard, the dew of it lies heavy over the ground. Something is drawn there, too, in the snow, a circle, and another shape inside it. A fire has been kindled nearby, but now it has burned low, and has a curious bluish tinge to it. All at once a wind begins to come through the forest. But it is not wind, not even storm. It is the soul of the forest, the spirit of the Wolfland.

Anna goes to her knees. She is afraid, but it is a new fear, an exulting fear. The stalks of the flowers whose heads she has eaten lie under her knees, and she raises her face like a dish to the moonlight.

The pines groan. They bend. Branches snap and snow showers down from them. The creature of the forest is coming, nearer and nearer. It is a huge single wing, or an enormous engine. Everything breaks and sways before it, even the moonlight, and darkness fills the glade. And out of the darkness Something whirls. It is difficult to see, to be sure—a glimpse of gold, two eyes like dots of lava seven feet in the air, a grey jaw, hung breasts which have hair growing on them, the long hand which is not a hand, lifting—And then every wolf in the forest seems to give tongue, and the darkness ebbs away.

Anna lies on her face. She is weeping. With terror. With—

It is night again, and the man of the house is coming home.

He swaggers, full of local beer, and eager to get to his

wife. He was angry, a short while since, because his carriage, which was to have waited for him outside the inn, had mysteriously vanished. There will be men to curse and brutalize in the courtyard before he goes up to his beloved Anna, a prelude to his final acts with her. He finds her a challenge, his wife. She seems able to withstand so much, looking at him proudly with horror in her eyes. It would bore him to break her. He likes the fact he cannot, or thinks he does. And tonight he has some good news. One of the paid men has brought word of their child. She is discovered at last. She can be brought home to the château to her father's care. She is two years old now. Strong and healthy. Yes, good news indeed.

They had known better in the village than to tell him he should beware on the forest track. He is not anxious about wolves, the distance being less than a mile, and he has his pistol. Besides, he organized a wolf hunt last month and cleared quite a few of the brutes off his land. The area about the château has been silent for many nights. Even Anna went walking without a servant—though he had not approved of that and had taught her a lesson. (Sometimes it occurs to him that she enjoys his lessons as much as he enjoys delivering them, for she seems constantly to seek out new ways to vex him.)

He is about a quarter of a mile from the château now, and here a small clearing opens off on both sides of the track. It is the night after the full moon, and her disc, an almost perfect round, glares down on the clearing from the pine tops. Anna's husband dislikes the clearing. He had forgotten he would have to go through it, for generally he is mounted or in the carriage when he passes the spot. There is some old superstition about the place. He hates it, just as he hates the stinking yellow flowers that grew in it before he burned them out. Why does he hate them? The woman who nursed him told him something and it frightened him, long ago. Well, no matter. He walks more quickly.

How quiet it is, how still. The whole night like a pane of black-white silence. He can hardly hear his own noisy footfalls. There is a disturbance in the snow, over there, a mark like a circle.

Then he realizes something is behind him. He is not sure how he realizes, for it is quite soundless. He stops, and turns, and sees a great and ghostly wolf a few feet from him on the track.

In a way, it is almost a relief to see the wolf. It is alone, and it is a natural thing. Somehow he had half expected something unnatural. He draws his pistol, readies it, points it at the wolf. He is a fine shot. He already visualizes lugging the bloody carcass, a trophy, into the house. He pulls the trigger.

A barren click. He is surprised. He tries again. Another click. It comes to him that his servant has emptied the chamber of bullets. He sees a vision of the park gates a quarter of a mile away, and he turns immediately and runs toward them.

Ten seconds later a warm and living weight crashes against his back, and he falls screaming, screaming before the pain even begins. When the pain does begin, he is unable to scream for very long, but he does his best. The final thing he sees through the haze of his own blood, which has splashed up into his eyes, and the tears of agony and the enclosing of a most atrocious death, are the eyes of the wolf, gleaming coolly back at him. He knows they are the eyes of Anna. And that it is Anna who then tears out his throat.

The small crystal goblet slipped out of Lisel's hand, empty, and broke on the floor. Lisel started. Dazed, she looked away from the fire, to Anna the Matriarch.

Had Lisel been asleep and dreaming? What an unpleasant dream. Or had it been so unpleasant? Lisel became aware her teeth were clenched in spiteful gladness, as if on a bone. If Anna had told her the truth, that man—that *thing*—had deserved it all. To be betrayed by his servants, and by his wife, and to perish in the fangs of a wolf. A werewolf.

Grandmother and granddaughter confronted each other a second, with identical expressions of smiling and abstracted malice. Lisel suddenly flushed, smoothed her face, and looked down. There had been something in the drink after all.

"I don't think this at all nice," said Lisel.

"Nice isn't the word," Anna agreed. Beautiful reclined at her feet, and she stroked his hair. Across the big room, the stained-glass window was thickening richly to opacity. The sun must be near to going down.

"*If* it's the truth," said Lisel primly, "you will go to hell."

"Oh? Don't you think me justified? He'd have killed your mother at the very least. *You* would never have been born."

Lisel reviewed this hypothetical omission. It carried some weight.

"You should have appealed for help."

"To whom? The marriage vow is a chain that may not be broken. If I had left him, he would have traced me, as he did the child. No law supports a wife. I could only kill him."

"I don't believe you killed him as you say you did."

"Don't you, m'mselle? Well, never mind. Once the sun has set, you'll see it happen before your eyes." Lisel stared and opened her mouth to remonstrate. Anna added gently: "And, I am afraid, not to myself alone."

Aside from all reasoning and the training of a short lifetime, Lisel felt the stranglehold of pure terror fasten on her. She rose and squealed: "What do you mean?"

"I mean," said Anna, "that the liqueur you drank is made from the same yellow flowers I ate to give me the power of transmogrification. I mean that the wolf-magic, once invoked, becomes hereditary, yet dormant. I mean that what the goddess of the Wolfland conveys must indeed be paid for at the hour of death—unless another will take up the gift."

Lisel, not properly understanding, not properly believing, began to shriek wildly. Anna came to her feet. She crossed to Lisel and shook the shrieks out of her, and when she was dumb, thrust her back in the chair.

"Now sit, fool, and be quiet. I've put nothing on you that was not already yours. Look in a mirror. Look at your hair and your eyes and your beautiful teeth. Haven't you always preferred the night to the day, staying up till the morning, lying abed till noon? Don't you love the cold forest? Doesn't the howl of the wolf thrill you through with fearful delight? And why else should the Wolfland accord you an escort, a pack of wolves running by you on the road. Do you think you'd have survived if you'd not been one of their kind, too?"

Lisel wept, stamping her foot. She could not have said at all what she felt. She tried to think of her father and the ballrooms of the city. She tried to consider if she credited magic.

"Now listen to me," snapped Anna, and Lisel muted her sobs just enough to catch the words. "Tonight is full moon, and the anniversary of that night, years ago, when I made my pact with the wolf goddess of the north. I have good cause to suspect I shan't live out this year. Therefore, tonight is the last chance I have to render you in my place into her charge. That frees me from her, do you see? Once you have swallowed the flowers, once she has acknowledged you, you belong to her. At death, I escape her sovereignty, which would otherwise bind me forever to the earth in wolf form, phantom form. A bargain: You save me. But you too can make your escape, when the time comes. Bear a child. You will be mistress here. You can command any man to serve you, and you're tolerable enough the service won't be unwilling. My own child, your mother, was not like me at all. I could not bring her to live with me, once I had the power. I was troubled as to how I should wean her to it. But she died, and in you I saw the mark from the first hour. You are fit to take my place. Your child can take yours."

"You're hateful!" shrieked Lisel. She had the wish to laugh.

But someone was flinging open the doors of the hall. The cinnamon light streamed through and fell into the fire and faded it. Another fire, like antique bronze, was quenching itself among the pines. The dying of the sun.

Anna moved toward the doors and straight out onto the snow. She stood a moment, tall and amazing on the peculiar sky. She seemed a figment of the land itself, and maybe she was.

"Come!" she barked. Then turned and walked away across the park.

All the servants seemed to have gathered like bats in the hall. They were silent, but they looked at Lisel. Her heart struck her over and over. She did not know what she felt or if she believed. Then a wolf sang in the forest. She lifted her head. She suddenly knew frost and running and black stillness, and a platinum moon, red feasts and wild hymnings, lovers with quicksilver eyes and the race of the ice wind and stars smashed under the hard soles of her four feet. A huge white ballroom opened before her, and the champagne of the air filled her mouth.

Beautiful had knelt and was kissing the hem of her red cloak. She patted his head absently, and the gathering of the servants sighed.

Presumably, as Anna's heiress, she might be expected to

live on in the forest, in the château which would be hers. She could even visit the city, providing she was home by sunset.

The wolf howled again, filling her veins with lights, raising the hair along her scalp.

Lisel tossed her head. Of course, it was all a lot of nonsense.

She hastened out through the doors and over the winter park and followed her grandmother away into the Wolfland.

Black As Ink

The chateau, dove-grey, nested among dark green trees. Lawns like marzipan sloped to a huge lake like a silver spoon, the farther end of which held up an anchored fleet of islands. Pines and willows framed the watery vistas. There were swans. It was hopelessly idyllic and very quickly bored him.

"Paris," he occasionally said, a kind of comma to everything. And now and then, in desperation, "Oslo. Stockholm."

His mother and his uncle glanced up from their interminable games of chess or cards, under the brims of their summer-walking hats, through the china and the crystal-ware, astonished.

"He is scarcely here," Ilena said, "and he wishes to depart."

"I was the same at his age," said Janov. "Nineteen. Oh my God, I was just the same."

"Twenty," said Viktor.

"What would you do in the city, except idle?" said Ilena.

"Exactly as I do here."

"And get drunk," said Janov. "And gamble."

"I told you about the business venture I—"

"And lose money. My God, I was just the same."

"I—"

"Hush, Viktor," said Ilena. "You should be sketching. This is what you're good at, and what you should do."

"Or take one of the horses. Ride it somewhere, for God's sake."

"Where?"

"Or the boat. Exercise."

Fat Janov beamed upon his slender nephew, flexing the bolster muscles of his arms, his coat-seams creaking.

Viktor remembered the long white car left behind in the town, cafés, theater, discourse far into the night. The summer was being wasted, ten days of it were already gone forever.

He thought he understood their delight in the chateau, the home of childhood lost, suddenly returned into their possession. Seeing his elegant mother, a fragile fashion-plate with a hidden framework of steel, drift through these rooms exclaiming, recapturing, he had been indulgent—"Do you recall, Jani, when we were here, and here, and did this, and did that?" And the gales of laughter, and the teasing, somewhat embarrassing to watch. Yes, indulgent, but already nervous at intimations of ennui, Viktor had planned a wild escape. Then all at once the plan had failed. And as the short sweet summer clasped the land, here he found himself, after all, trapped like a fly in honey.

"Just the place," Janov said, "for you to decide what you mean to do with yourself. Six months out of the university. Time to look about, get your bearings."

He had, dutifully, sketched the lake. He had ridden the beautiful horses, annoyed at his own clumsiness in the saddle, for he was graceful in other things. The boat he ignored. No doubt it let water. He observed Janov, snoring gently under a cherry tree, his straw hat tilted to his nose.

"I could, of course," said Viktor, "drown myself in the damn lake."

"Such language before your mother," said Ilena, ruffling his hair in a way that pleased or irritated him, depending on the weather of his mood, and which now maddened so that he grit his teeth. "Ah, so like me," she murmured with a callous, selfish pride. "Such impatience." And then she told him again how, as a girl, she had danced by the shore of the lake, the colored lamps bright in the trees above, trembling in the water below. They had owned the land in those days. Even the islands had belonged to her father. And now, there were alien houses built there. She could see the roofs of them and pointed them out to him with contempt. *"Les Nouveaux,"* she called them. In winter, when the trees lost their leaves, the houses of the Invader would be more apparent yet. Only the pines would shield her then from the uncivilized present.

Viktor imagined a great gun poised on the lawn, shells blasting the bold aliens into powder. He himself, with no comparative former image to guide him, could not even make them out.

Presently she reverted to her French novel, and he left her.

He walked down into a grove of dripping willows and began to make fresh plans to escape—a make-believe attack of appendicitis, possibly, was the only answer. . . .

When he awoke, the sun was down in the lake, a faded-golden upturned bowl. Through the willow curtains, the lawns were cool with shadows, and deserted.

Yes, he supposed it was truly beautiful. Something in the strange light informed him, the long northern sunset that separated day from dark, beginning now slowly to envelop everything in the palest, thinnest amber ambience, occluding foliage, liquid and air. One broad arrow of jasper-colored water flared away from the sun, and four swans, black on the glow, embarked like ships from the shelter of the islands. The islands were black, too, banks and spurs of black, and even as he looked at them he heard, with disbelief, a cloud of music rise from one of them and echo to him all the way across the lake. An orchestra was playing over there. Viktor heard rhythm and melody for the briefest second. Not the formal mosaic of Beethoven or Mozart, nor some ghost mazurka from Ilena's memory—this was contemporary dance music, racy and strong, spice on the wind, then blown away.

Just as he had instantly imagined the gun shelling the island, so another vision occurred to him, in its own manner equally preposterous.

As he rose, loafed into the enormous house, found his way upstairs unmolested, and dressed sloppily for dinner, so the idea went with him, haunting him. Before the sonorous gong sounded, he leaned a long while at his window, watching the last of the afterglow, now the color of a dry sherry, still infinitesimally diminishing. A white moon had risen to make a crossbow with a picturesque branch: how typical. Yet the phantom movements of the swans far out on the sherry lake had begun to fascinate him. The music, clearly, had disturbed them. Or were they always nocturnally active? Viktor recalled one of Janov's stories, which concerned a swan in savage flight landing with a tremendous thud on the roof of their father's study. The swans were supposed to be eccentric. They fled with summer, always returning with the spring, like clockwork things. Ilena said they sang when they died and she had heard one do so. Viktor did not really believe her, though as a child, first learning the tale, he had conjured a swan, lying in the rushes, haranguing with a coloratura voice.

The gong resounded, and with sour contempt, he went downstairs to the china and crystal, the food half the time lukewarm from its long journey out of the kitchen, and the presiding undead of old suppers, banquets. "Do you remember, Jani, when—?" "Do you recall, Vena, the night—?"

The idea of the boat stayed with him there. He took soup and wine and a tepid roast and some kind of preserve and a fruit pastry and coffee, and over the low cries of their voices he distinguished the lake water slapping the oars, felt the dark buoyancy of it, and all the while the music on the island came closer.

Of course, it was a stupid notion. Some inane provincial party or other, and he himself bursting in on it through the bushes. We owned this island once, he could say, erupting into the midst of *Les Nouveaux*. Yet, the boat rowed on in his thoughts, the swans drifting by, turning their snakelike necks away from him. The music had stopped in his fancy because he was no longer sure what he had heard at all. Maybe he had imagined everything.

"How silent Viktor is," said Ilena.

"Sulking," said Janov. "When I was eighteen, I was just the same."

"Yes," said Viktor, "I'm sulking. Pass the brandy."

"Pass the brandy," said Janov. "Eighteen and pass the brandy."

"Twenty and I'm going upstairs to read. Good night, Maman. Uncle."

Ilena kissed his cheek. Her exquisite perfume surrounded her, embraced him, and was gone.

"Do we play?" said Ilena.

"A couple of games," said Janov.

As Viktor went out there came the click of cards.

He waited in his room for an hour, reading the same paragraph carefully over and over. Once he got up and hurried toward the door. Then the absurdity swept him under again. He paced, found the window, stared out into the dark which had finally covered everything.

The moon had begun to touch the lake to a polished surface, like a waxed table. Nothing marred its sheen. There were no lights discernible, save the sparse lights of the chateau round about.

Viktor took his book downstairs and sat brooding on it in a corner of the salon, so he could feel superior as his mother and his uncle squabbled over their cards.

At midnight, he woke to find the salon empty. From an adjacent room the notes of the piano softly came for a while, then ceased. "Go to bed, *mon fils*," she called to him, followed by invisible rustlings of her garments as she went away. Tied to the brandy decanter, with the velvet ribbon she had worn at her throat, was a scrap of paper which read: *Un peu*. Viktor grimaced and poured himself one very large glass.

Presently he went out with the brandy onto the lawn before the house, and scanned again across the lake for pinpricks of light in the darkness. Nothing was to be seen. He thought of the boat, and wandered down the incline, between the willows, to the water's edge, thinking of it, knowing he would not use it.

"Paris," he said to his mother in his head. "Next year," she said. "Perhaps." A wave of sorrow washed over him. Even if he should ever get there, the world, too, might prove a disappointment, a crashing bore.

The brandy made him dizzy, heavy and sad.

He turned to go in, defeated. And at that moment, he saw the white movement in the water, troubling and beautiful. About ten boat-lengths away, a girl was swimming, slowly on her back, toward him. With each swanlike stroke of her arms, there came a white flash of flesh. It seemed she was naked. Amazed, Viktor stepped up into the black recess of the hanging trees. It was an instinct, not a wish to spy so much as a wish not to be discovered and reckoned spying. She had not seen him, could not have seen him. As the water shallowed toward the shore, she swung aside like a fish. Amongst the fronded trailers of the willows, not ten yards from him now, she raised her arms and effortlessly rose upright.

Her hair was blond, darkened and separated by water, and streaked across her body so her slender whiteness was concealed in hair, in leaves, in shadows. The water itself ringed her hips. She was naked, as he had thought. She parted the willow fronds with her hands, gazing between them, up the lawn toward the chateau, or so it seemed. It was pure luck she had beached exactly where he stood.

He was afraid she would hear his breathing. But she seemed wrapped in her own silence, so sure she was alone, she had remained alone, even with his eyes upon her.

Another whiteness flashed, and Viktor jumped upsetting the brandy, certain now she had heard him, his heart in his mouth. But she gave no sign of it. A swan cruised by her and between the willows, vanishing. A second bird, like a lily, floated far off.

A white girl swimming among the swans.

The water broke in silver rings. She had dived beneath the shallows and he had not seen it. He stared, and beheld her head, like a drowned moon, bob to the surface some distance off, then the dagger-cast of her slim back.

Without sound, she swam away toward the islands of invasion.

"My God," he whispered. But it was not until he was in his room again that he dared to laugh, congratulating himself, unnerved. Lying down, he slept uneasily.

He was already in the grip, as Ilena would have said, of one of his obsessions.

A day like any other day spread over the lake and the chateau, plaiting the willow trees with gold. Before noon, Viktor had one of the horses out and was riding on it around the lake, trying to find if the islands—her island—was accessible from shore. But it was not.

From a stand of birch trees it was just possible, however, to see the roofs of a house, and a little pavilion like white matchsticks near the water.

Viktor sat looking at it, in a sort of mindless reverie.

When he was thirteen years old, he had fallen wildly in love with one of the actresses in a minor production of *The Lady from the Sea*. This infatuation, tinged by tremors of earliest sexuality, but no more than tinged by them, was more a languid desperate ecstasy of the emotional parts, drenching him in a sort of rain—through which he saw the people he knew, and over the murmur of which he heard their voices, yet everything remote, none of it as real as the pale rouged face, the cochineal gown and thunderous hair. Never since had he felt such a thing for anyone. Not even that hoard of young women he had gazed after, then forgotten. Certainly not in the few, merely physical, pleasures he had experienced with the carefully selected paid women his walk of life gave access to.

But preposterously this—this was like that first soaring love. It was the artist in him, he supposed helplessly. For however poor his work, his soul was still that of the artist. The dazzle of pure whiteness on the dark lake, accented by swans, the sinking moon. He had been put in mind of a *rusalka*, the spirit of a drowned girl haunting water in a greed for male victims. And in this way, to his seemingly asexual desire was added a bizarre twist of dread, not asexual in the least.

"Been riding?" said Uncle Janov on his return. "Good, good."

"I thought I might try the boat this afternoon," said Viktor, with a malicious sense of the joy of implicit and unspoken things.

But he did not take the boat. He lay on the grass of the lawn, now, staring through the willows, over the bright water, toward the islands, all afternoon. In his head he attempted to compose a poem. White as snow, she moves among the swans . . . the snow of her hands, falling. . . . Disgusted with it, he would not even commit it to paper. Nor did he dare to make a drawing. His mother's parasoled shadow falling over him at intervals as she patrolled the lawns, made any enterprise save thought far too conspicuous. Even to take the boat could be a disaster. "Where is that boy going? He's too far out—"

Sugaring her conversation, as ever, fashionably with French, Ilena somehow made constant references to love throughout dinner. By a sort of telepathic means, she had lit on something to make Viktor suddenly as excruciatingly uncomfortable as a boy of thirteen. Finally she sought the piano, and played there, with Chopinesque melancholy and Mozartian frills, the old ballads of romance: *Desirée, Hèlas,*

J'ai Perdu. She could, of course, in fact know nothing. He himself scarcely knew. What on earth had got hold of him?

It was inevitable. To be so bored, so entrapped. There must be something to be interested in. He sprawled in a chair as Ilena plunged into *Lied*, trying longingly to remember the features of the girl's face.

When the house was quiet, save for some unaccountable vague noise the servants were making below, Viktor came downstairs and went out. He dragged the boat from its shed, pushed through the reeds, and started to row with a fine defiance.

There was no moon, which was excellent, even though he could not see where he was going.

An extraordinary scent lay over the lake, a smell of sheer openness. At first it went to his head. He felt exhilarated and completely in command of everything, himself, the night. He rowed powerfully, and the chateau, a dark wash of trees against the star-tipped sky, drew away and away. Then, unused to this particular form of labor, his arms and his back began to ache and burn. He became suddenly physically strained to the point of nausea, and collapsed on the oars, only too aware he would have to return by this modus operandi, and already certain he could not make another stroke in any direction.

But the rim of the island was now much closer than the far shore. He could distinguish the matchstick pavilion. Something white in the water shot blood through him like a charge of electricity, but it was only one of the swans mysteriously feeding or drinking from the lake.

Cursing softly, his teeth clenched, Viktor resumed work with the oars and pulled his way through the water until the boat bumped softly into the side of the island.

There was a post there among the reeds, sodden and rotted, but he tied the boat to it. The swan drifted away, weightless as if hollow.

Viktor scrambled up the incline. He stood beside the little pavilion, back broken, and full of a sinister excitement, trespassing and foolish and amused, and dimly afraid.

There was no music now, only the sound the lake made, and a soft intermittent susurrous of the leaves. Viktor glanced into the summer house, which was romantically neglected, conceivably even dangerous. Then, without hesitation, he began to make a way between the stalks of pine trees, and over the mounds of the grass, passing into the utter blankness of moonless overgrowth which had somehow seemed to make this venture permissible.

Beyond the trees was a house, surrounded by a wild lawn and a clutter of outbuildings. Viktor took a sudden notion of dogs, and checked, appalled, but nothing barked or scrabbled to get out at him.

There was something reassuringly ramshackle about the place. Even the house, far younger than the chateau, had a weird air of desuetude and decline. Viktor walked nearer and nearer through the rogue grass, passed under a rose-wine unraveling on a shed. A few feet from the veranda, in a clump of bushes, he came on a small china animal of indistinct species lying on its side as if dead, beside a wooden pole stuck in the ground. The purpose of the pole was moot. For the running up of a flag, perhaps?

Viktor laughed aloud, unable to prevent himself. To his outraged horror there came an echo, a feminine laughter that pealed out instantly upon his own.

"Good God," he said.

"Good God," said the voice.

Viktor, struck dumb, pulled himself together with an effort at the moment the echo voice said clearly: "Why don't you come here?"

"Where?" said Viktor.

"Wait," said the voice.

It seemed it was above him, and throwing back his head in a gesture of unnecessary violence, he noted a pale thing like tissue-paper in the act of turning away from a window. A moment later, he saw a light spring up and go traveling across the house. The impulse to flee was very strong. A lack of social etiquette had brought him here, but now the trauma of good manners, of all things, restrained him from flight. He felt a perfect fool. What would he say when the door opened? I was shipwrecked on your island by this terrible storm that has been silently and invisibly happening for the past hour?

Then the door opened and the light of a small oil lamp opened likewise, a large pale yellow chrysanthemum across the wooden veranda. There was a hammock strung there, and a little table, and in the dark oblong of the doorway, the lamp in her hand, the girl he had seen swimming, naked as a swan, in the lake.

Of course, he had known the second he heard her voice that it was she, no other.

"My God," he said again. He had an insane impulse to tell her how he had looked on her before, and choked it back with the utmost difficulty.

"Won't you come in?" said the girl.

He stared.

She wore a white frock, white stockings and shoes, her blond hair pinned on her head in an old-fashioned rather charming way, and in the thick yellow light she glowed. Her face was not pretty, but had an exquisite otherworldliness.

"I was looking for—that is, I think I have the wrong house—" he blurted.

"Well, never mind. Since you're here, why don't you come in?" And when he still hesitated, she said with the most winning innocence, devoid of all its implications, "There's no one here but myself. My uncle is in town on business."

Viktor discovered himself walking toward her. She smiled encouragement. There was not a trace of artifice about her, not even a hint of the powder he had learned to recognize, on her eggshell face.

She led him inside, and he had the impression of one space tumbling over into another in a melange of panellings and furnishings, and huge crazed shadows flung by the lamp. Then he was himself falling over a little card table, righting it, glimpsing the open window framed in the wings of opened shutters, the tassel of the blind swinging idly in the night air. He saw the lawn he had stood upon, the flagpole and the dead china animal. It was uncanny, surreal almost to him in that moment, to see from her viewpoint the spot he had only just vacated. She was saying something.

"—Russian tea," she finished. He turned too quickly, and observed a samovar. "Will you take some?" And he thought of Circe. He would drink the tea and change into a pig.

"Thank you."

And beyond the samovar, a beast with a monstrous horn. He noted the source of yesterday's music with another small shock. Not an orchestra at all. Of course not.

She had set the oil lamp on the card table, and the light

had steadied. Presently they sat down and drank the dark sweet tea, looking at each other neatly over the rims of the cups. There was nothing special about the room. He had seen many rooms like it. It was rather untidy, that was all, and the paper on the walls was distressfully peeling, due to damp he supposed. But the room smelled of water, not dampness, and of the tea, and of some elusive perfume which he wondered about, for it did not seem to be hers.

They did not speak again for a long while. It was so absurd, the whole thing. He did not know what to say. And was afraid besides of letting slip some reference to her nocturnal swim.

But he must say *something*—

"The chateau—" he said.

She smiled at him, polite and friendly, hanging graciously on his words.

"My mother," he said. "She owns—we live at the chateau."

"Yes?" she said. "How nice."

"And you," he fumbled.

"I live here," she said.

This was quite inane.

"It's very beautiful here," he said, inanely.

"Oh, yes."

"You must be wondering," he said, oddly aware she was not, "why I came up here."

"You said you thought it was another house. Someone you were looking for."

"Did I say that?" Yes, he had said it. "I'm afraid it was a lie. I came here out of curiosity. We used to own this land." Oh God, how pompous. "I say 'we.' I mean my mother's family. And I was . . . curious."

She smiled enigmatically. He finished the scalding tea at a gulp that seared his throat and stomach. Oink?

"Well," she said, standing up as if at a signal. "It was kind of you to call." She held out her hand and, disbelievingly, he rose and took it. Was she dismissing him?

"Well . . ." he repeated. Unsure, he felt in that instant another very strong urge to escape. "I suppose I should go back. Thank you for being so hospitable to a lawless trespasser." The words, gallant, buccaneering, pleased him. Cheered, he allowed her to lead him out to the veranda. "I heard your gramophone," he said, "the other night. Sound carries sometimes over the lake."

"Good-bye," she said.

He was on the lawn, and she stood above him on the veranda steps, white against the dark. He wanted to say: Do you often swim? And a vague wave of desire curled through him, making him tingle, and with it a strange aversion, drawing him away. But he said, without thinking, suddenly, "May I come back tomorrow?"

"Oh, no," she said. Nothing else. He stood waiting for almost a minute, waiting for there to *be* something else, some explanation, excuse, equivocation, or some softening reversal: Well, perhaps. . . . But there was nothing. She stood there kindly smiling upon him, and presently he said, like a fool, "Good night, then." And walked off across the lawn.

When he came to the trees, he looked back. She had gone in, and the door was shut on the lamp, the peeling paper. It occurred to him for the first time that, before he had been seen, she had sat there in that large decaying house in the darkness. As if his arrival alone had woken her, brought her to life along with the bubbling samovar.

He was disgusted with it all, himself, her. She was that vile and typically bourgeois combination of the nondescript and the obscure. He climbed in the boat, loosed it, and pushed away from shore.

As he rowed, inflamed muscles complaining, he cursed over and over. What on earth had happened? What had it been for? She bored him.

By the time he reached the willow banks of the chateau he was exhausted. He dragged the boat into its shed with an embarrassed need to hide his escapade, and went in through one of the unlocked little side entrances of his mother's ancestral house. He threw himself on his bed fully clothed and began in sheer bewilderment to read a novel.

He fell asleep with his cheek on the open book, dissatisfied and disapointed.

The dawn woke him, stiff and cramped from the night's exercise. The long resinous light filled him with a terrible religious hunger for unspecified things. He thought of the nameless girl and how she had bored him, and her peculiar demeanor, and her slender pallor, and the moment of stupid desire. And realized in astonishment that it was the depression of jail he was feeling. He was certainly in love with her.

Halfway through the afternoon, as Viktor was lying encushioned on the lawn in an anguish of stiffness, dreading movement of any kind, a strange man appeared, walking around the chateau from the pine trees with a determined air.

Viktor sensed imminence at once. He hauled himself painfully into a sitting position. Ilena and her parasol, an odd creature from another planet, its second stalk-necked head twirling so far above the first, was parading gracefully up and down a long way off. Janov was indoors, engaged in billiards.

The stranger approached.

"Young man," he said.

He towered over Viktor on the grass, an awful figure incongruously done up, even in the summer heat, in a black greatcoat caped like wings, and a tall black hat. A red beard streaked with darker red frothed between the two blacknesses, and a set of beautiless features, beaklike nose, small cold eyes of a yellowish, weaselish tinge.

"What do you want?" Viktor inquired haughtily.

The stranger considered.

"You, I think. I think I want you."

"What do you mean?"

"Get up, if you please. We must have words, you and I."

Viktor flushed with nerves.

"I don't think so."

"*I* think so."

"And who the hell are you," Viktor cried, "to think anything?"

The man's gelid face did not alter. Only the mouth moved, as if the rest of the countenance were a mask. But he pointed inexorably out across the lake.

"Over there," he said. "The house on the island. You know it?"

"Do I?"

"Yes, you know it. In the night, a visitor. You."

Viktor sneered. He was still sitting, helpless from the stiffness of that illicit row which now loomed above him, it seemed, in the retributive person of the red-bearded man.

"I will say this," said the man, "I do not like my niece disturbed when I am away. I do not like it. You hear me?"

Viktor stared arrogantly into the distance, blind. He could not bring himself to any more fruitless denials, or to argue.

"No further visits," said the man. "You will leave my niece alone. You hear me?"

Viktor stared. He was appalled but not entirely astonished, when the ghastly black thing swooped on him like a bird of prey, close to his ear, hissing, "You *hear* me?"

"I hear," said Viktor, coldly, feeling an inner trembling start.

"Otherwise," said the man, "I shall not be responsible for anything I may do."

Miles off, in some other country, Ilena had turned, her parasol tilting like a fainting flower. "Viktor!" she called.

"You hear me?" the man said again.

"Yes."

"Good," said the man. He rose up and his shadow withdrew. He moved in short powerful strides, across the lawn, away into the pine trees.

Viktor, crouched in an agony of muscles and inarticulate fury, watched him go. The mystery of the whole momentary episode added to its horror. That the man was uncle to the white girl in the house—very well, one could accept that. That he had reached the shore, rowing an unseen boat himself in his heavy unsuitable garments—this seemed unlikely. But how else had he come here, save by flight? And the threats, out of all proportion to anything—Viktor became aware he should have stood up, threatened in turn, gone for one of the servants. That the very activity for which he was accused—yes, *accused*—had kept him riveted to the earth, seemed damning.

And the girl. She must have reported his coming to the island. Said she did not care for it, was afraid. Ridiculous horrid little bourgeoise. Since dawn, he had been thinking of her, wondering if he could bear to woo her, and how it might be done, tactfully and pleasantly. Wondering too with romantic dread if she were a ghost, brought to quickness only by his arrival, swirling into a tomb at his retreat. A vampire who would drink his blood, a *rusalka* who would drown him. . . . And then, hammered flat across these sexually charged, yearning images, this beastly ordinary evil thing, the uncle like an indelible black stamp.

"Who was that man?" Ilena said, manifesting abruptly at his side.

"I don't know, Maman." Not quite a lie. No name had been given.

"Viktor, you are white as death. What did he say? Is it something you've done? Tell me. Some gambling debt—*Viktor!*"

"No, Maman. He was looking for another house, and asked the way."

"Then why," she said, "are you so pale?"

"I feel rather sick." That was sure enough.

"You drank too much at dinner," she said.

"Yes, Maman. Probably."

"What am I to do with you?" she asked.

"Send me back to the city?" he cried imploringly, the perpetual pleading shooting out of him when he least expected it to do so, had not even been thinking of it at all.

"Don't be foolish," she said. "In the city you would drink twice as much, gamble, do all manner of profligate idiotic things." She was smiling, teasing, yet in earnest. It was all true. Under her fragile cynicism her fear for him lurked like a wolf. She was afraid he would destroy himself as his father had done. And he caught her fear suddenly, fear of some lightless vortex; he did not even know its name.

"All right," he said, "all right, Maman. I'll stay here. I'll be good."

"There's my sensible darling."

When she had gone, he flopped on his face. Images of his father, a drunken man who died in Viktor's childhood, rose and faded. He recalled the lamps burning low on a winter's afternoon, and being told to play very quietly. And later, men in black at the door, and a white wax face in a long box that did not look remotely like anyone Viktor had ever seen before in his life.

But he was not his father. And abruptly there came an awful suspicion. That he had been brought here for no other reason than to be protected from the city, from all cities, to be *protected* from the long, animated discussions and card games that ran into the early hours, from the theaters, the cafés, the pure excitement that a city symbolized. A prisoner. In that moment he thought of the girl again, and a strange revelation swept over him with a maddening sense of relief.

Could it be she too was kept as a prisoner? That the loathsome man had brought her there and shut her up there, keeping all company away from her. Perhaps she had mentioned Viktor innocently, hoping for a repetition, and the devilish uncle had flown at her, battering her with the vulture's wings of his cape—No, no, you must go nowhere, see no one. I shall make sure he never comes here again.

But Viktor was powerless to alleviate her destiny. Powerless to alleviate his own.

He wondered which wine would be served with luncheon.

By the time the sun set on the lake he was very drunk. Somehow, he had contrived to be drinking all day. He did not know why this had seemed necessary, had not even thought about it. His mother's fear for him had begun it, and his fear for himself. As if by dipping into the vortex now and then, he could accustom himself to it, make it natural and mundane.

When the gong sounded for dinner he did not go down. He was afraid of Ilena seeing him as he was. But of course she came up, touched his forehead to see if he had a fever, gazed at him with her deep remorseless eyes. If she smelled the wine on his breath he was not certain, he tried not to let her, muffling himself in the counterpane from the bed, protesting he had a slight cold, wanted only to sleep—finally she left him. He lay and giggled, curled on his side, laughed at her a long while, then found himself crying.

He was surprised and shocked. He knew he was going to do something stupid, then, and such was his mental confusion that it was only two glasses of wine later that he realized what.

Rowing this drunk was much easier. He scarcely felt it at all, the grisly laboring drags and thrustings. Nor did he feel any anticipatory unease.

It was quite late, overcast, and a wind rising and falling. This would account perhaps for his only suddenly hearing the music that came from the island, when he was about a hundred yards from the reeds and the summer house. The gramophone. So near, it was obviously no orchestra, tinny and hesitant, cognisant of the little box that held it, and the big horn that let it out. Did the fact that the gramophone was playing mean the man was away? The man in the hat and greatcoat, the man like a black vulture? Or home?

What would Viktor do if he met the man?

Call his hand, of course. Just what he should have done before.

But really there was no need, if Viktor were careful, if he used the qualities of cunning and omnipotence he now felt stirring within himself, no need to meet the man.

Gently now. The reeds moved about him in a wave and the boat jumped jarringly against the rotted post. With the drunkard's lack of coordination and contrastingly acute assessment, he had seen landfall and planned for it and messed it up, all in a space of seconds. With an oath and some mirth, he tethered the boat and got ashore on the island.

No swans. Just the music. And, as he passed the pavilion, the music ran down and went out. He had reached the edge of the lawn before it started up again, a cheerful frivolous syncopation that sounded macabre, suddenly, in the dark.

But there were lights in the house, two windows a thick deep amber behind drawn blinds. They were on the other side of the veranda from the window she had called him from, the window of the room into which she had subsequently led him for a few minutes of reasonless dialogue, and a burning mouthful of tea.

The out buildings loomed. He ducked under the rose vine, stepped over the china animal still lying there, and beneath the flagpole. He went toward the lighted windows, and paused, pressed against the veranda rail. Through the music he could hear the murmur of voices, or of a single voice. And now he could see that one of the blinds was not quite level with the sill. A trio of inches gaped, a deeper gold, showing slyly into the nakedness of the house.

Viktor advanced onto the veranda, crossed to the window and kneeled down, putting his face close to the pane. It was as simple as that. He saw directly into the room.

It was an amazing sight, a scene from a farce. He had no urge to laugh.

To the jolting beat of a dance melody, a couple moved about between the furniture. A huge oil lamp threw light upon them, leaving the corners of the room in a magenta vignette. The girl was white, white hair, white dress; the man a black creature, clutching her close. The tall hat was gone from his head, which was covered with a snarled bush of reddish hair similar to that which sprang from the face. This face, that was for one instant in view on a turn, vanished on another, came in view again, was steeled in concentration, looking blindly away with its weasel eyes. Now and then the mouth spoke. Viktor found himself able to lip-read, with the slight aid of muffled sounds through the glass, and realized his adversary was counting out the beats. The girl's face was blank. Neither danced with pleasure or interest and yet, oddly, they danced quite well, the man surprisingly fluid, the girl following like a doll.

Like a doll, yes, that was exactly what she was like.

Abruptly the dance ended. The man let go and stood back, and the gramophone ran down. In the silence, the voice spoke, quite audible now.

"Better. You are better. But you must smile while you dance."

The girl was facing in Viktor's direction. He saw her face at once break into a soulless grimace.

"No, no." The man was displeased. "A smile. Soft, flexible. Like this."

He turned away, and any smile that face could conjure, how could it be at all appealing? And yet the girl presumably copied his expression. And now, agitated, Viktor saw her smile limpidly and beautifully. He was charmed by her smile, mimicked incredibly from the monster.

"Better," the monster said again. There was a trace of accent, had been when he spoke to Viktor earlier in the day, unnoticed then in the alarm of the interview. What was it? Germanic, perhaps. "Now, sit down. Walk to that chair and sit on it. As I have shown you."

The girl, still with a trace of the magical smile on her lips, went to the chair, and seated herself, ladylike and graceful.

"Good, that is good. Now we will talk."

The girl waited obediently, her eggshell face uplifted.

"The gardens. A bench," said the man. Viktor noted, all at once, that along with everything else incongruous, the foreigner still wore his greatcoat, securely fastened. "It is late in the morning. I have sat beside you. Good-day, m'mselle."

"Good day," she replied aloofly, turning her head a little away.

"I hope I do not disturb you?"

"No. Not at all."

"Have I seen you here before, m'mselle?"

"It's possible. Sometimes I walk my dog here."

"Ah, yes. Your dog. A delightful little fellow."

"I am training him to shake hands. He loves to show off to strangers. Perhaps you would be so kind—"

"But of course. Ah! How clever he is."

"Thank you. I should be very lonely without him."

"But are you alone, m'mselle? A lady like yourself. . . ."

"Quite alone." The girl sighed softly. Her eyes were lowered. The extraordinary playacting went on and on. "My uncle, you understand, has business affairs which take him often from home."

"Then, you spend all day in an empty flat?"

"Just so. It is very tiresome, I'm afraid."

"But then, m'mselle, might I ask you to take luncheon with me?"

"Why—" the girl hesitated. Her eyes fluttered upward, and stayed, their attention distracted. It took Viktor several moments, so objective had he become, to understand it was on him her gaze had faltered and then adhered. She had seen him peering in under the blind.

Stricken with dismay, he seemed changed to stone. But the man, with a flap of his black wings, paid no heed to the *direction* of her eyes.

"Continue," he barked sharply. "Go on, go on!"

The white girl only gazed into Viktor's horrified stare. Then suddenly she began to laugh, rocking herself, clasping her hands—delighted wild laughter.

"On! On!" She cried. She bubbled, almost enchanting, somehow not. "On!"

The man reached her in two strides, and shook her.

"Be quiet. Quiet!" The girl stopped laughing. She became composed, and so remained as he coldly and intently ranted at her. "Was it for this I bought you in that slum, sores and verminous bites all over you, for this? You will be still. You will attend. You will *learn*. You hear me?"

The effect of those repeated words upon Viktor was awful. They seemed to deprive him of all the strength of his inebriation. Stunned and totally unnerved, he came noiselessly to his feet. He crossed the veranda, praying she would say nothing of having seen him. But she would not, surely. She was not quite normal, not even quite sane—He reached the veranda step and misjudged it, saw his misjudgment in the moment he made it, could alter nothing, and fell heavily against the railing.

The clamor seemed to throb through every wooden board and timber of the house. Before he could regain enough balance to break into a run, something crashed over in the lighted room, and then the main door flew open and a black beast came out of it.

He had known this would happen. Somehow he had come here for this—this goal of self-destruction.

"What are you doing?" the thing demanded. It caught hold of him, and he was brought about to face it again. All the rich light was behind the man now, full on Viktor. There were no excuses to be made. He flinched from the man's odorless cold breath. "You are here? You dared to come back?"

Viktor pulled some part of himself together.

"Of course I dared. Why shouldn't I?"

"You trespass."

"No. I came to see you."

"Why? This island is private. You were told to keep away."

"You have no right to—"

"Every right. It is mine. I warned you."

"Go to hell," said Viktor. He was afraid. Could not control his limbs, barely his voice and the slurred movements of his mouth.

"No," said the man. "It is you who will go there. I will send you there." And with no further preliminary, he punched Viktor in the arm and, as he stumbled away grunting with shocked pain, on the side of the jaw. Viktor fell backward in the grass, and saw through a sliding haze, the man coming on at him.

As he rolled bonelessly against the legs of the veranda, the man kicked him in the side. The impact was vicious, filling him now with terror more than pain. Somehow, Viktor came to his feet.

"No," he said, and put up his arm. Like a big black bear the man lunged at him, bringing down both his fists together, sweeping away the protective arm as if it were a rag. The pain was awful this time, and the blow had been meant, clearly, for his head. Viktor had an impulse to curl up on the turf, allowing the man to beat him until he wearied himself and left his victim alone. Instead, Viktor's own fist lashed out. He caught the man on the nose, which began at once to bleed dark runnels of blood. But the madman scarcely hesitated. He flung his whole body after Viktor and caught him round the waist.

For a moment then Viktor felt himself trapped, and envisaged dying. To be weary would not be enough for his enemy. Only death could turn him aside. The man was squeezing him, choking him; stars burst in Viktor's brain.

"I warned you," said the man.

Some remnant of self-preservation—actually a story told him once by a prostitute—caused Viktor spontaneously to knee the hugging bear in its groin.

There was a dreadful sound, a sort of implosion, and the paws let him go. Staggering, Viktor ran.

There followed a nightmare sequence during which the china animal in the bushes tried to trip him, the grass and tree roots likewise. Then he plunged into water, found a rope, tore it free, and collapsed into the boat, crying for mercy to the darkness.

Somehow he made the oars work, and somehow the man did not come after him. Yet it was with the utmost fear that Viktor thrashed his way toward the midst of the lake. There, sobbing for breath, he lay still on the oars, and the great night grew still about him.

It seemed to be a long while afterward that he began to row for the chateau. And by then he seemed, too, to be quite sober, but perhaps he was not, his feelings a slow chilled turmoil where nothing anymore made sense. *My little dog does tricks—Ah what a clever fellow—better, m'mselle, better—* And in the middle of it all, something came over the last stretch of water from the shore, from the lawns where the chateau stood, serene and dislocated from reality.

It was a white something, and for a demented moment he thought the girl had jumped into the lake and swum out ahead of him. But no, it was a swan.

Feeling ill, he leaned on the oars, drifting, watching the swan come toward him. He became aware he must have disturbed it. It did not move like a ship but ran at him standing up on the water, flapping its wings which suddenly seemed enormous, like two white sheets. And abruptly the swan was beside him, hissing like a snake, smiting the boat, the air, his flesh—

He tried frantically to beat it off, to make for shore. This second nightmare sequence had no logic and afterward he did not properly remember it. All at once the boat slewed and he was in the water. It was colder than before, and an agonizing something had happened to his arm. He no longer had any control at all.

The first time he sank into the lake he shouted in terror, but the water was so very cold he could not shout again. And then he was falling down through it, knowing he was about to die, in absolute horror and despair, unable to save himself.

A month later he learned a servant, smoking a cigarette on the lawn near to the water, had seen the swan attack, and the accident with the boat. The man had leapt heroically into the lake and saved Viktor, while the swan faded away into the dark.

The broken arm and the fever had debilitated Viktor, and as soon as he was well enough his mother returned them all to the city.

"A terrible thing," Ilena said. "You might well have been drowned. I remember a story of a boy drowned in that lake. Whatever possessed you?"

"I don't know," Viktor said listlessly, propped up in bed, surrounded by the depressing medicines, the dreary novels.

Ilena said nothing at all, but weeks after, apropos another matter, Janov mentioned a man who had kept his mistress on one of the islands, a young girl reckoned to be simple. It seemed they had packed up suddenly and gone away, and the house was in a nasty state, full of damp and mice.

It was half a year before any of them thought Viktor fully recovered. He had begun to play cards with Uncle Janov, and next, billiards. Viktor had stopped drinking beyond the merest glass at dinner; he had taken a dislike for light and noise, painting and discussion. And so Ilena sent him to Paris, when he no longer wanted to go.

It was more than fifteen years later that he saw the girl again.

In the winter of the northern city, the ice lay in blue rifts upon the sea, and a copper sun bled seven degrees above the horizon. He had been to visit his mother, cranky and bemused, in the house on Stork Street. Such visits, as the years went by, had become increasingly bizarre. Something was happening to Ilena. Arthritis, for one thing, had crippled her, twisting her elegant figure like the stem of a slender blasted tree. Betrayed by her bones, her sensibilities gave way. She made demands on Viktor and on everyone, calling the servants constantly: Bring me that pomander, that box of cigarettes. I want tea. I want my book of cuttings. She drove them mad, and she drove Viktor mad, also. Uncle Janov was dead. He had died ten months before, sitting bolt upright at the card table, without a sound. No one realized he had absented himself until he refused to play his hand.

There had been a war, too, setting the whole world on its ear. Somehow, some had escaped the worst of that.

To Viktor himself, time had offered a few patronizing gifts. He had published four novels with reasonable success. More than anything, writing, which he performed indifferently now, and no longer with any pleasure, gave him an excuse for doing nothing else. He had become, he was afraid, the perfect archetype of what the masses reckoned an author to be: one too lazy to attempt anything more valuable. The family meanwhile remained wealthy; he really had no need to do anything at all, except, possibly, to marry, which he had idly been considering. A much-removed cousin had been presented as a candidate, a lushly attractive young woman, with indeed some look of Viktor himself. She was a nice girl, quite intelligent and entertaining, and maternally adequate, being ten years his junior. An ideal match. It would soothe Ilena, giving her the sense that the family continued, giving her, too, something fresh to criticize. For himself, the proposed liaison was rather like his "work." Something to give him an excuse to attempt nothing else. His libido, having reached a peak in his early twenties, was already diminishing. Sex had already lost all its alluring novelty. He had ceased to fall in love, and beyond a very occasional evening with one of the city's hetaeras, he had put all that away, as it were, in some cabinet of his physical emotions.

And then, he saw the girl again.

It would not have been true to say he had often thought of her. He had scarcely thought of her at all as the years went by. And despite a fleeting reference to the peculiar events on the island inserted into his first book, he had never really reexamined the case. It had seemed to him very quickly that nothing much had happened at all. It had been merely a series of coincidental occurrences, made dramatic only by his state of mind and the ultimate plunge into the lake. The fact that he had never returned to the chateau did not strike him as particularly ominous. He had been bored there. Just as he had mostly been bored in Paris and was now bored almost all the time and almost everywhere. The only difference was that his fear of boredom had gone away. He was accustomed to it now and expected nothing else. It had come to fit him, suit him quite comfortably, like a well-worn dressing gown.

He was walking through one of the sets of gardens that bordered the museum and art gallery, on his way to a luncheon engagement at the literary club. And suddenly he saw a small black shape, rather like an animated sausage, trotting across the whiteness of the snow. It was a little dog, seemingly inpervious to the cold, a very black, very purposeful little dog, that he followed with his eyes intuitively. And then a woman came out between the white trees, against an oval of brown sky. She was fashionably dressed, at the height of fashion indeed, and maybe not warmly enough for the season. Yet like the dog, which was obviously hers, she seemed untroubled by the cold. Like the dog too, she wore black—jet black—save for the tall scarlet feather in her hat and a pair of blinding scarlet gloves, and the scarlet of her lips.

Perhaps it was the maquillage on her face that prevented his immediately knowing her, or maybe only the fifteen years that had separated those three brief glimpses he had formerly had of her from this. Then something, the turn of her head, her gesture to the dog as it bounced up to her, jogged his memory.

For a full minute he stared at her, unable to say a word. She did not seem to see him at all, and yet something in her manner told him she knew quite well a man stood watching her, as she picked up and petted the dog. And then, irresistibly, he found he had gone over.

And he heard himself saying, as if by rote, for all at once he remembered the words: "Good day, m'mselle."

And aloofly she replied, "Good day," just as on the island, through the window.

"Forgive me for disturbing you. But I was intrigued by your little dog."

"Oh yes. I am training him to do tricks, to shake hands. He loves to show off to strangers. Look at him! He's trying to attract your attention."

And Viktor found himself pulling off one glove and extending his hand to take the icy little paw, shaking it.

"How clever he is," said Viktor.

"Thank you." The smiling face, pretty in its makeup, lowered mascaraed lids. No wonder she looked different. The dark lashes, the black eyebrows. "I should be very lonely without him."

Viktor almost choked, but he managed the words: "I find it hard to believe you're alone."

"Quite alone," she said. She sighed, petting the black little dog with scarlet fingers.

"Your uncle is often away from home," said Viktor, between sneering and joking and embarrassment.

"Why yes," she said. She looked at him wonderingly. "Do you know my uncle?"

"I met him, once," said Viktor. "Perhaps that gives me the right to presume. Will you have lunch with me?"

"Why—" she said. She lifted her pale eyes and looked at him. "Why, of course."

She put her red hand through his arm as they walked, holding the dog with the other. He felt hilarious, and had already dismissed the other lunch engagement from his mind.

In the restaurant he talked to her randomly, hypnotized by the perfection of her answers. She replied to all, elaborated sometimes, giving the impression of an utterly charming negative neutrality, restful and obliging. And the little dog was a model of decorum, even when she awarded it a spoonful of the hot chocolate sauce. He marveled at its training, and hers.

Framed in the black bell of her hat, her face fascinated him with its changes, but he longed for her to remove the hat, to show him if her hair, now obviously very short, was still blond. As blond as when she had swum in the lake among the swans.

After lunch, he escorted her, naturally, to her flat. It was on a quiet street, between the ordinary and the modish.

Flowerpots stood on the windowsills, winter bald. There was a plush carpet when, just as naturally, she invited him to enter and he did so.

They went upstairs to the second floor. She opened a door. It was much unlike the wild house with its peeling walls and oil lamps. The paper on the wall was a subtle cream and beige brocade, quite dry. At the touch of a switch the warmth of electricity flooded the rosy chairs, the deep blue rugs.

At this point, supposedly, the true meaning of their adventure would drift to the surface. It did so. Putting down the dog, she returned to Viktor across the pleasant room. Her gloves were gone, and she laid the smooth skin of her hand on his lapel.

"You've been very kind," she said. Her eyes were brimming with invitation. From now on her clients would, probably, become more businesslike. And he remembered how she had dismissed him the first time, on the island, trained also to that.

With a strange sensation, Viktor lowered his head toward her. Her mouth was cool and perfumed with lip paint, curiously uninvolved as it yielded first to the caress and then to the invasion. What did she feel? Nothing? And he, what did he feel? He was unsure. He had persuaded himself to love her, once, the love of the unknown thing. He remembered her white body in the water and a sudden pang of sexuality shot through him, startling him.

The girl drew gently away. "Come with me," she said secretively. And led him into her bedroom.

It was an ordinary chamber, in good taste, nothing lewd or even merely garish, no pictures of frolics intended to arouse or amuse, none of the bric-a-brac of the whore, except a heap of silken cushions.

"Take off your hat," he said to her. "Take off all your clothes. I want to watch you."

The girl laughed, and flirted with her eyes. The correct response. No doubt, his request was not unusual.

She stood then at the center of a red and black autumn of falling garments, and mesmerized, he did watch her, his heart ludicrously in his mouth as once before so long ago, and still the bell-shaped hat was left in place, even now she stood in her slip—he gestured to the hat, unable to vocalize, and she smiled and drew it upward from her head.

Her hair was black. Black as ink. He had not expected such a thing, it stunned him, and he felt again the water of the lake filling his nostrils, his throat, and the old break in his arm, which for years had promised the ultimate penance of Ilena's arthritis, burned and ached.

"Your hair," he said, forcing out the words, his excitement quite dead.

It was smooth and short and black, so black, as if a cupful of paint had been poured over her skull. Fashionable, and horrible.

She did not seem disturbed by his reaction, but went on archly smiling at him, trained as she was—this outcry of his was too far removed from her training to facilitate one of her closet-full of suitable responses.

It was only then, glaring at her, the cameo of black silk and blonde flesh, that he saw she had not changed at all, was just as he recalled, the ink blackness only an overlay. There was not a line that he could see in her smooth face, on her neck, her breast—these fifteen years, which had touched everything, had not touched her at all.

He went forward, and she, thinking equilibrium restored, invited with eyes and lips. But he did not take her to him, only stared at her. It was true. She was unmarked. He put one finger to her cheek, running it across her flesh that was as smooth as wax—And the bedroom door opened behind him.

Her hand flew to her scarlet mouth. It was another learned response, not real. Viktor could see that quite clearly. And he himself turned without any surprise and saw a man in a black greatcoat filling the doorway, his small eyes widened with outrage.

"What is this? I must ask you, sir—"

The voice was less foreign, the accent polished and succinct. The coat was of more recent cut, the face shaven, only a little red moustache and red hairs glinting in the flared nostrils. Nothing had faded, there was no grey. But the lines had deepened, quite normally.

Viktor felt a surge of relief. Yes, relief, that he would not have to go on with this absurd play, that he did not have to have her, the unobtainable, now ruined, thing.

He walked toward the man, who barked at her: "Get dressed!" And retreated out into the sitting room of the flat.

The bedroom door clipped shut. The black figure loomed before the mantelpiece.

"What am I to think?" the man said. "I come home unexpectedly, and I find my niece, and I find you, sir—and she is in her underwear—"

"What indeed," said Viktor. He knew the game, who would not? Once in Paris, he had almost been caught in such a way, if a chance acquaintance had not warned him: the flighty young woman, her husband bursting in—

"And she is a little—how shall I say this?—a little naïve in her wits, sir."

"An idiot," said Viktor.

"And you, taking advantage of such a thing, her plight—I see you are a man of substance, sir. What would your associates think, should they learn what you did this afternoon, how you tried to abuse a young girl of less than average mental capacity. Making her drunk, bringing her to her own home, with the purpose of satisfying your desires."

The voice went on. Now and then, almost smothered, Viktor noted the hint of the foreignness, still extant. He had known, probably, at some level of consciousness, from the moment he saw her in the garden. On an armchair, the little black dog slept, unperturbed by this rehearsal of fierce anger it had no doubt heard a hundred times.

Viktor sighed. He felt nothing anymore, not even satisfaction. Where was the island, the darkness? Where was twenty, now?

"Shut up," he broke in, loudly, but without emphasis.

The monstrous beaked thing did indeed fall silent.

"I do know your intention," said Viktor, calmly. "And I have a piece of news for you. I intend to pay you nothing. Nothing. Do you hear?" But not even this parody of the man's speech pleased him. Viktor went on, replacing his gloves as he did so. "If you wish, you may tell the world at large that you found me in the bedroom with your undressed niece, who is not your niece, but who you—let me get it right—bought in a slum, covered with sores and bites. And whom you taught to behave as she does, in gardens, ballrooms, and God knows where else, on an island, fifteen years ago."

The man's face had set, drawing in about itself, becoming unreadable, and most attentive.

"All of which," Viktor said, "I too am willing to reveal in my turn. Rather a blight on a profitable trade, I would think. And now," he found himself at the door, "good afternoon."

No move was made to stop him. He passed into the lobby and down the stairs, and on to the street.

Standing before the apartment house, Viktor paused and lit a cigarette, as if permitting pursuit to catch him up. But no one came, no window was flung wide, not even a flowerpot hurled. He wondered if the man even remembered him.

With a little shrug, Viktor turned to walk away. He felt a sullen disappointment which soon faded, slipping back into the worn dressing gown of boredom.

It was three nights later, strolling home alone from a dinner party, that someone came behind him on a deserted street, and brutally beat him, leaving him unconscious in the snow. It might only have been a coincidence.

He was presently found and taken home, but the episode resulted in a bout of pneumonia.

"My dear, you are so young, so young," said Ilena, holding his hand. She seemed quite her old self, dressed in inspiring pastel colors, somehow here and seated by the bed, not demanding, not complaining at all, only coaxing him. He smiled at her, to show her he was pleased she had come. He felt a remote tenderness, but somehow could not summon the strength to say one word to her. She spoke of his cousin, the one he was to marry. "She will be here directly. But the trains are so slow. The weather—"

Across from the bed, the wall went on slowly dissolving, as it had been doing now for almost an hour, a soft sweet dissolution, like melting snow.

The doctor shook his head at Ilena, gently. She stopped speaking and only held the hand of her son, who, at thirty-six, it seemed, was about to die. Some fundamental weakness in his constitution had finished him. His lungs were filled by fluid, he was drowning, there was no hope at all. Ilena, who had railed and wept in the corridor, was now calm and tactful in the face of another's agony. Her own, like the pain of her crippling disease, she would ignore for the present. Janov had spared her this. Even now, she did not quite believe that Janov had died, or that Viktor was dying. The whole world had paid with death for its dreams, its youthful mistakes, and was not done paying yet. But not her son, her son.

Somewhere a clock ticked. One of Viktor's clocks. A miracle would happen soon, and he would get better.

Viktor watched the melting of the wall, and saw the long lawns of the chateau appear. Three years ago, the chateau had been sold again, lost again, but that did not matter now. The house was dim beyond the wall, vanishing. A thick mist lay everywhere, swathing the great stretch of water that must be the lake, a surface of dark silver, with one blank tear of soft white light across it. Beautiful, serene and melancholy, the light, the lake, and then a dark movement far away, something a mile out on the glacial water.

"Your last book," Ilena said, unable to restrain her words despite herself. "I was reading it again, just yesterday. What a curious, clever book it is. High time you wrote another, my dear. Perhaps, in the spring—"

Yes, Maman, he said. But he said nothing. He stared away beyond the wall and saw the shape of the darkness on the water drifting nearer. He could see what it was, now. A swan, a black swan, floating like a ship toward him over the utter silence of the winter lake.

"Do you remember," Ilena said, "when we were at the chateau and that silly thing happened with the boat?" It was the way she had been used to speak to Janov: *Do you recall, Nani, when we were here, and did this and did that?* Viktor smiled at her, but he did not smile.

The black swan came nearer and nearer, black as night, black as ink, and it seemed to him he heard it sing.

"You musn't leave me," Ilena whispered, knowing he no longer heard her. "What shall I do, alone?"

But the shadow of the black swan had filled the room. She was alone already.

Beauty

1

His hundred and fifty-first birthday dawned aboard the sleek ship from Cerulean, high above the white-capped ocean that was the earth. By nightfall he would be at home, in his beautiful robot-run house. Beyond the tall windows a landscape of the western hemisphere would fall away, pure with snow, to a frozen glycerine river. Far from the weather control of the cities, the seasons came and went there with all the passion and flamboyance of young women. And in the house, the three young women came and went like the seasons.

Dark slender Lyra with her starry eyes and her music—well-named; Joya, much darker, ebony skinned and angel-eyed, full of laughter—well-named, too. And the youngest, his only born child, made with a woman from whom he had long since parted: Estár, with her green-brown hair the color of the summer oak woods, and her unrested turbulent spirit—ill-named for a distant planet, meaning the same as the Greek word *psyche*.

It seemed his seed made daughters, either mixed with the particles of unknown women in crystal tubes, or mingled in a human womb. They were his heirs, both to his mercantile fortune and to his treasures of art and science. He loved each of them, and was loved in turn. But sometimes Estár filled him with a peculiar fear. Her life would never be simple, and perhaps never happy. He did not like to think of her, maybe far from the shelter of the house, the shelter he could give her. In fifty, sixty more years, he might be dead. What then?

Tonight, there was the ceremonial dinner party to welcome him home, and to mark his birthday. A few charming guests would be there, delighting in the golden rooms. There would be the exchange of presents, for, with every birthday, gifts were given as well as received. This time, they had told him those three, laughing, what they wanted. "Natural things!" they had cried. Lyra wished for pearls, *real* pearls, the kind only to be taken from oysters which had died, neither cultured nor killed for. And Joya had demanded a dress of silk, an old dress made before the ending of the silkworm trade. Estár, he guessed, had subconsciously put them up to it, and when her turn came he had waited, uneasy in some way he could not explain. "A rose," she said, "a grown rose. But something from a hothouse or a city cultivatory won't do."

"In all this snow –" exclaimed Joya.

"I can send to the east," he said.

"No," said Estár, all too quietly. "You must pluck it yourself."

"But then," said Lyra, "he would have to detour from Cerulean. He'll never be home in time for the dinner party to give you such a present."

Estár smiled. "It seems I've posed you a riddle, Papa."

"It seems you have," he said, wincing a little at the title "Papa" which she had adopted from some book. His other daughters called him by his name, graciously, allowing him to be a person, not merely an adjunctive relation. "Well, I'll keep my eyes wide for roses in the snow."

Yet how ominous it had seemed, and not until the ship landed at the huge western terminus did he discover why.

"Mercator Levin? Would you be good enough to step this way?"

The attendant was human, a courteous formality that boded ill.

"Is anything worng?" he asked. "My cargo?"

"Is quite in order, I assure you. The commissioner wishes to speak with you, on another matter."

Perplexed, he followed, and presently entered the circular office with its panoramic views of the landing fields. Dusk was immanent, and the miles of ground constellated by lights. Far away, little flaming motes, the ships sank slowly down or up.

He was offered wines, teas, coffees, and other social stimulants. He refused them all, his oppression growing. The commissioner, a few years his junior, was patently troubled, and paving the way—to something. At last he leaned back in his chair, folded his hands and said,

"Depending on how you see your situation, Mercator Levin, it is my duty to inform you that either a great honor, or a great annoyance, is about to befall your family."

"What can you mean?"

"This, sir, has been placed in our care, for you."

He watched, he looked, he saw, and the control and poise of one and a half centuries deserted him. Risen from a recess in the desk, a slim crystal box stood transparent in the solarized light. A heap of soil lay on the floor of the box. Growing straight up from it was a translucent stem only faintly tinged with color, and leafless. At the head of the stem there blossomed a rose slender as a tulip, its petals a pale and singing green. There were no thorns, or rather only one and that metaphysical, if quite unbearably penetrating.

"I see it is not an honor," said the commissioner, so softly Levin was unsure if he were dealing with a sadist or a man of compassion. In any event, that made no odds. "I'm very sorry, Mercator. But I had no choice. And you, as you know, have none either. As you see, the name and code stamped into the crystal are your own."

"Yes," he said.

"So, if you would be so kind. I am to act as the witness, you understand, of your acceptance."

"But I don't accept," Levin said.

"You know, sir, that failure to comply—"

"I know. I'll do it. But *accept*? How could I?"

"No." And the commissioner lowered his eyes.

When he was within a foot of the desk and the box, the crystal opened for him. Levin reached in and took the smooth stem of the green rose in his fingers. The roots broke away with a crisp snap, like fresh lettuce, and a sweet aroma filled the air. It was the most disgusting, nauseating scent he had ever smelled.

Homecoming, normally so full of pleasure, was now resonant with dread. He dismissed the snow-car at the edge of the hill, and climbed, as he always did, toward the lovely, sprawling house. Most of it was of one-story construction in deference to the high winds that blew here in winter and often in the spring also, and all weatherproofed in a wonderful plasteel that made its walls seem to catch the prevailing light within themselves, glowing now a soft dull silver like the darkening sky. It had been turned into lace besides by the hundred golden windows—every illuminator was on to welcome him.

Inside, the house was warm and fragrant, old wood, fine synthetics. The robot servants had laid everything ready in his rooms, even to the selection of bedside books and music. His luggage was here ahead of him. He prepared himself, dressed for the party, went down. He had hurried to do so, but without eagerness. The glass of spirit he left untouched.

The main communal room of the house was some forty square meters, summer-heated from the floor, and also by the huge open central fire of natural coals, its suspended chimney like the glass pillar of an hallucination floating just above. How that chimney had fascinated Lyra and Joya as children. Something in its strength and exquisite airy unactuality—

For a while, the scene held in the room. They had not noticed him yet, though they expected him at any second. Lyra was playing the piano in a pool of light. What would it mean to her to be sent away? She was studying with two of the greatest musicians of the age, and already her compositions—three concertos, a symphony, song cycles, sonatas—were phenomenal and unique. She promised so much to herself, to her world. And she was, besides, in love. The young man who stood by the piano, watching her white hands, her face. Levin looked at him with a father's jealousy and a father's pride that the lover of his daughter should be both handsome and good. The Asiatic blood that showed in his amber skin, the carven features and slanting eyes, the violinist's hands, the talent of his calling—all these were charming and endearing things.

And then, standing listening by the fire, Joya, jet-black on the redness of the coals, no longer fascinated by the chimney, fascinating instead her two admirers, one male and one female. They were her friends, poets, a little eccentric as all Joya's friends turned out to be. It had alarmed him at first. He had feared she would be forced to change. But Joya had not altered, only extending her sunshine to others, giving them a steadiness they lacked, herself losing none. And she was now four months pregnant. She had told him her news the day he left, her eyes bright. It was splendid, enchanting. The thought of her as the mother of children filled him with painful happiness. She did not know who had fathered the child, which would be a son, nor did she care, had not bothered with the tests to discover. He had chided her gently, since the father had every right to know, and Joya had laughed: "Later. For now he's only mine."

And to send Joya away, two lives now—No! No, no.

Seated between the fire and the piano, the other guests were also listening to the music, four contemporaries of Levin's, well-known, stimulating and restful people of experience, and, in one case, genius, and three well-liked others, mutual acquaintances of them all. And there, on the periphery of the group, alone, his third daughter, his born daughter, and he grew cold at the perfection of the omens. The apple tint she used upon her brown hair had been freshly enhanced. Her dress, of the fashion known as Second Renascence, was a pale and singing green. She played with a glass of wine in her left hand, twirling the stem between her fingers. The translucent stem. It was as if she had known. He had heard rumors of such things before. It was ironical, for just now he recalled, of course, that she had almost never *been* born, her mother's frenetic life-style having brought on the preliminaries of an accidental abortion—the child had been saved, and had continued to grow inside the woman's womb to a well coordinated seventh-month term. But how nearly—

Estár seemed to feel his eyes on her. She looked about, and, not speaking to anyone, got up and came noiselessly over to him in the doorway. She was tall and slim, and almost a stranger.

"Welcome home, Papa." She did not reach to kiss him as the others did, restrained, perhaps inhibited. He had noticed it with many born children. Those not carried in flesh seemed far easier with the emotional expressions of the flesh, a paradox. "Did you," said Estár, "find my rose?"

He looked at her in devastating sadness.

"At first, I thought I'd have to fail you," he said. "But in the end—look. Here it is."

And he held the green flower out to her in silence.

She gazed at it, and her pale face whitened. She knew it, and if by prescience she had foretold it, then that clearly had not been with her conscious mind. For a long while she did not take the rose, and then she reached out and drew it from his hand. The music was ending in the room. In another moment the others would become aware of his arrival, of this scene at the door.

"Yes," Estár said. "I see it must be me. *They* are your daughters. I'm only your guest."

"Estár," he said. "What are you saying?"

"No," she said, "I'm sorry. I meant only I have nothing to lose, or little—a nice home, a kind father—but they have everything to lose . . . love, children, brilliance—No, it has to be me, doesn't it?"

"I intend to petition," he began, and stopped.

"You know that everyone petitions. And it does no good at all. When do I have to leave?"

"The usual period is a month. Oh Estár—if there were anything at all—"

"You'd do it. I know. You're marvelous, but there are limits. It's not as if I'll never see you again. And, I respect your judgment. I do. To choose me."

The music ended. There was applause and laughter, and then the first cry of his name across the room.

"You fool," he said to his youngest daughter, "don't you know that I chose you—not because I consider you expendable—but because I love you the best?"

"Oh," she said. Her eyes filled with tears, and she lowered her head, not letting him see them.

"That is the decision this thing forces us to," he said. "To sacrifice in blood. Could I ask you the unforgivable thing—not to tell the others until this wretched party is over?"

"Of course," she said. "I'll go to my rooms for a little, ten minutes, perhaps. Then I'll come back, bright as light. Watch me. You'll be proud. Tell them I went to put your—your gift in water."

Levin had been a child five years old when the planet of his birth received its first officially documented visit from the stars. The alien ships fell like a summer snow, a light snow; there were not many. The moon cities, Martian Marsha, and the starry satellite colonies that drifted between, these the aliens by-passed. They came to the home world and presented it with gifts, clean and faultless technologies, shining examples of intellect and industry, from a culture similar to, much advanced on, greatly differing from, the terrestrial. And later, like wise guests not outstaying their welcome, the ships, and most of the persons who came with the ships, went away. Their general purpose was oblique if altruistic. The purpose of those who remained less so, more so. At first they were seen in the capacity of prefects. To some extent, Earth had been conquered. Left free, no doubt she must still answer now and then to her benign superiors. But the remaining aliens required neither answers nor menials. It seemed they stayed only because they wished to, in love with Earth, tired of journeying . . . something of this sort. Perfectly tended by their own machineries, setting up their own modest estates far from the cities and the thoroughfares of popular life, they appropriated nothing and intruded not at all. They seemed content merely to be there. It was easy, for the most part, to forget them.

And then, about the time that Levin ended his adult education, around twenty-six or so, the first roses were sent. Immersed in a last fascinating study of something he had now quite forgotten, he missed the event. Only common outcry had alerted him. He remembered ever after the broodingly sinister concern that overcame him. It seemed the aliens in fact had decided to demand one thing. Or rather, they asked, courteously and undeniably. Somehow, without any threat, it was made clear that they could take *without* asking, that to ask was their good manners. The rose was a gracious summons, and with the first roses an explanation went of what the gracious summons entailed. Despite the outcry, despite petitionings, letters, speeches loudly made in the senates and councils of every nation and every ethnic alliance of the world, the summonses were obeyed. There was no other choice. *I will not,* had been replied to, gently, illimitably: *You will.*

Without force, without threat, by unspoken undemonstrated implication only. The Earth was in fee to her friends. Stunned at the first, the only blow, there was, finally, no battle. The battles came later, seventy years later, when the second wave of roses—those alien roses from gardens blooming with the seeds of another planet, roses purple, azure, green—was dashed across humanity's quietude. Some resorted to concealment, then, and some fought. Some simply refused, standing firm; alone. But once again the inexorable pressure, invisibly and indecipherably applied, undid them. Men found themselves in conflict only with other men. The aliens did not attack them or seize from them. But they waited and were felt to be waiting. Roses thrown on fire were found not to burn. Roses flung among garbage were mysteriously returned, all burnished. The aliens made no other demand. The first demand was always enough. Without their gifts, humanity would not thrive quite as it did. Gradually, persuaded by their own kind, bamboozled, worn out with beating their heads on the hard walls of censure, those who had hidden and fought and stood alone, crumbled, gave in, let go.

And it was a fact, in all the first two waves of the sending of the roses, and in all the sporadic individual sendings that had followed in these fifty years after the two waves, nothing had ever been asked of those who could not spare the payment. It had a kind of mathematical soulless logic, hopelessly unhuman—*in*human.

Always the families to whom the roses went were rich—not prosperous, as almost all men were now prosperous—but something extra. Rich, and endowed with friends and kin, abilities of the mind and spirit: consolations for the inevitable loss. The loss of one child. A son, or a daughter, whichever of the household was best suited to be sent, could most easily be spared, was the most likely to find the prospect challenging or acceptable, or, endurable.

He remembered how at twenty-six it had suggested to him immolations to Moloch and to Jupiter, young children given to the god. But that was foolish, of course. They did not, when they went to the alien estates, go there to die, or even to worship, to extend service. They were neither sacrifices nor slaves. They had been seen quite often after, visiting their families, corresponding with them. Their lives continued on those little pieces of alien ground, much as they had always done. They were at liberty to move about the area, the buildings, the surrounding landscapes, at liberty to learn what they wished of the aliens' own world, and all its facets of science and poetry.

There was only discernible in them, those ones who went away, a distancing, and a dreadful sourceless silence, which grew.

The visits to their homes became less. Their letters and video-ings ceased. They melted into the alien culture and were gone. The last glimpses of their faces were always burdened and sad, as if against advice they had opened some forbidden door and some terrible secret had overwhelmed them. The bereaved families knew that something had consumed their sons and daughters alive, and not even bones were left for them to bury.

It was feared, though seldom spoken of, that it was natural xenophobia, revulsion, which destroyed and maybe killed the hearts of humanity's children. They had grown with their own kind, and then were sent to dwell with another kind. Their free revisitings of family and friends would only serve to point the differences more terribly between human and alien. The aliens—and this was almost never spoken of—were ugly, were hideous. So much had been learned swiftly, at the very beginning. Out of deference to their new world, out of shame, perhaps, they covered their ugliness with elegant garments, gloves, masking draperies, hoods and visors. Yet, now and then, a sighting—enough. They were like men or women, a little taller, a slender, finely muscled race . . . But their very likeness made their differences the more appalling, their loathsomeness more unbearable. And there were those things which now and then must be revealed, some inches of pelted hairy skin, the gauntleted over-fingered hands, the brilliant eyes empty of white, lensed by their yellow conjunctiva.

These, the senders of roses.

It seemed, without knowing, Levin always had known that one day the obscene sacrifice would be asked of him. To one of these creatures would now travel his youngest daughter Estár, who wore by choice the clothing of reborn history.

While she ordered the packing of her luggage, he wrote letters and prepared tapes of appeal and righteous anger.

Both knew it to be useless.

Somewhere in the house, Joya and Lyra wept.

On the first day of Midwinter, the snow-car stood beside the porch.

"Good-bye," she said.

"I will—" he began.

"I know you'll do everything you can." She looked at her sisters, who were restraining their frightened tears with skill and decorum so that she should not be distressed. "I shall see you in the spring. I'll make sure of that," she said. It was true, no doubt. Joya kissed her. Lyra could not risk the gesture, and only pressed her hand. "Good-bye," Estár said again, and went away.

The snow sprang in two curved wings from the car. In ten seconds it was a quarter of a mile away. The snow fell back. The sound of crying was loud. Levin took his two remaining daughters in his arms and they clung to him. Catching sight of them all in a long mirror, he wryly noted he and they were like a scene from an ancient play—Greek tragedy or Shakespeare: Oedipus and Antigone, Lear with Cordelia lost—*A Winter's Tale*.

He wondered if Estár cried, now that she was in private and unseen.

2

Estár had not cried; she was sickened from fear and rage. Neither of these emotions had she expressed, even to herself, beyond the vaguest abstracts. She had always been beset by her feelings, finding no outlet. From the start, she had seen Lyra express herself through music, Joya through communicatino. But Estár had been born with no creative skills and had learned none. She could speak coherently and seemingly to the point, she could, if required to, write concise and quite interesting letters, essays and fragments of descriptive poetry. But she could not convey *herself* to others. And *for* herself, what she was aware of, suffered, longed for—these concepts had never come clear. She had no inkling as to what she wanted, and had often upbraided herself for her lack of content and pleasure in the riches fate had brought her, her charming family, the well-ordered beauty of her world. At fifteen, she had considered a voluntary term at Marsha, the

Martian colonial belt, but had been disuaded by physical circumstance. It seemed her lungs, healthy enough for Earth, were not of a type to do well for her in the thin half-built atmosphere of Mars. She had not grieved, she had not wanted to escape to another planet any more than she wanted anything else. There had simply been a small chance that on Mars she might have found a niche for herself, a *raison d'Estár*.

Now, this enforced event affected her in a way that surprised her. What did it matter after all if she were exiled? She was no ornament at home to herself or others and might just as well be placed with the ambiguous aliens. She could feel, surely, no more at a loss with this creature than with her own kind, her own kin.

The fear was instinctive, of course, she did not really question that. But her anger puzzled her. Was it the lack of choice? Or was it only that she had hoped eventually to make a bond between herself and those who loved her, perhaps to find some man or woman, one who would not think her tiresome and unfathomable and who, their novelty palling, she would not come to dislike. And now these dreams were gone. Those who must live with the aliens were finally estranged from all humanity, that was well known. So, she had lost her own chance at becoming human.

It was a day's journey. The car, equipped with all she might conceivably need, gave her hot water and perfumed soap, food, drink, played her music, offered her books and films. The blue-white winter day only gradually deepened into dusk. She raised the opaque blinds of the forward windows and looked where the vehicle was taking her.

They were crossing water, partly frozen. Ahead stood a low mountain. From its conical exaggerated shape, she took it to be man-made, one of the structured stoneworks that here and there augmented the Earth. Soon they reached a narrow shore, and as the dusk turned gentian, the car began to ascend.

A gentle voice spoke to her from the controls. It seemed that in ten minutes she would have arrived.

There was a tall steel gate at which the snow-car was exchanged for a small vehicle that ran on an aerial cable.

Forty feet above the ground, Estár looked from the window at the mile of cultivated land below, which was a garden. Before the twilight had quite dispersed, she saw a weather control existed, manipulating the seasons. It was autumn by the gate and yellow leaves dripped from the trees. Later, autumn trembled into summer, and heavy foliage swept against the sides of the car. It was completely dark when the journey ended, but as the car settled on its platform, the mild darkness and wild scents of spring came in through its opening doors.

She left the car and was borne down a moving stair, a metal servant flying leisurely before with her luggage. Through wreaths of pale blossom she saw a building, a square containing a glowing orb of roof, and starred by external illuminators.

She reached the ground. Doors bloomed into light and opened.

A lobby, quite large, a larger room beyond. A room of seductive symmetry—she had expected nothing else. There was no reason why it should not be pleasant, even enough like other rooms she had seen as to appear familiar. Yet, too, there was something indefinably strange, a scent, perhaps, or some strain of subsonic noise. It was welcome, the strangeness. To find no alien thing at once could have disturbed her. And maybe such psychology was understood, and catered to.

A luminous bead came to hover in the air like a tame bird.

"Estár Levina," it said, and its voice was like that of a beautiful unearthly child. "I will be your guide. A suite has been prepared for you. Any questions you may wish—"

"Yes," she broke in, affronted by its sweetness, "when shall I meet—with your controller?"

"Whenever you desire, Estár Levina."

"When *I* desire? Suppose I have no desire *ever* to meet—him?"

"If such is to be your need, it will be respected, wherever possible."

"And eventually it will no longer be possible and I shall be briskly escorted into his presence."

The bead shimmered in the air.

"There is no coercion. You are forced to do nothing which does not accord with your sense of autonomy."

"But I'm here against my will," she said flatly.

The bead shimmered, shimmered.

Presently she let it lead her silently across the symmetrical alien room, and into other symmetrical alien rooms.

Because of what the voice-bead had said to her, however, she kept to her allotted apartment, her private garden, for a month.

The suite was beautiful, and furnished with all she might require. She was, she discovered, even permitted access, via her own small console, to the library bank of the house. Anything she could not obtain through her screen, the voice-bead would have brought for her. In her garden, which had been designed in the manner of the Second Renascence, high summer held sway over the slender ten-foot topiary. When darkness fell, alabaster lamps lit themselves softly among the foliage and under the falling tails of water.

She wondered if she was spied on. She acted perversely and theatrically at times in case this might be so. At others she availed herself of much of what the technological dwelling could give her.

Doors whisked open, clothes were constructed and brought, baths run, tapes deposited as though by invisible hands. It was as if she were waited on by phantoms. The science of Earth had never quite achieved this fastidious level, or had not wanted to. The unseen mechanisms and energies in the air would even turn the pages of books for her, if requested.

She sent a letter to her father after two days. If read simply:

I am here and all is well. Even to her the sparseness was disturbing. She added a postscript: *Joya must stop crying over me or her baby will be washed away.*

She wondered, as her letter was wafted out, if the alien would read it.

On the tenth day, moodily, she summoned from the library literature and spoken theses on the aliens' culture and their world.

"Curiosity," she said to the walls, "killed the cat."

She knew already, of course, what they most resembled—some species of huge feline, the hair thick as moss on every inch of them save the lips, the nostrils, the eyes, and the private areas of the body. Though perhaps ashamed of their state, they had never hidden descriptions of themselves, only their actual selves, behind the visors and the draperies.

She noted that while there were many three-dimensional stills of their planet, and their deeds there and elsewhere, no moving videos were available, and this perhaps was universally so.

She looked at thin colossal mountain ranges, tiny figures in the foreground, or sporting activities in a blur of dust—the game clear, the figures less so. Tactfully, no stress was laid even here, in their own habitat, on their unpalatable differences. What Earth would see had been vetted. The sky of their planet was blue, like the sky of Earth. And yet utterly alien in some way that was indecipherable. The shape of the clouds, maybe, the depth of the horizon. . . . Like the impenetrable differences all about her. Not once did she wake from sleep disoriented, thinking herself in her father's house.

The garden appealed to her, however; she took aesthetic comfort from it. She ate out on a broad white terrace under the leaves and the stars in the hot summer night, dishes floating to her hands, wine and coffees into her goblet, her cup, and a rose-petal paper cigarette into her fingers.

Everywhere secrets, everywhere the concealed facts.

"If," she said to the walls, "I am observed, are you enjoying it, O Master?" She liked archaic terms, fashions, music, art, attitudes. They had always solaced her, and sometimes given her weapons against her own culture which she had not seemed to fit. Naturally, inevitably, she did not really feel uneasy here. As she had bitterly foreseen, she was no more un-at-home in the alien's domicile than in her father's.

But why was she here? The ultimate secret. Not a slave, not a pet. She was free as air. As presumably all the others were free. And the answers that had come from the lips and styluses of those others had never offered a satisfactory solution. Nor could she uncover the truth, folded in this privacy.

She was growing restless. The fear, the rage, had turned to a fearful angry ache to know—to seek her abductor, confront him, perhaps touch him, talk to him.

Curiosity. . . . If by any chance he did not spy on her, did not nightly read reports on her every action from the machines of the house, why then the Cat might be curious too.

"How patient you've been," she congratulated the walls, on

the morning of the last day of the month. "Shall I invite you to my garden? Or shall I meet you in yours?" And then she closed her eyes and merely thought, in concise clipped words within her brain: *I will wait for you on the lawn before the house, under all that blossom. At sunset.*

And there at sunset she was, dressed in a version of Earth's fifteenth century, and material developed from Martian dust crystals.

Through the blossoming spring trees the light glittered red upon her dress and on her, and then a shadow came between her and the sun.

She looked up, and an extraordinary sensation filled her eyes, her head, her whole torso. It was not like fear at all, more like some other tremendous emotion. She almost burst into tears.

He was here. He had read her mind. And, since he had been able to do that, it was improbable he had ever merely spied on her at all.

"You admit it," she said. "Despite your respect for my—my privacy—how funny!—you admit I have *none*!"

He was taller than she, but not so much taller that she was unprepared for it. She herself was tall. He was covered, as the aliens always covered themselves, totally, entirely. A glint of oblique sun slithered on the darkened face-plate through which he saw her, and through which she could not see him at all. The trousers fit close to his body, and the fabric shone somewhat, distorting, so she could be sure of nothing. There was no chink. The garments adhered. Not a centimeter of body surface showed, only its planes, male and well-formed: familiar, alien—like the rooms, the skies of his world. His hands were cased in gauntlets, a foolish, inadvertent complement to her own apparel. The fingers were long. There were six of them. She had seen a score of photographs and threedems of such beings.

But what had happened. That was new.

Then he spoke to her, and she realized with a vague shock that some mechanism was at work to distort even his voice so it should not offend her kind.

"That I read your thoughts was not an infringement of your privacy, Estár Levina. Consider. You intended that they should be read. I admit, my mind is sensitive to another mind which signals to it. You signaled very strongly. Almost, I might say, with a razor's edge."

"*I*," she said, "am not a telepath."

"I'm receptive to any such intentional signal. Try to believe me when I tell you I don't, at this moment, know what you are thinking. Although I could guess."

His voice had no accent, only the mechanical distortion. And yet it was—charming—in some way that was quite ab-human, quite unacceptable.

They walked awhile in the outer garden in the dusk. Illuminators ignited to reveal vines, orchids, trees—all of another planet, mutating gently among the strands of terrestrial vegetation.

Three feet high, a flower like an iris with petals like dark blue flames allowed the moon to climb its stem out of the valley below.

They barely spoke. Now and then she asked a question, and he replied. Then, somewhere among a flood of Earthly sycamores, she suddenly found he was telling her a story, a myth of his own world. She listened, tranced. The weird voice, the twilight, the spring perfume, and the words themselves made a sort of rhapsody. Later that night, alone, she discovered she could not remember the story and was forced to search it out among the intellectual curios of the library bank. Deprived of his voice, the garden and the dusk, it was a very minor thing, common to many cultures, and patently more than one planet. A quest, a series of tasks. It was the multitude of plants which had prompted the story, that and the rising of a particular star.

When they reentered the house, they went into an upper room, where a dinner was served. And where he also ate and drank. The area of the facial mask which corresponded with his lips incredibly somehow was not there as he raised goblet or fork toward them. And then, as he lowered the utensil, it *was* there once more, solid and unbreachable as ever. Not once, during these dissolves of seemingly impenetrable matter, did she catch a glimpse of what lay beyond. She stared, and her anger rose like oxygen, filling her, fading.

"I apologize for puzzling you," he said. "The visor is constructed of separable atoms and molecules, a process not yet in use generally on Earth. If this bothers you, I can forgo my meal."

"It bothers me. Don't forgo your meal. Why," she said, "are you able to eat Earth food? Why has this process of separable atoms not been given to Earth?" And, to her astonishment, her own fragile glass dropped from her hand in pieces that never struck the floor.

"Have you been cut?" his distorted voice asked her unemphatically.

Estár beheld she had not.

"I wasn't," she said, "holding it tightly enough for that to happen."

"The house is eager to serve you, unused to you, and so misunderstands at times. You perhaps wanted to crush something?"

"I should like," she said, "to return to my father's house."

"At any time, you may do so."

"But I want," she said, "to stay there. I mean that I don't want to come back here."

She waited. He would say she had to come back. Thus, she would have forced him to display his true and brutal omnipotence.

He said, "I'm not reading your mind, I assure you of that. But I can sense instantly whenever you lie."

"Lie? What am I lying about? I said, I want to go home."

" 'Home' is a word which has no meaning for you, Estár Levina. This is as much your home as the house of your father."

"This is the house of a beast," she said, daringly. She was very cold, as if winter had abruptly broken in. "A superior, wondrous monster." She sounded calm. "Perhaps I could kill it. What would happen then? A vengeance fleet dispatched from your galaxy to destroy the terrestrial solar system?"

"You would be unable to kill me. My skin is very thick and resilient. The same is true of my internal structure. You could, possibly, cause me considerable pain, but not death."

"No, of course not." She lowered her eyes from the blank shining mask. Her pulses beat from her skull to her soles. She was ashamed of her ineffectual tantrum. "I'm sorry. Sorry for my bad manners, and equally for my inability to murder you. I think I should go back to my own rooms."

"But why?" he said. "My impression is that you would prefer to stay here."

She sat and looked at him hopelessly.

"It's not," he said, "that I disallow your camouflage, but the very nature of camouflage is that it should successfully wed you to your surroundings. You are trying to lie to yourself, and not to me. This is the cause of your failure."

"Why was I brought here?" she said. "Other than to be played with and humiliated." To her surprise and discomfort, she found she was being humorous, and laughed shortly. He did not join in her laughter, but she sensed from him something that was also humorous, receptive. "Is it an experiment in adaptation; in tolerance?"

"To determine how much proximity a human can tolerate to one of us?"

"Or vice versa."

"No."

"Then what?"

There was a pause. Without warning, a torrent of nausea and fear swept over her. Could he read it from her? Her eyes blackened and she put one hand over them. Swiftly, almost choking, she said, "If there is an answer, don't, please don't tell me."

He was silent, and after a few moments she was better. She sipped the cool wine from the new goblet which had swum to her place. Not looking at him at all, she said, "Have I implanted this barrier against knowledge of that type, or have you?"

"Estár," she heard him say, far away across the few yards of the table, "Estár, your race tends sometimes to demand too little or too much of itself. If there's an answer to your question, you will find it in your own time. You are afraid of the *idea* of the answer, not the answer itself. Wait until the fear goes."

"How can the fear go? You've condemned me to it, keeping me here."

But her words were lies, and now she knew it.

She had spoken more to him in a space of hours than to any of her own kind. She had been relaxed enough in his company almost to allow herself to faint, when, on the two other occasions of her life that she had almost fainted, in company with Levin, or with Lyra, Estár had clung to consciousness in horror, unreasonably terrified to let go.

The alien sat across the table. Not a table knife, not an angle of the room, but was subtly strange in ways she could not place or understand. And he, his ghastly nightmarish ugliness swathed in its disguise. . . .

Again with no warning she began to cry. She wept for three minutes in front of him, dimly conscious of some dispassionate compassion that had nothing to do with involvement. Sobbing, she was aware after all he did not read her thoughts. Even the house did not, though it brought her a foam of tissues. After the three minutes she excused herself and left him. And now he did not detain her.

In her rooms, she found her bed blissfully prepared and lay down on it, letting the mechanisms, visible and invisible, undress her. She woke somewhere in the earliest morning and called the bead like a drop of rain and sent it to fetch the story he had told her.

She resolved she would not go near him again until he summoned her.

A day passed.

A night.

A day.

She thought about him. She wrote a brief essay on how she analyzed him, his physical aura, his few gestures, his inherent hideousness to which she must always be primed, even unknowingly. The distorted voice that nevertheless was so fascinating.

A night.

She could not sleep. He had not summoned her. She walked in her private garden under the stars and found a green rose growing there, softly lighted by a shallow lamp. She gazed on the glow seeping through the tensed and tender petals. She knew herself enveloped in such a glow, a light penetrating her resistance.

"The electric irresistible charisma," she wrote, "of the thing one has always yearned for. To be known, accepted, and so to be at peace. No longer unique, or shut in, or shut *out*, or alone."

A day.

She planned how she might run away. Escaping the garden, stumbling down the mountain, searching through the wilderness for some post of communications or transport. The plan became a daydream and he found her.

A night.

A day.

That day, she stopped pretending, and suddenly he was in her garden. She did not know how he had arrived, but she stepped between the topiary and he was there. He extended his hand in a formal greeting; gloved, six-fingered, not remotely unwieldy. She took his hand. They spoke. They talked all that day, and some of the night, and he played her music from his world and she did not understand it, but it touched some chord in her, over and over with all of its own fiery chords.

She had never comprehended what she needed of herself. She told him of things she had forgotten she knew. He taught her a board game from his world, and she taught him a game with dots of colored light from Earth.

One morning she woke up singing, singing in her sleep. She learned presently she herself had invented the fragment of melody and the handful of harmonies. She worked on it alone, forgetting she was alone, since the music was with her. She did not tell him about the music until he asked her, and then she played it to him.

She was only ashamed very occasionally, and then it was not a cerebral, rather a hormonal thing. A current of some fluid nervous element would pass through her, and she would recall Levin, Lyra, Joya. Eventually something must happen, for all that happened now was aside from life, unconnected to it.

She knew the Alien's name by then. It had no earthly equivalents, and she could not write it, could not even say it; only think it. So she thought it.

She loved him. She had done so from the first moment she had stood with him under the spring trees. She loved him with a sort of welcome, the way diurnal creatures welcome the coming of day.

He must know. If not from her mind, then from the manner in which, on finding him, she would hurry toward him along the garden walks. The way she was when with him. The flowering of her creativity, her happiness.

What ever would become of her?

She sent her family three short noncommittal soothing letters, nothing compared to the bulk of their own.

When the lawns near the house had altered to late summer, it was spring in the world and, as she had promised, Estár went to visit her father.

3

Buds like emerald vapor clouded the boughs of the woods beyond the house. The river rushed beneath, heavy with melted snows. It was a windless day, and her family had come out to meet Estár. Lyra, a dark note of music, smiling, Joya, smiling, both looking at her, carefully, tactfully, assessing how she would prefer to be greeted, not *knowing*. How could they? Joya was slim again. Her child had been born two weeks ago, a medically forward seven-month baby, healthy and beauteous—they had told her in a tape, the most recent of the ten tapes they had sent her, along with Lyra's letters. . . . Levin was standing by the house door, her father.

They all greeted her, in fact, effusively. It was a show, meant to convey what they were afraid to convey with total sincerity.

They went in, talking continuously, telling her everything. Lyra displayed a wonderful chamber work she and Ekosun, her lover, were at work on—it was obvious he had been staying with her here, and had gone away out of deference to Estár's return, her need for solitary confinement with her family. Joya's son was brought, looking perfectly edible, the color of molasses, opening on a toothless strawberry mouth and two wide amber eyes. His hair was already thick, the color of corn. "You see," said Joya, "I know the father now, without a single test. This hair—the only good thing about *him*."

"She refuses even to let him know," said Levin.

"Oh, I will. Sometime. But the child will take my name, or yours, if you allow it."

They drank tea and ate cakes. Later there came wine, and later there came dinner. While there was food and drink, news to tell, the baby to marvel at, a new cat to play with—a white cat, with a long grey understripe from tail to chin-tip—a new picture to worship, Lyra's music to be heard—

while there was all this, the tension was held at bay, almost unnoticeable. About midnight, there came a lull. The baby was gone, the cat slept, the music was done and the picture had faded beyond the friendly informal candlelight. Estár could plead tiredness and go to bed, but then would come tomorrow. It must be faced sometime.

"I haven't," she said, "really told you anything about where I've been."

Joya glanced aside. Lyra stared at her bravely.

Levin said, "In fact, you have."

She had, he thought, told them a very great deal. She was strangely different. Not actually in any way he might have feared. Rather, she seemed more sure, quieter, more still, more absorbent, more favorably aware of them than ever in the past. One obvious thing, something that seemed the emblem of it all, the unexpected form of this change in her—her hair. Her hair now was a calm pale brown, untinted, no longer green.

"What have I told you then?" she said, and smiled, not intending to, in case it should be a smile of triumph.

"At least," he said, "that we needn't be afraid for you."

"No. Don't be. I'm really rather happy."

It was Lyra who burst out, unexpectedly, shockingly, with some incoherent protest.

Estár looked at her.

"He's—" she sought a word, selected one, "interesting. His world is interesting. I've started to compose music. Nothing like yours, not nearly as complex or as excellent, but it's fulfilling. I like doing it. I shall get better."

"I'm so sorry," said Lyra. "I didn't mean—it's simply—"

"That I shouldn't be happy because the situation is so unacceptable. Yes. But it isn't. I'd never have chosen to go there, because I didn't know what it would entail. But, in fact, it's exactly the sort of life I seem to need. You remember when I meant to go to Marsha? I don't think I would have done as much good there as I'm doing here, for myself. Perhaps I even help him in some way. I suppose they must study us, benignly. Perhaps I'm useful."

"Oh, Estár," Lyra said. She began to cry, begged their pardon and went out of the room, obviously disgusted at her own lack of finesse. Joya rose and explained she was going to look after Lyra. She too went out.

"Oh dear," said Estár.

"It's all right," Levin said. "Don't let it trouble you too much. Over-excitement. First a baby invades us, then you. But go on with what you were saying. What do you do on this mountain?"

He sat and listened as she told him. She seemed able to express herself far better than before, yet even so he was struck by the familiarity rather than the oddness of her life with the alien. Really, she did little there she might not have done here. Yet here she had never done it. He pressed her lightly, not trusting the ice to bear his weight, for details of the being with whom she dwelled.

He noticed instantly that, although she had spoken of him freely, indeed very often, in the course of relating other things, she could not seem to speak of him directly with any comfort. There was an embarrassment quite suddenly apparent in her. Her gestures became angular and her sentences dislocated.

Finally, he braced himself. He went to the mahogany cabinet that was five hundred years old, and standing before it pouring a brandy somewhat younger, he said, "Please don't answer this if you'd rather not. But I'm afraid I've always suspected that, despite all genetic, ethnic or social disparity, those they selected to live with them would ultimately become their lovers. Am I right, Estár?"

He stood above the two glasses and waited.

She said, "Nothing of that sort has ever been discussed."

"Do you have reason to think it will be?"

"I don't know."

"I'm not asking out of pure concern, nor out of any kind of prurient curiosity. One assumes, judging from what the others have said or indicated, that nobody has ever been raped or coerced. That implies some kind of willingness."

"You're asking me if I'd be willing to be his lover?"

"I'm asking if you are in love with him."

Levin turned with the glasses, and took her the brandy. She accepted and looked at it. Her face, even averted, had altered, and he felt a sort of horror. Written on her quite plainly was that look he had heard described—a deadly sorrow, a drawing inward and away. Then it was gone.

"I don't think I'm ready to consider that," she said.

"What is it," he said, "that gives you a look of such deep pain?"

"Let's talk about something else," she said.

Merchant and diplomat, he turned the conversation at once, wondering if he were wrong to do so.

They talked about something else.

It was only much later, when they parted for the night, that he said to her, "Anything I *can* do to help you, you've only to tell me."

And she remembered when he brought the rose and gave it to her, how he had said he loved her the best. She wondered if one always loved, then, what was unlike, incompatible.

"This situation has been rather an astonishment to us all," he added now. She approved of him for that, somehow. She kissed him good night. She was so much easier with him, as if estrangement had made them closer, which it had not.

Two weeks passed, Lyra and Joya laughed and did not cry. There were picnics, boat rides, air trips. Lyra played in live concert, and they went to rejoice in her. Things now seemed facile enough that Ekosun came back to the house, and after that a woman lover of Joya's. They breakfasted and dined in elegant restaurants. There were lazy days too, lying on cushions in the communal rooms listening to music tapes or watching video plays, or reading, or sleeping late, Estár in her old rooms among remembered things that no longer seemed anything to do with her. The green rose of her summons, which would not die but which had something to do with her, had been removed.

It was all like that now. A brightly colored interesting adventure in which she gladly participated, with which she had no link. The very fact that their life captivated her now was because of its—*alienness*. And her family, too. How she liked and respected them all at once, what affection she felt for them. And for the same reason.

She could not explain it to them, and would be ill-advised to do so even if she could. She lied to herself, too, keeping her awareness out of bounds as long as she might. But she sensed the lie. It needed another glass of wine, or another chapter of her book, or a peal of laughter, always something, and then another thing and then another, to hold it off.

At the end of two weeks her pretense was wearing thin and

she was exhausted. She found she wanted to cry out at them: I know who you are! You are my dear friends, my dazzling idols—I delight in you, admire you, but I am sometimes uneasy with you. Now I need to rest and I want to go—

Now I want to go home.

And then the other question brushed her, as it must. The house on the mountain was her home because he (she wordlessly expressed his name) was there. And because she loved him. Yet in what way did she love him? As one loved an animal? A friend? A lord? A teacher? A brother? Or in the way Levin had postulated, with a lover's love? And darkness would fall down on her mind and she would close the door on it. It was unthinkable.

When she devised the first tentative move toward departure, there was no argument. They made it easy for her. She saw they had known longer than she that she wanted to leave.

"I almost forgot to give you these. I meant to the first day you came back. They're fawn topaz, just the color your hair is now."

On Joya's smoky palm, the stones shone as if softly alight.

"Put your hair back, the way you had it at the concert, and wear them then."

"Thank you," said Estár. "They're lovely."

She reached toward the earrings and found she and her sister were suddenly holding hands with complete naturalness. At once she felt the pulse under Joya's skin, and a strange energy seemed to pass between them, like a healing touch.

They laughed, and Estár said unthinkingly, "But when shall I wear them on the mountain?"

"Wear them for him," said Joya.

"For—"

"For him," said Joya again, very firmly.

"Oh," Estár said, and removed her hand.

"No, none of us have been debating it when you were out of the room," said Joya. "But we do know. Estár, listen to me, there's truly nothing wrong in feeling emotion for this—for him, or even wanting him sexually."

"Oh really, *Joya.*"

"*Listen.* I know you're very innocent. Not ignorant, innocent. And there's nothing wrong in that either. But now—"

"Stop it, Joya." Estár turned away, but the machines packing her bag needed no supervision. She stared helplessly at the walls. Joya would not stop.

"There is only one obstacle. In your case, not culture or species. You know what it is. They way they *look*. I'm sorry, I'm sorry, Estár. But this is the root of all your trouble, isn't it?"

"How do I know?" She was exasperated.

"There is no way you can know. Unless you've seen him already, without that disguise they wear. Have you?"

Estár said nothing. Her silence, obviously, was eloquent enough.

"Go back then," said Joya, "go back and make him let you see him. Or find some way to see him when he doesn't realize you can. And then you *will* know."

"Perhaps I don't want to know."

"Perhaps not. But you've gone too far."

"You're trying to make me go too far. You don't understand."

"Oh, don't I?"

Estár rounded on her, and furiously saw only openness.

"You might possibly," said Estár, "want to spoil—something—"

"I might. But what does that matter? He—it—whatever the alien is, he's real and living and male and you're committed to him, and until you see him and know if you can bear it, how can you *dare* commit yourself?"

"But they're ugly," Estár said flatly. The words, she found, meant very little.

"Some humans are ugly. They can still be loved, loving."

"Suppose somehow I do see him—and I can't think how I would be able to—and suppose then I can't stand to look at him—"

"Then your feelings will undergo some kind of alternate channeling. But the way you are now is absurd."

"Oh prithee, sweet sister," Estár snarled, "let me be. Or, blameless one, throw thou the first stone."

Joya looked bemused. Then she said, "I did, didn't I? Two of them. You caught them, too."

And went out of the room, leaving the brown topaz earrings in Estár's hand.

It was so simple to return in the end it was like being borne away by a landslide.

All at once she was in a vehicle, the house flowing off behind her to a minuscule dot, and so to nothing. Then she was alone and sat down with her thoughts to consider everything—and abruptly, before she was ready, the conical mountain loomed before her.

There was a ghost of winter frost in the garden by the gate. Further on, the banana-yellow leaves were falling. She had seen many places anachronized by a weather control, yet here it seemed rather wonderful . . . for no reason at all.

The blossom was gone from about the building, but roses had opened everywhere. Alien roses, very tall, the colors of water and sky, not the blood and blush, parchment, pallor and shadow shades of Earth. She walked through a wheatfield of roses and in at the doors.

She went straight through all the intervening rooms and arrived in the suite the Alien called—had given her. There, she looked about her steadfastly. Even now, she was not entirely familiar with the suite, and unfamiliar with large sections of the house and gardenland.

Under such circumstances, it was not possible to recognize this place as her home. Even if, intellectually, she did so.

She wondered where he might be in the house. Surely he would know she had returned. Of course he would know. If she went out into her own garden, perhaps—

A word was spoken. It meant "yes." And although she did not know the word she knew its meaning for it had been spoken inside her head.

She waited, trembling. How close they were, then, if he could speak to her in such a way. She had been probing, seeking for him, her intuitive telepathy now quite strong, and she had touched him, and in turn been touched. There was no sense of intrusion. The word spoken in her head was like a caress, polite and very gentle.

So she went out into her garden, where is was beginning to be autumn now, and where the topiary craned black against the last of the day's sunlight. He stood just beyond the trees, by the stone basin with the colored fish. A heron made of blue steel balanced forever on the rim, peering downward, but the fish were sophisticated and unafraid of it, since it had never attacked them.

Suppose it was this way with herself? There he stood, swathed, masked, hidden. He had never given her cause to fear him. But was that any reason not to?

He took her hand; she gave her hand. She loved him, and was only frightened after all because he must know it. They began to talk, and soon she no longer cared that she loved him or that he knew.

They discussed much and nothing, and it was all she had needed. She felt every tense string of her body and her brain relaxing. All but one. What Levin, her father, had hinted, what Lyra had shied away from saying and Joya said. Could he perceive and sense this thing in her thoughts? Probably. And if she asked, in what way would he put her off? And could she ask? And would she ask?

When they dined that evening, high up in the orb of the roof, only the table lit, and the stars thickly clustered over the vanes above, she watched the molecules parting in his visor to accommodate cup or goblet or fork.

Later, when they listened to the music of his planet, she watched his long hands, cloaked in their gauntlets, resting so quiet yet so animate on the arms of a chair they were like sleeping cats.

Cat's eyes. If she saw them would she scream with horror? Yes, for weeks her sleep had been full of dreams of him, incoherent but sexual dreams, dreams of desire. And yet he was a shadow. She dreamed of coupling in the dark, blind, unseeing. She could hate Joya for being so right.

When the music ended, there came the slow turn of his head, and she beheld the graceful power of it, that concealed skull pivoted by that unseen neck. The cloaked hands flexed. The play of muscle ran down his whole body like a wave, and he had risen to his feet, in a miracle of coordinated movement.

"You're very tired, Estár," he said.

"But you know what I want to ask you."

"Perhaps only what you feel you should want to ask."

"To see you. As you are. It must happen, surely, if I live here with you."

"There's no need for it to happen now. Sometimes, with those others like yourself who are the companions of my kind, it only happens after many years. Do you comprehend, Estár? You're not bound to look at me as I am."

"But," she said, "you would allow it?"

"Yes."

She stared at him and said, "When?"

"Not tonight, I think. Tomorrow, then. You recall that I swim in the mornings. The mechanism that waits on you will bring you to my pool. Obviously, I swim without any of this. You can look at me, see me, and after that stay or go away, as you wish."

"Thank you," she said. Her head began to ache and she felt as if some part of her had died, burned out by the terror of what she had just agreed to.

"But you may change your mind," he said. "I won't expect you."

There was no clue in his distorted, expressive voice. She wondered if he, too, was afraid.

She made all the usual preparations for bed and lay down as if tonight were like any other, and did not sleep. And in the morning, she got up and bathed and dressed, as if it were any other morning. And when the machines had washed and brushed her hair, and enhanced her face with pastel cosmetics, she found she could not remember anything of the night or the routines of waking, bathing, dressing or anything at all. All she could remember was the thing to come, the moment when she saw him as he truly was. That moment had already happened to her maybe five thousand times, over and over, as she conjured it, fled from it, returned to it, in her mind.

And therefore, was he aware of all she had pictured? If he had not sensed her thoughts, he must deduce her thoughts.

She drank scalding tea, glad to be burned.

The voice-bead hovered, and she held out her hand. It came to perch on her fingers, something which she liked it to do, a silly affectionate ruse, her pretense, its complicity, that it was somehow creaturally alive.

"Estár, when shall I take you to the indoor pool?"

"Yes," she said. "Take me there now."

It was a part of the house she had not been in very much, and then, beyond a blank wall which dissolved as the molecules in his visor had done, a part of the house she had never entered. *His* rooms.

They opened one from another. Spare, almost sparse, but supple with subtle color, here and there highlighted by things which, at some other time, she would have paused to examine in fascinated interest—musical instruments from his world, the statue of a strange animal in stranger metal, an open book on whose surfaces he had written by hand in the letters of an alien alphabet. But then doors drew aside, and the bead glimmered before her out into a rectangular space, open above on the skies of Earth, open at its center on a dense blue water. Plants grew in pots along the edges of the pool, huge alien ferns and small alien trees, all leaning lovingly to the pool which had been minerally treated to resemble the liquids of their home. With a very little effort, Estár might imagine it was his planet she saw before her, and that dark swift shape sheering through the water, just beneath its surface, that shape was the indigenous thing, not the *alien* thing at all. Indeed, she herself was the alien, at this instant.

And at this instant, the dark shape reached the pool's end, only some ten feet from her. There came a dazzle across the water as he broke from it. He climbed from the pool and moved between the pots of ferns and trees, and the foliage and the shadow left him, as the water had already done. It was as he had told her. She might see him, unmasked, naked, open-eyed.

She stared at him until she was no longer able to do so. And then she turned and walked quickly away. It was not until she reached the inner rooms that she began to run.

She re-entered the suite he had given her, and stayed there only for an hour before she sent the voice-bead to him with her request. It returned with his answer inside five minutes. This time, there was no telepathic communion. She could not have borne it, and he had recognized as much.

4

"Please don't question me," she said. "Please."

Her family who, not anticipating her arrival on this occasion, had not been waiting to meet her—scattered like blown leaves about the room—acquiesced in gracious trouble monosyllables.

They would realize, of course, what must have occurred. If any of them blamed themselves was not apparent. Estár did not consider it, would consider nothing, least of all that she was bound, eventually, to return to the place she had fled.

She went to her apartment in Levin's house, glanced at its known unknown angles and objects, got into the remembered unremembered bed. "Bring me something to make me sleep," she said to the household robots. They brought it to her. She drank the cordial and sank thousands of miles beneath some sea. There were dreams, but they were tangled, distant. Waking for brief moments she could not recall them, only their colors, vague swirlings of noise or query. They did not threaten her. When she woke completely, she had more of the opiate brought, and slept again.

Days and nights passed. Rousing, she would permit the machines to give her other things. She swallowed juices, vitamins and small fruits. She wandered to the bathroom, immersed herself in scented fluid, dried herself and returned to bed. And slept.

It would have to end, obviously. It was not a means of dying, merely of temporary oblivion, aping the release of death. The machineries maintained her physical equilibrium, she lost five pounds, that was all. No one disturbed her, came to plead or chide. Each morning, a small note or two would be delivered—Joya or Lyra—once or twice Levin. These notes were handwritten and full of quiet solicitude. They were being very kind, very patient. And she was not behaving well, to worry them, to throw her burden upon them second hand in this way. But she did not care very much about that. What galvanized her in the end, ousted her from her haven of faked death, was a simple and inevitable thing. Her dreams marshalled themselves and began to assume coherence. She began to dream of him. Of the instant when he had left the water and she had seen him as he was. So they condemned her to relive, over and over again, that instant, just as she had lived it over and over before it had happened. Once the dreams were able to do this to her, naturally, there was no point in sleeping any longer. She must wake up, and find a refuge in the alternative of insomnia.

Seven days had gone by. She emerged from the depths a vampire, eager to feed on each of the other living things in the house, to devour their lives, the world and everything, to cram her mind, her consciousness. Again, they humored her. None of them spoke of what must have caused this, but the strain on them was evident. Estár liked them more each second, and herself less. How could she inflict this on them? She inflicted it. Three days, three nights went by. She did not sleep at any time.

Catching the atmosphere like a germ, Joya's son became fractious. The cat leapt, its fur electric, spitting at shadows. A terrible recurring headache, of which she did not speak but which was plain in her face, began to torment Lyra. Her lover was absent. Estár knew Ekosun would dislike her for consigning her sister to such pain. Finally Joya broke from restraint, and said to her, "I'm sorry. Do you believe that?" Estár ignored the reference, and Joya said, "Levin's in contact with the Mercantile Senate. They have a great deal of power. It may be possible to force the issue." "No one has ever been able to do anything of the sort." "What would you like me to do?" said Joya. "Throw myself from a great height into the river?" Estár laughed weakly. She took Joya in her arms. "It wasn't you. I would have had to—you were right. Right, right." "Yes," said Joya, "I was right. Perhaps one of the most heinous crimes known to humanity."

When Estár courteously excused herself and went away, Joya did not protest. Joya did not feel guilty, only regretful at the consequences of an inevitable act. Clean of conscience, she in turn set no further conflict working in Estár—the guilty are always the most prone to establish complementary guilt, and the most unforgiving thereafter.

And so Estár came to spend more and more time with Joya, but they did not speak of him once.

On the twelth day Estár fell asleep. She dreamed and saw him, framed by the pool and the foliage of his planet, and she started awake with a cry of loud anger.

It seemed she could never forget the awfulness of the revelation, could not get away from it. And therefore she might as well return to the mountain. Probably he would leave her very much alone. Eventually, it might be possible for her to become reconciled. They might meet again on some level of communication. Eventually. Conceivably. Perhaps.

That evening she spent in one of the communal rooms of her family's house. She tried to repay their sweetness and their distress with her new calm, with gentle laughter, thanking them with these things, her reestablished sense of self, her resignation tinged by intimations of hope, however dull, and by humor coming back like a bright banner.

They drank cold champagne and vodka, and the great fire roared under the transparent column, for like the drinks still the nights were cold. Estár had grown in this house, and now, quite suddenly and unexpectedly, she remembered it. She smiled at her father who had said he loved her the best of his daughters. She knew it was untrue, and yet that he had said it to her had become a precious thing.

There was a movement, a flicker like light. For a moment she thought it came from the fire, or from some mote traveling across the air of the room, the surface of her eye. And then she knew it had moved within her brain. She knew that he had spoken to her, despite the miles between them, and the manner in which she had left him. There were no words at all. It was like a whisper, or the brush of a low breeze across the plateaux of her mind. She felt a wonderful slowness fill her, and a silence.

One hour later a message came for her, delivered to the house by a machinery only glimpsed in the gusty evening. She opened the synthetic wrapper. She had anticipated, nor was she wrong to have done so. There was one line of writing, which read: *Estár. Tomorrow, come back to the mountain.* And he had signed it with that name she could not read or speak, yet which she knew now as well, maybe better, than her own. She looked a long while at the beautiful unhuman letters.

They watched her, and she said to them, "Tomorrow I am going back to the mountain. To him."

There was again that expression on her face; it had been there, mostly, since she had reentered Levin's house on this last visit. (*Visit.* She did not belong to them anymore.) The expression of the children of Earth sacrificed to monsters or monstrous gods, given in their earthly perfection to dwell with beasts. That dreadful demoralizing sadness, that devouring fading in the face of the irreparable. And yet there was nothing in her voice, and as she left the room her step was untrammelled and swift. And Levin recollected, not wanting to, the story of lemmings rushing in blithe tumult toward the ocean to be drowned.

A peacock-green twilight enclosed the mountain garden

and the building. Estár looked at it in wonder; it transformed everything. It seemed to her she was on some other planet, neither her own nor his.

A capsule had given her sleep throughout the journey. Drowsily serene she walked into the building and the voice-bead played about her, as if glad she had returned. They went to her suite and she said, "Where is he?" And opened her door to find him in the room.

She started back. In the blue-green resin of the dusk she saw at once that he was dressed in the garments of his own world, which concealed hardly anything of him.

She turned away and said coldly: "You're not being fair to me."

"It will soon be dark," he said. "If you leave the lamps unlit, you won't see me well. But you have seen me. The pretense is finished." There was no distortion to his voice. She had never really heard *him* speak before.

She came into the room and sat down beside a window. Beyond the glassy material, the tall topiary waved like seaweed in the sea of sky. She looked at this and did not look at him.

Yet she saw only him.

The water-sky dazzled as the pool had done, and he stepped out of the sky, the pool, and stood before her as in all her dreams, unmasked, naked, open-eyed. The nature of the pool was such, he was not even wet.

The hirsute pelt which covered his kind was a reality misinterpreted, mis-explained. It was most nearly like the fur of a short-haired cat, yet in actuality resembled nothing so much as the nap of velvet. He was black, like her sister Joya, yet the close black nap of fur must be tipped, each single hair, with amber; his color had changed second to second, as the light or dark found him, even as he breathed, from deepest black to sheerest gold. His well-made body was modeled from these two extremes of color, his fine musculature, like that of a statue, inked with ebony shadows, and highlighted by gilding. Where the velvet sheathing faded into pure skin, at the lips, nostrils, eyelids, genitals, the soles of the feet, palms of the hands, the flesh itself was a mingling of the two shades, a somber cinnamon, couth and subtle, sensual in its difference, but not shocking in any visual or aesthetic sense. The inside of his mouth, which he had also contrived to let her see, was a dark golden cave, in which conversely the humanness of the white teeth was in fact itself a shock. While at his loins the velvet flowed into a bearded blackness, long hair like unraveled silk; the same process occurred on the skull, a raying mane of hair, very black, very silken, its edges burning out through amber, ochre, into blondness—the sunburst of a black sun. The nails on his six long fingers, the six toes of his long and arched feet, were the tint of new dark bronze, translucent, bright as flames. His facial features were large and of a contrasting fineness, their sculptured quality at first obscured, save in profile, by the sequential ebb and flare of gold and black, and the domination of the extraordinary eyes. The long cinnamon lids, the thick lashes that were not black but startingly flaxen—the color of the edges of the occipital hair—these might be mistaken for human. But the eyes themselves could have been made from two highly polished citrines, clear saffron, darkening around the outer lens, almost to the cinnamon shade of the lids, and at the center by curiously blended charcoal stages to the ultimate black of the pupil. Analogously, they were like the eyes of a lion, and perhaps all of him lionlike, maybe, the powerful body, its skin unlike a man's, flawless as a beast's skin so often was, the pale-fire edged mane. Yet he was neither like a man not an animal. He was like himself, his kind, and his eyes were their eyes, compelling, radiant of intellect and intelligence even in their strangeness, and even in their beauty. For he *was* beautiful. Utterly and dreadfully beautiful. Coming to the Earth in the eras of its savagery, he would have been worshipped in terror as a god. He and his would have been forced to hide what they were for fear the true sight of it would burn out the vision of those who looked at them. And possibly this was the reason, still, why they had hidden themselves, and the reason too for the misunderstanding and the falsehoods. To fear to gaze at their ugliness, that was a safe and sensible premise. To fear their grandeur and their marvel—that smacked of other emotions less wise or good.

And she herself, of course, had run from this very thing. Not his alien hideousness—his beauty, which had withered her. To condescend to give herself to one physically her inferior, that might be acceptable. But not to offer herself to the lightning bolt, the solar flame. She had seen and she had been scorched, humiliated and made nothing, and she had run away, ashamed to love him. And now, ashamed, she had come back, determined to put away all she had felt for him or begun to feel or thought to feel. Determined to be no more than the companion of his mind, which itself was like a star, but, being an invisible, intangible thing, she might persuade herself to approach.

But now he was here in a room with her, undisguised, in the gracious garments of his own world and the searing glory of his world's race, and she did not know how she could bear to be here with him.

And she wondered if he were pleased by her suffering and her confusion. She wondered why, if he were not, he would not let her go forever. And she pictured such an event and wondered then if, having found him, she *could* live anywhere but here, where she could not live at all.

The sky went slowly out, and they had not spoken any more.

In the densening of the darkness, those distant suns, which for eons had given their light to the Earth, grew large and shining and sure.

When he said her name, she did not start, nor did she turn to him.

"There is something which I must tell you now," he said to her. "Are you prepared to listen?"

"Very well."

"You think that whatever I may say to you must be irrelevant to you, at this moment. That isn't the case."

She was too tired to weep, or to protest, or even to go away.

"I know," he said quietly. "And there's no need for you to do any of these things. Listen, and I shall tell you why not."

As it turned out, they had, after all, a purpose in coming to the Earth, and to that other handful of occupied planets they had visited, the bright ships drifting down, the jewels of their technology and culture given as a gift, the few of their species left behind, males and females, dwellers in isolated mansions, who demanded nothing of their hosts until the first flowering of alien roses, the first tender kidnappings of those worlds' indigenous sons and daughters.

The purpose of it all was never generally revealed. But power, particularly benign power, is easily amalgamated and countenanced. They had got away with everything, always. And Earth was no exception.

They were, by the time their vessels had lifted from the other system, a perfect people, both of the body and the brain; and spiritually they were more nearly perfect than any other they encountered. The compassion of omnipotence was intrinsic to them now, and the generosity of wholeness. Yet that wholeness, that perfection had had a bizarre, unlooked-for side effect. For they had discovered that totality can, by its very nature, cancel out itself.

They had come to this awareness in the very decades they had come also to know that endless vistas of development lay before them, if not on the physical plane, then certainly on the cerebral and the psychic. They possessed the understanding, as all informed creatures do, that their knowledge was simply at its dawn. There was more for their race to accomplish than was thinkable, and they rejoiced in the genius of their infancy, and looked forward to the limitless horizons—and found that their own road was ended, that they were not to be allowed to proceed. Blessed by unassailable health, longevity, strength and beauty, their genes had rebelled within them, taking this peak as an absolute and therefore as a terminus.

Within a decade of their planetary years, they became less fertile, and then sterile. Their bodies could not form children, either within a female womb or externally, in an artificial one. Cells met, embraced, and died in that embrace. Those scarcity of embryos that were successfully grown in the crystalline generative placentae lived, in some cases, into the Third Phase, approximate to the fifth month of a human pregnancy—and then they also died, their little translucent corpses floating like broken silver flowers. To save them, a cryogenic program was instituted. Those that lived, on their entry to the Third Phase, were frozen into stasis. The dream persisted that at last there would be found some way to realize their life. But the dream did not come true. And soon even the greatest and most populous cities of that vast and blue-skied planet must report that, in a year twice the length of a year of the Earth, only eight or nine children had been saved to enter even that cold limbo, which now was their only medium of survival.

The injustice of fate was terrible. It was not that they had become effete, or that they were weakened. It was their actual peerlessness which would kill the race. But being what they were, rather than curse God and die, they evolved another dream, and before long pursued it across the galaxies. Their natural faculties had remained vital as their procreative cells had not. They had conceived the notion that some other race might be discovered, sufficiently similar to their own that—while it was unlikely the two types could mingle physically to produce life—in the controlled environment of a breeding tube such a thing might be managed. The first world that offered them scope, in a system far beyond the star of Earth, was receptive and like enough that the first experiments were inaugurated. They failed.

And then, in one long night, somewhere in that planet's eastern hemisphere, a female of that race miscarrying and weeping bitterly at her loss, provided the lamp to lead them to their dream's solution.

With the sound and astounding anatomical science of the mother world, the aliens were able to transfer one of their own children, one of those embryos frozen in cryogenesis for fifty of their colossal years, into the vacated womb.

And, by their science too, this womb, filled and then despoiled, was repaired and sealed, brought in a matter of hours to the prime readiness it had already achieved and thought to abandon. The mother was monitored and cared for, for at no point was she to be endangered or allowed to suffer. But she thrived, and the transplanted child grew. In term, the approximate ten-month term normal to that planet, it was born, alive and whole. It had come to resemble the host race almost exactly; this was perhaps the first surprise. As it attained adulthood, there was a second surprise. Its essence resembled only the essence of its parental race. It was alien, and it pined away among the people of its womb-mother. Brought back to its true kind, then, and only then, it prospered and was happy and became great. It seemed, against all odds, their own were truly their own. Heredity had told, not in the physical, but in the ego. It appeared the soul of their kind would continue, unstoppable. And the limitless horizons opened again before them, away and away.

By the date in their travels when they reached Earth, their methods were faultless and their means secret and certain. Details had been added, refining details typical of that which the aliens were. The roses were one aspect of such refinements.

Like themselves, the plants of the mother world were incredibly long-lived. Nourished by treated soil and held in a vacuum—as the embryos were held in their vacuum of coldness—such flowers could thrive for half an Earth century, even when uprooted.

Earth had striven with her own bellicosity and won that last battle long before the aliens came. Yet some aggression, and some xenophobic self-protective pride remained. Earth was a planet where the truth of what the aliens intended was to be guarded more stringently than on any other world. A woman miscarrying her child in the fourth or fifth month, admitted to a medical center, and evincing psychological evidence of trauma—even now it happened. This planet was full of living beings, a teeming globe prone still to accident and misjudgment. As the woman lay sedated, the process was accomplished. In the wake of the dead and banished earthly child, the extra-terrestrial embryo was inserted, and anchored like a star. Women woke, and burst into tears and tirades of relief—not knowing they had been duped. Some not even remembering, for the drugs of the aliens were excellent, that they had ever been close to miscarrying. A balance was maintained. Some recalled, some did not. A sinister link would never be established. Only the eager and willing were ever employed.

There was one other qualification. It was possible to predict logistically the child's eventual habitat, once born. Since the child would have to be removed from that habitat in later years, the adoptive family were chosen with skill. The rich—who indeed tended more often to bear their children bodily—the liberated, the open-minded, the un-lonely. That there might be tribulation at the ultimate wrenching away was unavoidable, but it was avoided or lessened wherever and however feasible. Nor was a child ever recalled until it had reached a level of prolonged yearning, blindly and intuitively begging to be rescued from its unfitted human situation.

Here the roses served.

They in their crystal boxes, the embryos frozen in their crystal wombs. With every potential child a flower had been partnered. The aura of a life imbued each rose. It was the aura, then, which relayed the emanations of the child and the adult which the child became. The aura which told, at last, this telepathically sensitive race, when the summons must be sent, the exile rescued.

The green rose now flourishing in her garden here was Estár's own rose, brought home.

The woman who had carried Estár inside her, due to her carelessness, had aborted Levin's child, and received the alien unaware. The woman had needed to bear a child, but not to keep the child. Levin had gladly claimed what he took to be his own.

Estár, the daughter of her people, not Levin's daughter, not Lyra's sister or Joya's either. Estár had grown up and grown away, and the green rose which broadcast her aura began to cry soundlessly, a wild beacon. So they had released her from her unreal persona, or let her release herself.

And here she was now, turning from the window of stars to the invisible darkness of the room, and to his invisible darkness.

For a long while she said nothing, although she guessed—or telepathically she knew—he waited for her questions. At last one came to her.

"Marsha," she said. "They disqualified me from going there."

"A lie," he said. "It was arranged. In order that your transposition should be easier when it occurred."

"And I—" she said, and hesitated.

"And you are of my kind, although you resemble the genera which was your host. This is always the case. I know your true blood line, your true father and mother, and one day you may meet them. We are related, you and I. In the terminology of this world, cousins. There is one other thing."

She could not see him. She did not require to see him with her eyes. She now waited, for the beauty of his voice.

"The individual to whom you are summoned—this isn't a random process. You came to me, as all our kind return, to one with whom you would be entirely compatible. Not only as a companion, but as a lover, a bonded lover—a husband, a wife. You see, Estár, we've learned another marvel. The changes that alter our race in the womb of an alien species, enable us thereafter to make living children together, either bodily or matrically, whichever is the most desired."

Estár touched her finger to the topaz in her left ear.

"And so I love you spontaneously, but without any choice. Because we were chosen to be lovers?"

"Does it offend you?"

"If I were human," she said, "it might offend me. But then."

"And I, of course," he said, "also love you."

"And the way I am—my looks. . . . Do you find me ugly?"

"I find you beautiful. Strangely, alienly lovely. That's quite usual. Although for me, very curious, very exciting."

She shut her eyes then, and let him move to her across the dark. And she experienced in her own mind the glorious wonder he felt at the touch of her skin's smoothness like a cool leaf, just as he would experience her delirious joy in the touch of his velvet skin, the note of his dark and golden mouth discovering her own.

Seeing the devouring sadness in her face when she looked at them, unable to reveal her secret, Estár's earthly guardians would fear for her. They would not realize her sadness was all for them. And when she no longer moved among them, they would regret her, and mourn for her as if she had died. Disbelieving or forgetting that in any form of death, the soul—Psyche, Estár, (well-named)—refinds a freedom and a beauty lost with birth.